One Summer

David Baldacci is a worldwide bestselling novelist. With his books published in over 45 different languages and in more than 80 countries, and with over 110 million copies in print, he is one of the world's favourite storytellers. His family foundation, the Wish You Well Foundation, a non-profit organization, works to eliminate illiteracy across America. Still a resident of his native Virginia, he invites you to visit him at www.DavidBaldacci.com, and his foundation at www.WishYouWellFoundation.org, and to look into its programme to spread books across America at www.FeedingBodyandMind.com.

ALSO BY DAVID BALDACCI

The Camel Club series
The Camel Club
The Collectors
Stone Cold
Divine Justice
Hell's Corner

Sean King and Michelle Maxwell series
Split Second
Hour Game
Simple Genius
First Family

Shaw series
The Whole Truth
Deliver Us From Evil

Other novels
True Blue
Absolute Power
Total Control
The Winner
The Simple Truth
Saving Faith
Wish You Well
Last Man Standing
The Christmas Train

DAVID BALDACCI

One Summer

MACMILLAN

First published 2011 by Grand Central Publishing, USA

This edition published 2011 by Macmillan
an imprint of Pan Macmillan, a division of Macmillan Publishers Limited
Pan Macmillan, 20 New Wharf Road, London N1 9RR
Basingstoke and Oxford
Associated companies throughout the world
www.panmacmillan.com

ISBN 978-0-230-75328-0

Copyright © 2011 by Columbus Rose, Ltd.

The right of David Baldacci to be identified as the
author of this work has been asserted by him in accordance
with the Copyright, Designs and Patents Act 1988.

This book is a work of fiction. Names, characters, places, and incidents are
the product of the author's imagination or are used fictitiously. Any resemblance
to actual events, locales, or persons, living or dead, is coincidental.

All rights reserved. No part of this publication may be
reproduced, stored in or introduced into a retrieval system, or
transmitted, in any form, or by any means (electronic, mechanical,
photocopying, recording or otherwise) without the prior written
permission of the publisher. Any person who does any unauthorized
act in relation to this publication may be liable to criminal
prosecution and civil claims for damages.

The Macmillan Group has no responsibility for the information provided by
any author websites whose address you obtain from this book ('author websites').
The inclusion of author website addresses in this book does not constitute
an endorsement by or association with us of such sites or the content,
products, advertising or other materials presented on such sites.

1 3 5 7 9 8 6 4 2

A CIP catalogue record for this book is available from
the British Library.

Printed in the UK by CPI Mackays, Chatham ME5 8TD

Visit **www.panmacmillan.com** to read more about all our books
and to buy them. You will also find features, author interviews and
news of any author events, and you can sign up for e-newsletters
so that you're always first to hear about our new releases.

*To Spencer, my little girl all grown up.
And I couldn't be prouder of the
person you've become.*

One Summer

1

Jack Armstrong sat up in the secondhand hospital bed that had been wedged into a corner of the den in his home in Cleveland. A father at nineteen, he and his wife, Lizzie, had conceived their second child when he'd been home on leave from the army. Jack had been in the military for five years when the war in the Middle East started. He'd survived his first tour in Afghanistan and earned a Purple Heart for taking one in the arm. After that he'd weathered several tours of duty in Iraq, one of which included the destruction of his Humvee while he was still inside. That injury had won him his second Purple. And he had a Bronze Star on top of that for rescuing three ambushed grunts from his unit and nearly getting killed in the process. After all that, here he was, dying fast in his cheaply paneled den in Ohio's Rust Belt.

His goal was simple: just hang on until Christmas. He sucked greedily on the oxygen coming from the line in his nose. The converter that stayed in the corner of the small room was on maximum production, and Jack knew that one day soon it would be turned off because he'd be dead. Before Thanksgiving he was certain he could last another month. Now Jack was not sure he could make another day.

But he would.

I have to.

In high school the six-foot-two, good-looking Jack had varsity lettered in three sports, quarterbacked the football team, and had his pick of the ladies. But from the first time he'd seen Elizabeth "Lizzie" O'Toole, it was all over for him in the falling-in-love department. His heart had been won perhaps even before he quite realized it. His mouth curled into a smile at the memory of seeing her for the first time. Her family had come from South Carolina. Jack had often wondered why the O'Tooles had moved to Cleveland, where there was no ocean, a lot less sun, a lot more snow and ice, and not a palm tree in sight. Later, he'd learned it was because of a job change for Lizzie's father.

She'd come into class that first day, tall, with long auburn hair and vibrant green eyes, her face already mature and lovely. They had started going together in high school and had never been separated since, except long enough for Jack to fight in two wars.

"Jack; Jack honey?"

Lizzie was crouched down in front of him. In her hand was a syringe. She was still beautiful, though her looks had taken on a fragile edge. There were dark circles under her eyes and recently stamped worry lines on her face. The glow had gone from her skin, and her body was harder, less supple than it had been. Jack was the one dying, but in a way she was too.

"It's time for your pain meds."

He nodded, and she shot the drugs directly into an access

line cut right below his collarbone. That way the medicine flowed directly into his bloodstream and started working faster. Fast was good when the pain felt like every nerve in his body was being incinerated.

After she finished, Lizzie sat and hugged him. The doctors had a long name for what was wrong with him, one that Jack still could not pronounce or even spell. It was rare, they had said; one in a million. When he'd asked about his odds of survival, the docs had looked at each other before one finally answered.

"There's really nothing we can do. I'm sorry."

"Do the things you've always wanted to do," another had advised him, "but never had the chance."

"I have three kids and a mortgage," Jack had shot back, still reeling from this sudden death sentence. "I don't have the luxury of filling out some end-of-life bucket list."

"How long?" he'd finally asked, though part of him didn't really want to know.

"You're young and strong," said one. "And the disease is in its early stages."

Jack had survived the Taliban and Al-Qaeda. He could maybe hold on and see his oldest child graduate from college. "So how long?" he'd asked again.

The doctor said, "Six months. Maybe eight if you're lucky."

Jack did not feel very lucky.

He vividly remembered the morning he started feeling not quite right. It was an ache in his forearm and a stab of pain in his right leg. He was a building contractor by trade, so aches and pains were to be expected. But things soon carried to a new level. His limbs would grow tired from three hours of physical labor as opposed to ten. The stabs of pain became more frequent, and his balance began to deteriorate. His back finally couldn't make it up the ladder with the stacks of shingles. Then it hurt to carry his youngest son around after ten minutes. Then the fire in his nerves started, and his legs felt like an old man's. And one morning he woke up and his lungs were like balloons filled with water. Everything had accelerated after that, as though his body had simply given way to whatever was invading it.

His youngest child, Jack Jr., whom everyone called Jackie, toddled in and climbed on his dad's lap, resting his head against his father's sunken chest. Jackie's hair was long and inky black, curled up at the ends. His eyes were the color of toast; his thick eyebrows nearly met in the middle, like a burly woolen thread. Jackie had been their little surprise. Their other kids were much older.

Jack slowly slid his arm around his two-year-old son. Chubby fingers gripped his forearm, and warm breath touched his skin. It felt like the pierce of needles, but Jack simply gritted his teeth and didn't move his arm because there wouldn't be many more of these embraces. He slowly turned his head and looked out the window, where the snow was steadily falling. South Carolina and palm trees had nothing on Cleveland when it came to the holidays. It was truly beautiful.

He took his wife's hand.

"Christmas," Jack said in a wheezy voice. "I'll be there."

"Promise?" said Lizzie, her voice beginning to crack.

"Promise."

2

Jack awoke, looked around, and didn't know where he was. He could feel nothing, wasn't even sure if he was still breathing.

Am I dead? Was this it?

"Pop-pop," said Jackie as he slid next to his father on the bed. Jack turned and saw the chubby cheeks and light brown eyes.

Jack stroked his son's hair. Good, thick strands, like he used to have before the disease had stolen that too. Curious, Jackie tried to pull out the oxygen line from his father's nose, but he redirected his son's hand and cupped it with his own.

Lizzie walked in with his meds and shot them into the access line. An IV drip took care of Jack's nutrition and hydration needs. Solid foods were beyond him now.

"I just dropped the kids off at school," she told him.

"Mikki?" said Jack.

Lizzie made a face. Their daughter, Michelle, would be turning sixteen next summer, and her rebellious streak had been going strong since she'd become a teenager. She was into playing her guitar and working on her music, wearing junky clothes, sneaking out at night, and ignoring the books. "At least she showed up for the math test. I suppose actually passing it would've been asking too much. On the bright side, she received an A in music theory."

Jackie got down and ran into the other room, probably for a toy. Jack watched him go with an unwieldy mixture of pride and sorrow. He would never see his son as a man. He would never even see him start kindergarten. That cut against the natural order of things. But it was what it was.

Jack had experienced an exceptionally long phase of denial after being told he had little time left. That was partially because he had always been a survivor. A rocky childhood and two wars had not done him in, so he had initially felt confident that despite the doctors' fatal verdict, his disease was beatable. As time went by, however, and his body continued to fail, it had become clear that this battle was not winnable. It had reached a point where making the most of his time left was more important to him than trying to beat his head against an impenetrable wall. Most significantly, he wanted his kids' memories of his final days to be as positive as possible. Jack had concluded that if he had to die prematurely, that was about as good a way to do so as there was. It beat being depressed and making everyone else around him miserable, waiting for him to die.

Before he'd gotten sick, Jack had talked to his daughter many times about making good life choices, about the importance of school, but nothing seemed to make a difference to the young woman. There was a clear disconnect now between father and daughter. When she'd been a little girl, Mikki had unconditionally loved her dad, wanted to be around him all the time. Now he rarely saw her. To her, it seemed to Jack, he might as well have been already dead.

"Mikki seems lost around me," he said slowly.

Lizzie sat next to him, held his hand. "She's scared and confused, honey. Some of it has to do with her age. Most of it has to do with..."

"Me." Jack couldn't look at her when he made this admission.

"She and I have talked about it. Well, I talked and she didn't say much. She's a smart kid, but she really doesn't understand why this is happening, Jack. And her defense mechanism is to just detach herself from it. It's not the healthiest way to cope with things, though."

"I can understand," said Jack.

She looked at him. "Because of your dad?"

He nodded and rubbed her hand with his fingers, his eyes moistening as he remembered his father's painful death. He took several long pulls on the oxygen. "If I could change things, I would, Lizzie."

She rested her body next to his, wrapped her arms around his shoulders, and kissed him. When she spoke, her voice was husky and seemed right on the edge of failing. "Jack, this is hard on everyone. But it's hardest on you. You have been so brave; no one could have handled—" She couldn't continue. Lizzie laid her head next to his and wept softly. Jack held her with what little strength he had left.

"I love you, Lizzie. No matter what happens, nothing will ever change that."

He'd been sleeping in the hospital bed because he couldn't make it up the stairs to their bedroom even with assistance. He'd fought against that the hardest because as his life dwindled away he had desperately wanted to feel Lizzie's warm body against his. It was another piece of his life taken from him, like he was being dismantled, brick by brick.

And I am, brick by brick.

After a few minutes, she composed herself and wiped her eyes. "Cory is playing the Grinch in the class play at the school on Christmas Eve, remember?"

Jack nodded. "I remember."

"I'll film it for you."

Cory was the middle child, twelve years old and the ham in the family.

Jack smiled and said, "Grinch!"

Lizzie smiled back, then said, "I've got a conference call in an hour, and then I'll be in the kitchen working after I give Jackie his breakfast."

She'd become a telecommuter when Jack had gotten ill. When she had to go out, a neighbor would come over or Lizzie's parents would stop by to help.

After Lizzie left, Jack sat up, slowly reached under the pillow, and pulled out the calendar and pen. He looked at the dates in December, all of which had been crossed out up to December twentieth. Over three decades of life, marriage, fatherhood, defending his country, and working hard, it had come down to him marking off the few days left. He looked out the window and to the street beyond. The snow had stopped, but he'd heard on the news that another wintry blast was expected, with more ice than snow.

There was a knock at the door, and a few moments later Sammy Duvall appeared. He was in his early sixties, with longish salt-and-pepper hair and a trim beard. Sammy was as tall as Jack, but leaner, though his arms and shoulders bulged with muscles from all the manual labor he'd done. He was far stronger than most men half his age and tougher than anyone Jack had ever met. He'd spent twenty years in the military and fought in Vietnam and done some things after that around the world that he never talked about. A first-rate, self-taught carpenter and all-around handyman, Sammy was the reason Jack had joined the service. After Jack left the army, he and Sammy had started the contracting business. Lacking a family of his own, Sammy had adopted the Armstrongs.

The military vets shared a glance, and then Sammy looked over all the equipment helping to keep his friend alive. He shook his head slightly and his mouth twitched. This was as close as stoic Sammy ever came to showing emotion.

"How's work?" Jack asked, and then he took a long pull of oxygen.

"No worries. Stuff's getting done and the money's coming in."

Jack knew that Sammy had been completing all the jobs pretty much on his own and then bringing all the payments to Lizzie. "At least half of that money is yours, Sammy. You're doing all the work."

"I got my Uncle Sam pension, and it's more than I need. That changes, I'll let you know."

Sammy lived in a converted one-car garage with his enormous Bernese mountain dog, Sam Jr. His needs were simple, his wants apparently nonexistent.

Sammy combed Jack's hair and even gave him a shave. Then the friends talked for a while. At least Sammy said a few words and Jack listened. The rest of the time they sat in silence. Jack didn't mind; just being with Sammy made him feel better.

After Sammy left, Jack lifted the pen and crossed out December twenty-first. That was being optimistic, Jack knew, since the day had really just begun. He put the calendar and pen away.

And then it happened.

He couldn't breathe. He sat up, convulsing, but that just made it worse. He could feel his heart racing, his lungs squeezing, his face first growing red and then pale as the oxygen left his body and nothing replenished it.

December twenty-first, he thought, *my last day.*

"Pop-pop?"

Jack looked up to see his son holding the end of the oxygen line that attached to the converter. He held it up higher, as though he were giving it back to his dad.

"Jackie!"

A horrified Lizzie appeared in the doorway, snatched the line from her son's hand, and rushed to reattach the oxygen line to the converter. A few moments later, the oxygen started to flow into the line and Jack fell back on the bed, breathing hard, trying to fill his lungs.

Lizzie raced past her youngest son and was by Jack's side in an instant. "Oh my God, Jack, oh my God." Her whole body was trembling.

He held up his hand to show he was okay.

Lizzie whirled around and snapped, "That was bad, Jackie, bad."

Jackie's face crumbled, and he started to bawl.

She snatched up Jackie and carried him out. The little boy was struggling to free himself, staring at Jack over her shoulder, reaching his arms out to his father. His son's look was pleading.

"Pop-pop," wailed Jackie.

The tears trickled down Jack's face as his son's cries faded away. But then Jack heard Lizzie sobbing and pictured her crying her heart out and wondering what the hell she'd done to deserve all this.

Sometimes, Jack thought, living was far harder than dying.

3

Jack awoke from a nap late the next day in time to see his daughter opening the front door, guitar case in hand. He motioned to her to come see him. She closed the door and dutifully trudged to his room.

Mikki had auburn hair like her mother's. However, she had dyed it several different colors, and Jack had no idea what it would be called now. She was shooting up in height, her legs long and slender and her hips and bosom filling out. Though she acted like she was totally grown up now, her face was caught in that time thread that was firmly past the little-girl stage but not yet a woman. She would be a junior in high school next year. Where had the time gone?

"Yeah, Dad?" she said, not looking at him.

He thought about what to say. In truth, they didn't have much to talk about. Even when he'd been healthy, their lives lately had taken separate paths. *That was my fault*, he thought. *Not hers.*

"Your A." He took a long breath, tried to smile.

She smirked. "Right. Music theory. My only one. I'm sure Mom told you that too. Right?"

"Still an A."

"Thanks for mentioning it." She looked at the floor, an awkward expression on her features. "Look, Dad, I gotta go. People are waiting. We're rehearsing."

She was in a band, Jack knew, though he couldn't recall the name of it just now.

"Okay, be careful."

She turned to leave, and then hesitated. Her fingers fiddled with the guitar case handle. She glanced back but still didn't meet his gaze. "Just so you know, when you were asleep I duct taped your oxygen line onto the converter so it can't be pulled off again. Jackie didn't know what he was doing. Mom didn't have to give him such a hard time."

Jack gathered more oxygen and said, "Thanks."

A part of him wanted her to look at him, and another part of him didn't. He didn't want to see pity in her eyes. Her big, strong father reduced to this. He wondered whom she would marry. Where would they live? Would it be far from Cleveland?

Will she visit my grave?

"Mikki?"

"Dad, I really got to go. I'm already late."

"I hope you have a great...day, sweetie."

He thought he saw her lips quiver for a moment, but then she turned and left. A few moments later, the front door closed behind her. He peered out the window. She hopped across the snow and climbed into a car that one of her guy friends was driving. Jack had never felt more disconnected from life.

After dinner that night, Cory, in full costume, performed

his Grinch role for his father. Cory was a chunky twelve-year-old, though his long feet and lanky limbs promised height later. His hair was a mop of brown cowlicks, the same look Jack had had at that age. Lizzie's parents had come over for dinner and to watch the show and had brought Lizzie's grandmother. Cecilia was a stylish lady in her eighties who used a walker and had her own portable oxygen tank. She'd grown up and lived most of her life in South Carolina. She'd come to live with her daughter in Cleveland after her husband died and her health started failing. Her laugh was infectious and her speech was mellifluous, like water trickling over smooth rocks.

Cecilia joked that Jack and she should start their own oxygen business since they had so much of the stuff. She was dying too, only not quite as fast as Jack. This probably would also be her last Christmas, but she had lived a good long life and had apparently made peace with her fate. She was uniformly upbeat, talking about her life in the South, the tea parties and the debutante balls, sneaking smokes and drinking hooch behind the local Baptist church at night. Yet every once in a while Jack would catch her staring at him, and he could sense the sadness the old lady held in her heart for his plight.

After Cory finished his performance, Cecilia leaned down and whispered into Jack's ear. "It's Christmas. The time of miracles." This was not the first time she'd said this. Yet for some reason Jack's spirits sparked for a moment.

But then the doctor's pronouncement sobered this feeling.

Six months, eight if you're lucky.

Science, it seemed, always trumped hope.

At eleven o'clock he heard the front door open, and Mikki slipped in. Jack thought he saw her glance his way, but she didn't come into the den. When Jack was healthy they had kept a strict watch over her comings and goings. And for months after he'd become ill, Lizzie had kept up that vigil. Now she barely had time to shower or snatch a meal, and Mikki had taken advantage of this lack of oversight to do as she pleased.

When everyone was asleep, Jack reached under his pillow and took out his pen. This time he wasn't crossing off dates on a calendar. He took out the piece of paper and carefully unfolded it. He spread it out on a book he kept next to the bed. Pen poised over the paper, he began to write. It took him a long time, at least an hour to write less than one page. His handwriting was poor because he was so weak, but his thoughts were clear. Eventually there would be seven of these letters. One for each day of the last week of his life, the date neatly printed at the top of the page—or as neatly as Jack's trembling hand could manage. Each letter began with "Dear Lizzie," and ended with "Love, Jack." In the body of the letter he did his best to convey to his wife all that he felt for her. That though he would no longer be alive, he would always be there for her.

These letters, he'd come to realize, were the most important thing he would ever do in his life. And he labored to make sure every word was the right one. Finished, he put the letter in an envelope, marked it with a number, and slipped it in the nightstand next to his bed.

He would write the seventh and last letter on Christmas Eve, after everyone had gone to bed.

Jack turned his head and looked out the window. Even in the darkness he could see the snow coming down hard.

He now knew how a condemned man felt though he had committed no crime. The time left to him was precious. But there was only so much he could do with it.

4

Jack marked off December twenty-fourth on his calendar. He had one letter left to write. It would go into the drawer with the number seven written on the envelope. After he was gone, Lizzie would read them, and Jack hoped they would provide some comfort to her. Actually, writing them had provided some comfort for Jack. It made him focus on what was really important in life.

    Jack's mother-in-law, Bonnie, had stayed with him while the rest of the family went to see Cory in the school play. Lizzie had put her foot down and made Mikki go as well. Bonnie had made a cup of tea and had settled herself down with a book, while Jack was perched in a chair by the window waiting for the van to pull up with Lizzie and the others.

    Sammy came by, stomping snow off his boots and tugging off his knit cap to let his long, shaggy hair fall out. He sat next to Jack and handed him a gift. When Jack opened it he looked up in surprise.

It was five passes to Disney World, good for the upcoming year.

Sammy gripped Jack by the shoulder. "I expect you and the family to get there."

Jack glanced over to see Bonnie shaking her head in mild reproach. Bonnie O'Toole was not a woman who believed in miracles. Yet Jack knew the man well enough to realize that Sammy fully believed he would use those tickets. He patted Sammy on the arm, smiled, and nodded.

After Sammy left, Jack glanced at the tickets. He appreciated his friend's confidence, but Jack was the only one who knew how close he was to the end. He had fought as hard as he could. He didn't want to die and leave his family, but he couldn't live like this either. His mind focused totally on the last letter he would ever compose. He knew when his pen had finished writing the words and the paper was safely in the envelope, he could go peacefully. It was a small yet obviously important benchmark. But he would wait until Christmas was over, when presents were opened and a new day had dawned. It was some comfort to know that he had a little control left over his fate, even if it was simply the specific timing of his passing.

He saw the headlights of the oncoming van flick across the window. Bonnie went to open the front door, and Jack watched anxiously from the window as the kids piled out of the vehicle. Lizzie's dad led them up the driveway, carrying Jackie because it was so slick out. The snow was still coming down, although the latest weather report had said that with the temperatures staying where they were, it was more ice than snow at this point, making driving treacherous.

His gaze held on Lizzie as she closed up the van, and then

turned, not toward the house, but away from it. Jack hadn't noticed the person approach her because his attention had been on his wife. The man came into focus; it was Bill Miller. They'd all gone to school together. Bill had blocked on the line for Jack the quarterback. He'd attended Jack and Lizzie's wedding. Bill was single, in the plumbing business, and doing well.

Jack pressed his face to the glass when he saw Bill draw close to his wife. Lizzie slipped her purse over her shoulder and swiped the hair out of her eyes. They were so close to one another, Jack couldn't find even a sliver of darkness between them. His breath was fogging the glass, he was so near it. He watched Bill lean in toward Lizzie. He saw his wife rise up on tiptoe. And then Bill staggered back as Lizzie slapped him across the face. Though he was weak, Jack reared up in his chair as though he wanted to go and defend his wife's honor. Yet there was no need. Bill Miller stumbled off into the darkness as Lizzie turned away and marched toward the house.

A minute later he heard Lizzie come in, knocking snow off her boots.

Lizzie strode into the den, first pulling off her scarf and then rubbing her hands together because of the cold. Her face was flushed, and she didn't look at him like she normally did. "Time for the presents; then Mom and Dad are going to take off. They'll be back tomorrow, okay, sweetie? It'll be a great day."

"How's your hand?"

She glanced at him. "What?"

He pointed to the window. "I think Bill's lucky he's still conscious."

"He was also drunk, or I don't think he would've tried that. Idiot."

Jack started to say something, but then stopped and looked away. Lizzie quickly picked up on this and sat next to him.

"Jack, you don't think that Bill and I—"

He gripped her hand. "Of course not. Don't be crazy." He kissed her cheek.

"So what then? Something's bothering you."

"You're young, and you have three kids."

"That I get." She attempted a smile that flickered out when she saw the earnest look on his face.

"You need somebody in your life."

"I don't want to talk about this." She tried to rise, but he held her back.

"Lizzie, look at me. Look at me."

She turned to face him, her eyes glimmering with tears.

"You will find someone else."

"No."

"You will."

"I've got a full life. I've got no room for—"

"Yes, you do."

"Do we have to talk about this now? It's Christmas Eve."

"I can't be picky about timing, Lizzie," he said, a little out of breath.

Her face flushed. "I didn't mean that. I...you look better tonight. Maybe...the doctors—"

"No, Lizzie. No," he said firmly. "That can't happen. We're past that stage, honey." He sucked on his air, his gaze resolutely on her.

She put a hand to her eyes. "If I think about things like that, then it means, I don't want to...You might..."

He held her. "Things will work out all right. Just take it

slow. And be happy." He made her look at him, and he brushed the tears from her eyes. He took a long pull on his oxygen and managed a grin. "And for God's sake, don't pick Bill."

She laughed. And then it turned into a sob as he held her.

When they pulled away a few moments later, Lizzie wiped her nose with a tissue and said, "I was actually thinking about next summer. And I wanted to talk to you about it."

Jack's heart was buoyed by the fact that she still sought out his opinion. "What about it?"

"You'll probably think it's silly."

"Tell me."

"I was thinking I would take the kids to the Palace."

"The Palace? You haven't been back there since—"

"I know. I know. I just think it's time. It's in bad shape from what I heard. I know it needs a lot of work. But just for one summer it should be fine."

"I know how hard that was for you."

She reached in her pocket and pulled out a photo. She showed it to Jack. "Haven't looked at that in years. Do you remember me showing it to you?"

It was a photo of the O'Tooles when the kids were all little.

"That's Tillie next to you. Your twin sister."

"Mom said she never could tell us apart."

Jack had to sit back against his pillow and drew several long breaths on his line while Lizzie patiently waited.

Finally he said, "She was five when she died?"

"Almost six. Meningitis. Nothing the doctors could do." She glanced briefly at Jack, and then looked away. Her unspoken thought could have been, *Just like you.*

"I remember my parents telling me that Tillie had gone to

Heaven." She smiled at the same time a couple of tears slid down her cheeks. "There's an old lighthouse on the property down there. It was so beautiful."

"I remember you telling me about it. Your grandmother... still owns the Palace, right?"

"Yes. I was going to ask her if it would be all right if we went down there this summer."

"The O'Tooles exchanging the sunny ocean for cold Cleveland?" He coughed several times, and Lizzie went to adjust his air level. When she did so he started breathing easier.

She said, "Well, I think leaving the Palace was because of me."

"What do you mean?"

"I never really told you about this before, and maybe I'd forgotten it myself. But I've been thinking about Tillie lately." She faltered.

"Lizzie, please tell me."

She turned to face him. "When my parents told me my sister had gone to Heaven, I...I wanted to find her. I didn't really understand that she was dead. I knew that Heaven was in the sky. So I started looking for, well, looking for Heaven to find Tillie."

"You were just a little kid."

"I would go up in the lighthouse. Back then it still worked. And I'd look for Heaven, for Tillie really, with the help of the light." She paused and let out a little sob. "Never found either one."

Jack held her. "It's okay, Lizzie; it's okay," he said softly.

She wiped her eyes on his shirt and said, "It became a sort of obsession, I guess. I don't know why. But every day that went by and I couldn't find her, it just hurt so bad. And when

I got older, my parents told me that Tillie was dead. Well, it didn't help much." She paused. "I can't believe I never told you all this before. But I guess I was a little ashamed."

His wife's distress was taking a toll on Jack. He breathed deeply for several seconds before saying, "You lost your twin. You were just a little kid."

"By the time we moved to Ohio, I knew I would never find her by looking at the sky. I knew she was gone. And the lighthouse wasn't working anymore anyway. But I think my parents, my mom especially, wanted to get me away from the place. She didn't think it was good for me. But it was just... silly."

"It was what you were feeling, Lizzie." He touched his chest. "Here."

"I know. So I thought I'd go back there. See the place. Let the kids experience how I grew up." She looked at him.

"Great idea," Jack gasped.

She rubbed his shoulder. "You might enjoy it too. You could really fix the place up. Even make the lighthouse work again." It was so evident she desperately wanted to believe this could actually happen.

He attempted a smile. "Yeah."

The looks on both their faces were clear despite the hopeful words.

Jack would never see the Palace.

5

Later that night his father-in-law helped Jack into a wheelchair and rolled him into the living room, where their little tree stood. It was silver tinsel with blue and red ornaments. Jack usually got a real tree for Christmas, but not this year of course.

The kids had hot chocolate and some snacks. Mikki even played a few carols on her guitar, though she looked totally embarrassed doing so. Cory told his dad about the play, and Lizzie bustled around making sure everyone had everything they needed. Then she played the DVD for Jack so he could see the performance for himself. Finally his in-laws prepared to leave. The ice was getting worse and they wanted to get home, they said. Lizzie's father helped Jack into bed.

At the front door Lizzie gave them each a hug. Jack heard Bonnie tell her daughter to just hang in there. It was always darkest before the dawn.

"The kids are the most important thing," said her dad. "Afterward, we'll be right here for you."

Next, Jack heard Lizzie say, "I was thinking about talking to Cee," referring to her grandmother Cecilia.

"About what?" Bonnie said quickly, in a wary tone.

"Next summer I was thinking of taking the kids to the Palace, maybe for the entire summer break. I wanted to make sure Cee would be okay with that."

There were a few moments of silence; then Bonnie said, "The Palace! Lizzie, you know—"

"Mom, don't."

"This is not something you need, certainly not right now. It's too painful."

"That was a long time ago," Lizzie said quietly. "It's different now. It's okay. I'm okay. I have been for a long time, actually, if you'd ever taken the time to notice."

"It's never long enough," her mother shot back.

"Let's not discuss it tonight. Not tonight," said Lizzie.

After her parents left, Jack listened as his wife's footsteps came his way. Lizzie appeared in the doorway. "That was a nice Christmas Eve."

He nodded his head dumbly, his gaze never leaving her face. The tick of the clock next to his bed pounded fiercely in Jack's head.

"Don't let her talk you out of going to the Palace, Lizzie. Stick to your guns."

"My mother can be a little..."

"I know. But promise me you'll go?"

She nodded, smiled. "Okay, I promise. Do you need anything else?" she asked.

Jack looked at the clock and motioned to the access line below his collarbone, where his pain meds were administered.

"Oh my gosh. Your meds. Okay." She started to the small

cabinet in the corner where she kept his medications. But then Lizzie stopped, looking slightly panicked.

"I forgot to pick up your prescription today. The play and...I forgot to get them." She checked her watch. "They're still open. I'll go get them now."

"Don't go. I'm okay without the meds."

"It'll just take a few minutes. I'll be back in no time. And then it'll just be you and me. I want to talk to you some more about next summer."

"Lizzie, you don't have to—"

But she was already gone.

The front door slammed. The van started up and raced down the street.

Later Jack woke, confused. He turned slowly to find Mikki dozing in the chair next to his bed. She must have come downstairs while he was asleep. He looked out the window. There were streams of light whizzing past his house. For a moment he had the absurd notion that Santa Claus had just arrived. Then he tried to sit up because he heard it. Sounds on the roof.

Reindeer? What the hell was going on?

The sounds came again. Only now he realized they weren't on the roof. Someone was pounding on the front door.

"Mom? Dad?" It was Cory. His voice grew closer. His head poked in the den. He was dressed in boxer shorts and a T-shirt and looked nervous. "There's someone at the door."

By now Mikki had woken. She stretched and saw Cory standing there.

"Someone's at the front door," her brother said again.

Mikki looked at her dad. He was staring out at the swirl of lights. It was like a spaceship was landing on their front lawn. *In Cleveland?* Jack thought he was hallucinating. Yet when he looked at Mikki, it was clear that she saw the lights too. Jack raised a hand and pointed at the front door. He nodded to his daughter.

Looking scared, she hurried to the door and opened it. The man was big, dressed in a uniform, and had a gun on his belt. He looked cold, tired, and uncomfortable. Mostly uncomfortable.

"Is your dad home?" he asked Mikki. She backed away and pointed toward the den. The police officer stamped off his boots and stepped in. The squeak of his gun belt sounded like a scream in miniature. He walked where Mikki was pointing, saw Jack in the bed with the lines hooked to him, and muttered something under his breath. He looked at Mikki and Cory. "Can he understand? I mean, is he real sick?"

Mikki said, "He's sick, but he can understand."

The cop drew next to the bed. Jack lifted himself up on his elbows. He was gasping. In his anxiety, his withered lungs were demanding so much air the converter couldn't keep up.

The officer swallowed hard. "Mr. Armstrong?" He paused as Jack stared up at him. "I'm afraid there's been an accident involving your wife."

6

Jack sat strapped into a wheelchair staring up at his wife's coffin. Mikki and Cory sat next to him. Jackie had been deemed too young to attend his mother's funeral; he was being taken care of by a neighbor. The priest came down and gave Jack and his children holy communion. Jack nearly choked on the host but finally managed to swallow it. Ironically, it was the first solid food he'd had in months.

At my wife's funeral.

The weather was cold, the sky puffy with clouds. The wind cleaved the thickest coats. The roads were still iced and treacherous. They'd been driven to the cemetery in the funeral home sedan designated for family members. His father-in-law, Fred, rode up front, next to the driver, while he and the kids were squeezed in the back with Bonnie. She had barely uttered a word since learning her youngest daughter had been instantly killed when her van ran a red light and was broadsided by an oncoming snowplow.

The graveside service was mercifully brief; the priest seemed to understand that if he didn't hustle things along, some of the older people might not survive the event.

Jack looked over at Mikki. She'd pinned her hair back and put on a black dress that hung below her knees; she sat staring vacantly at the coffin. Cory had not looked at the casket even once. As a final act, Jack was wheeled up to the coffin. He put his hand on top of it, mumbled a few words, and sat back, feeling totally disoriented. He had played this scene out in his head a hundred times. Only he was in the box and it was Lizzie out here saying good-bye. Nothing about this was right. He felt like he was staring at the world upside down.

"I'll be with you soon, Lizzie," he said in a halting voice. The words seemed hollow, forced, but he could think of nothing else to say.

As he started to collapse, a strong hand gripped him.

"It's okay, Jack. We'll get you back to the car now." He looked up into the face of Sammy Duvall.

Sammy proceeded to maneuver him to the sedan in record time. Before closing the door, he put a reassuring hand on Jack's shoulder. "I'll always be there for you, buddy."

They were driven home, the absence of Lizzie in their midst a festering wound that had no possible healing ointment. Jackie was brought home, and people stopped by with plates of food. An impromptu wake was held; devastated folks chatted in low tones. More than once Jack caught people gazing at him, no doubt thinking, *My God, what now?*

Jack was thinking the same thing. *What now?*

Two hours later the house was empty except for Jack, the kids, and his in-laws. The children instantly disappeared. Minutes later Jack could hear guitar strumming coming from Mikki's bedroom, the tunes melancholy and abbreviated.

Cory and Jackie shared a bedroom, but no sound was coming from them. Jack could imagine Cory quietly sobbing, while a confused Jackie attempted to comfort him.

Bonnie and Fred O'Toole looked as disoriented as Jack felt. They had signed on to help their healthy daughter transition with her kids to being a widow and then getting on with her life. Without the buffer that Lizzie had been, Jack could focus now on the fact that his relationship with his in-laws had been largely superficial.

Fred was a big man with a waistline large enough to portend a host of health problems down the road. He tended to defer to his wife in all things other than sports and selling cars, which was the line of work that had brought him to Cleveland. He was a man who would prefer to look at the floor rather than in your eye, unless he was trying to sell you the latest Ford F-150. Then he could be animated enough, at least until you signed on the dotted line and the financing cleared.

Bonnie was shorter than her daughter. The mother of four grown children, she was now well into her sixties, and her figure had lost its shape. Her waist and hips had turned into a solid wall of flesh. Her hair was white, cut short and rather brutally, and her eyeglasses filled most of her square face. Fred kept sighing, rubbing his big hands over his pressed suit pants, as though attempting to rub some dirt off his fingers. Bonnie, who had kept on her black outfit, was sitting very still on the couch, her gaze aimed at a corner of the ceiling but apparently not actually registering on it.

Fred sighed again, and this seemed to rouse Bonnie.

"Well," she said. "Well," she said again. Fred eyed her, as did Jack.

She looked over and gave Jack a quick glance that was undecipherable.

Then came more silence.

Finally, a few minutes later Fred helped Jack get into bed, and then he and Bonnie went up to Jack and Lizzie's room. They would be staying here full-time until other arrangements were made.

Jack lay in the dark staring at the ceiling. The days after Lizzie had died had been far worse than when he'd received his own death sentence. His life ending he'd accepted. Hers he had not. Could not. Mikki and Cory had barely spoken since the police officer had come with the awful news. Jackie had wandered the house looking for his mother and crying when he couldn't find her.

Jack slid open the drawer of the nightstand and took out the six letters. He obviously had not written one on Christmas Eve. In these pages he had poured out his heart to the person he cherished above all others. As he looked down at the pages, wasted pages now, his spirits sank even lower.

Jack rarely cried. He'd seen fellow soldiers die horribly in the Middle East, watched his father perish from lung cancer, and attended the funeral of his wife. He had shed a few tears at each of these events, but not for long and always in a controlled way. Now, staring at the ceiling, thinking a thousand anguished thoughts, he did weep quietly as it finally struck him that Lizzie was really gone.

7

The next morning Bonnie took charge. She came to see Jack with Fred in tow. "This won't be easy, Jack," she cautioned, "but we really don't have much time." She squared her shoulders and seemed to attempt a sympathetic look. "The children of course come first. I've talked to Becky and also to Frances several times."

Frances and Becky were Lizzie's older sisters, who lived on the West Coast. The only brother, Fred Jr., was on active military duty, stationed in Korea. He had not been able to make it to the funeral.

"Becky can take Jack Jr., and Frances has agreed to take Cory. That just leaves Michelle." Bonnie had never called her Mikki.

"*Just* Michelle?" said Jack.

Bonnie looked momentarily taken aback. When she spoke, her tone was less authoritative and more conciliatory. "This is hard on all of us. You know Fred and I had planned to move to Tempe next year after things were more settled with Lizzie and the kids. We were going this year, but then you got sick. And we stayed on, because that's what families do in those situations. We tried to do our best, for all of you."

"We couldn't have gotten on without you."

This remark seemed to please her, and she smiled and gripped his hand. "Thank you. That means a lot."

She continued, "We'll take Michelle with us. And because Jack Jr. will be in Portland with Becky and Cory in LA with Frances, they will all at least be on or near the West Coast. I'm sure they'll see each other fairly often. It's really the only workable solution that I can see."

"When?" Jack asked.

"The Christmas break is almost over, and we think we can get all the kids transitioned in the next month. We decided it was no good waiting until the fall, for a number of reasons. It'll be better all around for them."

"For you too," said Jack. As soon as he said it, he wished he hadn't.

Bonnie's conciliatory look faded. "Yes, us too. Jack, we're taking care of all the children. They'll all have homes with people they love and who love them. You can't have an issue with that."

Jack touched his chest. "And me?"

"Yes, well . . . I was getting to that, of course." She stood but didn't look at him. Instead, she stared at a spot right over his head. "Hospice. I'll arrange all the details." Now she looked at him, and Jack had to admit, she didn't look happy about this. "If we could take care of you, Jack, in the time that you have left, we would. But we're not young anymore, and taking in Michelle and all . . ."

Fred added, "And Lizzie dying."

Jack and Bonnie stared at him for an instant. Each seemed surprised the man was still there, much less that he had spoken. Bonnie said, "Yes, and Lizzie not...well, yes."

Jack drew a long breath and mustered his strength. He said, "*My* kids, *my* decision."

Fred looked at Jack and then over at his wife. Bonnie, though, had eyes only for Jack.

She said, "You can't care for the kids. You can't even take care of yourself. Lizzie did everything. And now she's gone." Her eyes glittered; her tone was harsh once more.

"Still my decision," he said defiantly. He had no idea where he was going with this, but the words had tumbled from his mouth.

"Who else will take three kids? If we do nothing, the matter is out of our hands and they'll go into foster care. They'll probably never see each other again. Is that what you want?" She sat down next to him, her face inches from his. "Is that really what you want?"

He sucked in some more air, his resolve weakening along with his energy. "Why can't I stay here?" he said. Another long inhalation. "Until the kids leave?"

"Hospice is much cheaper. I'm sorry if that sounds callous, but money is tight. Tough decisions have to be made."

"So I die alone?"

Bonnie looked at her husband. Clearly, from his expression, Fred sided with Jack on this point.

Fred said, "Doesn't seem right, Bonnie. Taking the family away like that. After all that's happened."

Jack shot his father-in-law an appreciative look.

Bonnie fidgeted. "I've been thinking about that, actually." She sighed. "Jack, I'm not trying to be heartless. I care about you. I don't want to do any of this." She paused. "But they just lost their mother." Bonnie paused but didn't continue.

It slowly dawned on Jack, what she was getting at.

"And to see me die too?"

Bonnie spread her hands. "But you're right. You are their father. So I'll leave it up to you. You tell me what to do, Jack, and I'll do it. We can keep the kids here until...until you pass. They can attend your funeral, and then we can make the move. They can be with you until the end." She looked at Fred, but he apparently had nothing to add.

Jack was surprised, then, when Fred said, "Anything you want, Jack, we'll take care of it. Okay?"

Jack was silent for so long that Bonnie finally rose, clutched her sweater more tightly around her shoulders and said, "Fine, we can have an in-home nursing service come. Lizzie had some life insurance. We can use those funds to—"

"Take the kids."

Fred and Bonnie looked at him. Jack said again, "Take the kids."

"Are you sure?" asked Bonnie. She seemed to be sincere, but Jack knew this way would take a lot of the pressure off her.

He struggled to say, "As soon as you can." *It won't be long,* Jack thought. *Not now. Not with Lizzie gone.*

When she turned to leave, Bonnie froze. Mikki and Cory were standing there.

Bonnie said nervously, "I thought you were upstairs."

"You don't think this concerns us?" Mikki said bluntly.

"I think the adults need to make the decisions for what's best for the children."

"I'm not a child!" Mikki snapped.

Bonnie said, "Michelle, this is hard on all of us. We're just trying to do the best we can under the circumstances." She paused and added, "You lost your mother and I lost my daughter." Bonnie's voice cracked as she added, "None of this is easy, honey."

Mikki gazed over at her father. He could feel the anger emanating from his oldest child. "You're all losers!" yelled Mikki. She turned and rushed from the house, slamming the door behind her.

Bonnie shook her head and rubbed at her eyes before looking back at Jack. "This is a big sacrifice, for all of us." She left the room, with Fred obediently trailing her. Cory just stood there staring at his dad.

"Cor," he began. But his son turned and ran back upstairs.

A minute went by as Jack lay there, feeling like a turtle toppled on its back.

"Jack?"

When he looked over, Bonnie was standing a few feet from his bed holding something in her hand.

"The police dropped this off yesterday." She held it up. It was the bag with Jack's prescription meds. "They found it in the van. It was very unfortunate that Lizzie had to go back out that night. If she hadn't, she'd obviously be alive today."

"I told her not to go."

"But she did. For you," she replied.

The tears started to slide down her cheeks as she hurried from the room.

8

The room was small but clean. That wasn't the problem. Jack had slept for months inside a shack with ten other infantrymen in the middle of a desert, where it was either too frigid or too hot. What Jack didn't like here were the sounds. Folks during their last days of life did not make pleasant noises. Coughs, gagging, painful cries—but mostly it was the moaning. It never ceased. Then there was the squeak of the gurney wheels as the body of someone who had passed was taken away, the room freshened up for the next terminal case on the waiting list.

Most patients here were elderly. Yet Jack wasn't the youngest person. There was a boy with final-stage leukemia two doors down. When Jack was being wheeled to his room he'd seen the little body in the bed: hairless head, vacant eyes, tubes all over him, barely breathing, just waiting for it to be over. His family would come every day; his mother was often here all the time. They would put on happy expressions when they were with him and then start bawling as soon as they left his side. Jack had witnessed this as they passed his doorway. All hunched over, weeping into their cupped hands. They were just waiting, too, for it to be over. And at the same time dreading when it would be.

Jack reached under his pillow and pulled out the calendar. January eleventh. He crossed it off. He had been here for five days. The average length of stay here, he'd heard, was three weeks. Without Lizzie, it would be three weeks too long.

He again reached under his pillow and pulled out the six now-crumpled envelopes with his letters to Lizzie inside them. He'd had Sammy bring them here from the house before it was listed for sale. He held them in his hands. The paper was splotched with his tears because he pulled them out and wept over them several times a day. What else did he have to do with his time? These letters now constituted a weight around his heart for a simple reason: Lizzie would never read them, never know what he was feeling in his last days of life. At the same time, it was the only thing allowing him to die with peace, with a measure of dignity. He put the letters away and just lay there, listening for the squeaks of the final gurney ride for another patient. They came with alarming regularity. Soon, he knew it would be his body on that stretcher.

He turned his head when the kids came in, followed by Fred. He was surprised to see Cecilia stroll in with her walker and portable oxygen tank resting in a burgundy sling. It was hard for her to go outside in the cold weather, yet she had done so for Jack. Jackie immediately climbed up on his dad's lap, while Cory sat on the bed. Arms folded defiantly over her chest, Mikki stood by the door, as far away from everyone as she could be. She had on faded jeans with the knees torn out, heavy boots, a sleeveless unzipped parka, and a black long-sleeve T-shirt that said, REMEMBER DARFUR. Her hair was now orange. The color contrasted sharply with the dark circles under her eyes.

Cory had been saying something that only now Jack focused on. His son said, "But, Dad, you'll be here and we'll be way out there."

"That's the way *Dad* apparently wants it," said Mikki sharply.

Jack turned to look at her. Father's and daughter's gazes locked until she finally looked away, with an eye roll tacked on.

Cory moved closer to him. "Look, I think the best thing we can do, Dad, is stay here with you. It just makes sense."

Jackie, who was struggling with potty training, slid to the side of the bed and got down holding his privates.

"Gramps," said Mikki, "Jackie has to go. And I'm not taking him this time."

Fred saw what Jackie was doing and scuttled him off to the bathroom down the hall.

As soon as he was gone, Jack said, "You have to go, Cor." He didn't look at Mikki when he added, "You all do."

"But we won't be together, Dad," said Cory. "We'll never see each other."

Cecilia, who'd been listening to all this, quietly spoke up. "I give you my word, Cory, that you will see your brother and sister early and often."

Mikki came forward. Her sullen look was gone, replaced with a defiant one. "Okay, but what about Dad? He just stays here alone? That's not fair."

Jack said, "I'll be with you. And your mom will too, in spirit," he added a little lamely.

"Mom is dead. She can't be with anyone," snapped Mikki.

"Mikki," said Cecilia reproachfully. "That's not necessary."

"Well, it's true. We don't need to be lied to. It's bad enough that I have to go and live with *them* in Arizona."

Tears filled Cory's eyes, and he started to sob quietly. Jack pulled him closer.

Jackie and Fred came back in, and the visit lasted another half hour. Cecilia was the last to leave. She looked back at Jack. "You'll never be alone, Jack. We all carry each other in our hearts."

Those words were nice, and heartfelt, he knew, but Jack Armstrong had never felt so alone as he did right now. He had a question, though.

"Cecilia?"

She turned back, perhaps surprised by the sudden urgency in his voice. "Yes, Jack?"

Jack gathered his breath and said, "Lizzie told me she wanted to take the kids to the Palace next summer."

Cecilia moved closer to him. "She told you that?" she asked. "The Palace? My God. After all this time."

"I know. But maybe...maybe the kids could go there sometime?"

Cecilia gripped his hand. "I'll see to it, Jack. I promise."

9

They all came in to visit Jack for the last time. They would be flying out later that day to their new homes. Bonnie was there, as was Fred. Cory and Jackie crowded around their father, hugging, kissing, and talking all at once to him.

Jack was lying in bed, dressed in a fresh gown. His face and body were gaunt; the machines keeping him comfortable until he passed were going full blast. He looked at each of his kids for what he knew would be the final time. He'd already instructed Bonnie to have him cremated. "No funeral," he'd told her. "I'm not putting the kids through that again."

"I'll call you as soon as I get there, Dad," said Cory, who wouldn't look away from his father.

"Me too!" chimed in Jackie.

Jack took several deep breaths as he prepared to do what had to be done. His kids would be gone forever in a few minutes, and he was determined to make these last moments as memorable and happy as possible.

"Got something for you," said Jack. He'd had Sammy bring the three boxes to him. He slowly took them from the cabinet next to his bed and handed one to Cory and one to Jackie. He held the last one and gazed at Mikki. "For you."

"What is it?" she asked, trying to seem disinterested, though he could tell her curiosity was piqued.

"Come see."

She sighed, strolled over, and took the box from her father.

"Open them," said Jack.

Cory and Jackie opened the boxes and looked down at the piece of metal with the purple ribbon attached.

Mikki's was different.

Fred said to her, "That's a Bronze Star. That's for heroism in combat. Your dad was a real hero. The other ones are Purple Hearts for being...well, hurt in battle," he finished, looking awkwardly at Cory and Jackie.

Jack said, "Open the box and think of me. Always be with you that way."

Even Bonnie seemed genuinely moved by this gesture, and she dabbed at her eyes with a tissue. But Jack wasn't looking at her. He was watching his daughter. She touched the medal carefully, and her mouth started to tremble. When she looked up and saw her dad watching her, she closed the box and quickly stuck it in her bag.

Cecilia was the last to leave. She sat next to him and patted his hand with her wrinkled one.

"How do you feel, Jack, really?"

"About dying or saying good-bye to my kids for the last time?" he said weakly.

"I mean, do you feel like you want to let go?"

Jack turned to face her. The confusion, and even anger, seeping into his features was met by a radiant calm in hers.

"I'm in hospice, Cee. I'm dead."

"Not yet you're not."

Jack looked away, sucked down a tortured breath. "Matter of time. Hours."

"Do you want to let go?" she asked again.

"Yes. I do."

"Okay, honey, okay."

After Cecilia left, Jack lay there in the bed. His last ties to his family had been severed. It was over. He didn't need to pull out the calendar. There would be no more dates to cross off. His hand moved to the call button. It was time now. He had prearranged this with the doctor. The machines keeping him alive would be turned off. He was done. It was time to go. All he wanted now was to see Lizzie. He conjured her face up in his mind's eye. "It's time, Lizzie," he said. "It's time." The sense of relief was palpable.

However, his hand moved away from the button when Mikki came back into the room and held up the medal. "I just wanted to say that... that this was pretty cool."

Father and daughter gazed awkwardly at each other, as though they were two long-lost friends reunited by chance. There was something in her eyes that Jack had not seen there for a long time.

"Mikki?" he said, his voice cracking.

She ran across the room and hugged him. Her breath burned against his cold neck, warming him, sending packets of energy, of strength, to all corners of his body. He squeezed back, as hard as his depleted energy would allow.

She said, "I love you so much. So much."

Her body shook with the pain, the trauma of a child soon to be orphaned.

When she stood, Mikki kept her gaze away from him. When she spoke, her voice was husky. "Good-bye, Daddy."

She turned and rushed from the room.

"Good-bye, Michelle," Jack mumbled to the empty room.

10

Jack lay there for hours, until day evaporated to night. The clock ticked, and he didn't move. His breathing was steady, buoyed by the machine that replenished his lungs, keeping him alive. Something was burning in his chest that he could not exactly identify or even precisely locate. His thoughts were focused on his last embrace with his daughter, her unspoken plea for him not to leave her. With the end of his life, with his last breath, the Armstrong children would be without parents. His finger had hovered over the nurse's call button all day, ready to summon the doctor, to let it be over. But he never pushed it.

As the clock ticked, the burn in Jack's chest continued to grow. It wasn't painful; indeed, it warmed his throat, his arms, his legs, his feet, his hands. His eyes became teary and then dried; became teary and then dried again. Sobs came and went. And still his mind focused only on his daughter. That last embrace. That last silent plea.

The nurses came and went. He was fed with liquid, shot like a bullet into his body. The clock ticked, the air continued to pour into him. At precisely midnight Jack started feeling odd. His lungs were straining, as they had been when Jackie had pulled the line out of the converter at home.

This might be it, Jack thought, button or no button; not even the machines could keep him alive any longer. He had wondered what the moment would actually feel like. Wedged in a mass of burning metal in Iraq after being blown up in his Humvee, he had wondered that too: whether his last moments on earth would be thousands of miles away from Lizzie and his kids. What it would feel like. What would be waiting for him.

Who would not be scared? Terrified even? The last journey. The one everyone took alone. Without the comfort of a companion. And, unless one had faith, without the reassurance that something awaited him at the end.

He took another deep breath, and then another. His lungs were definitely weakening. He could not drive enough oxygen into them to sustain life. He reached up and fiddled with the line in his nose. That's when he realized what the problem was. There was no airflow. He clicked on the bed light and turned to the wall. There was the problem; the line had come loose from the wall juncture. The pressure cuff had not come off, however, or he would've heard the air escaping into the room. He was about to press the call button but decided to see if he could push the line back in himself.

That's when it struck him.

How long have I been breathing on my own?

He glanced at the vitals monitor. The alarm hadn't gone off, though it should have. But as he gazed at the oxygen levels, he realized why the buzzer hadn't sounded. His oxygen levels hadn't dropped.

How was that possible?

He managed to push the line back in and took several deep breaths. Then he pulled the line out of his nose and breathed on his own for as long as he could. Ten minutes later, his lungs started to labor. Then he put the line back in.

What the hell is going on?

Over the next two hours, he kept pulling the line out and breathing on his own until he was up to fifteen minutes. His lungs normally felt like sacks of wet cement. Now they felt halfway normal.

At three a.m. he sat up in bed and then did the unthinkable. He released the side rail and swung around so his feet dangled over the sides of the bed. He inched forward until his toes touched the cold tile floor. Every part of him straining with the effort, little by little, Jack pushed himself up until most of his weight was supported by his legs. He could hold himself up for only a few seconds before collapsing back onto the sheets. Panting with the exertion, pain searing his weakened lungs, he repeated the movement twice more. Every muscle in his body was spasming from the strain.

Yet as the sweat cooled on his forehead, Jack smiled—for good reason.

He had just stood on his own power for the first time in months.

The next morning, after the hospice nurse had come through on her rounds, he edged to the side of the bed again, and his toes touched the floor. But then his hands slipped on the bedcovers and he crumpled to the floor. At first he panicked, his hand clawing for the call button, which was well out of reach. Then he calmed. The same methodical, practical nature that had carried him safely through Iraq and Afghanistan came back to him.

He grabbed the edge of the bed, tightened his grip, and pulled. His emaciated body slipped, slithered, and jerked until he was fully back on the bed. He lay there in quiet triumph, hard-earned sweat staining his hospice gown.

That night he half walked and half crawled to the bathroom and looked at himself in the mirror for the first time in months. It was not a pretty sight. He looked eighty-four instead of thirty-four. A sense of hopelessness settled over him. He was fooling himself. But as he continued to gaze in the mirror, a familiar voice sounded in his head.

You can do this, Jack.

He looked around frantically, but he was all alone.

You can do this, honey.

It was Lizzie. It couldn't be, of course, but it was.

He closed his eyes. "Can I?" he asked.

Yes, she said. *You have to, Jack. For the children.*

Jack crawled back to his bed and lay there. Had Lizzie really spoken to him? He didn't know. Part of him knew it was impossible. But what was happening to him seemed impossible too. He closed his eyes, conjured her image in his mind, and smiled.

The next night he heard the squeak of the gurney. The patient next door to him would suffer no longer. The person was in a better place. Jack had seen the minister walk down the hallway, Bible in hand. A better place. But Jack was no longer thinking about dying. For the first time since his death sentence had been pronounced, Jack was focused on living.

The next night as the clock hit midnight, Jack lifted himself off the bed and slowly walked around the room, supporting himself by putting one hand against the wall. He felt stronger, his lungs operating somewhat normally. It was as though his body was healing itself minute by minute. He heard a rumbling in his belly and realized that he was hungry. And he didn't want liquid pouring into a line. He wanted real food. Food that required teeth to consume.

Every so often he would smack his arm to make sure he wasn't dreaming. At last he convinced himself it was real. No, it wasn't just real.

This is a miracle.

11

Two weeks passed, and Jack celebrated the week of his thirty-fifth birthday by gaining four pounds and doing away with the oxygen altogether. Miracle or not, he still had a long way to go because his body had withered over the months. He had to rebuild his strength and put on weight. He sat up in his chair for several hours at a time. Using a walker, he regularly made his way to the bathroom all on his own. Another week passed, and four more pounds had appeared on his frame.

Things that Jack, along with most people, had always taken for granted represented small but significant victories in his improbable recovery. Holding a fork and using it to put solid food into his mouth. Washing his face and using a toilet instead of a bed pan. Touching his toes; breathing on his own.

The hospice staff had been remarkably supportive of Jack after it was clear that he was getting better. Perhaps it was because they were weary of people leaving this place solely on the gurney with a sheet thrown over their bodies.

Jack talked to his kids every chance he got, using his old cell phone. Jackie was bubbly and mostly incoherent. But Jack could sense that the older kids were wondering what was going on.

Cory said, "Dad, can't you come live with us?"

"We'll see, buddy. Let's just take it slow."

With the help of the folks at the hospice, Jack was able to use Skype to see his kids on a laptop computer one of the medical techs brought in. Cory and Jackie were thrilled to see their dad looking better.

Mikki was more subdued and cautious than her brothers, but Jack could tell she was curious. And hopeful.

"You look stronger, Dad."

"I'm feeling better."

"Does this mean?" She stopped. "I mean, will you...?"

Jack's real fear, even though he did believe he was experiencing a true miracle, was that his recovery might be temporary. He did not want to put his kids through this nightmare again. But that didn't mean he couldn't talk to them. Or see them.

"I don't know, honey. I'm trying to figure that out. I'm doing my best."

"Well, keep doing what you're doing," she replied. And then she smiled at him. That one look seemed to make every muscle in Jack's body firm even more.

One time Bonnie had appeared on the computer screen after Mikki had left the room. Her approach was far more direct, as she stared at Jack sitting up in bed. "What is going on?"

"I'm still here."

"Your hospice doctor won't talk to me. Privacy laws, he said."

"I know," Jack said. "But I can fill you in. I'm feeling better. Getting stronger. How're things working out with Mikki?"

"Fine. She's settled in, but we need to address *your* situation."

"I *am* addressing it. Every day."

And so it had gone, day after day, week after week. Using Skype and the phone, and answering all the kids' questions. Jack could see that more and more even Mikki was coming to grips with what was happening. Every time he saw her smile or heard her laugh at some funny remark he made, it seemed to strengthen him even more.

It was on a cold, blustery Monday morning in February that Jack walked down the hall under his own power. He'd gained five more pounds, his face had filled out, and his hair was growing back. His appetite had returned with a vengeance. They had also stopped giving him pain meds because there was no more pain.

The hospice doctor sat down with him at the end of the week. "I'm not sure what's going on here, Jack, but I'm ordering up some new blood work and other tests to see what we have. I don't want you to get your hopes up, though."

Jack simply stared at him, a spoonful of soup poised near his lips.

The doctor went on. "Look, if this continues, that's terrific. No one will be happier than me—well, of course, except for you. All of my patients die, Jack, to put it bluntly. And we just try to help them pass with dignity."

"But," said Jack.

"But your disease is a complicated one. And always a fatal one. This might just be a false remission."

"Might be."

"Well, without dashing your hopes, it probably is."

"Have others in my condition had a remission?"

The doctor looked taken aback. "No, not to my knowledge."

"That's all I needed to know."

The doctor looked confused. "Needed to know about what?"

"I know I was dying, but now I'm not."

"How can you be so sure?"

"Sometimes you just know."

"Jack, I have to tell you that what's happening to you is medically impossible."

"Medicine is not everything."

The doctor looked him over and saw the new muscle, the fuller face, and the eyes that burned with a rigid intensity.

"Why do you think this is happening to you, Jack?" he finally asked.

"You're a doctor; you wouldn't understand."

"I'm also a human being, and I'd very much like to know."

Jack reached in his drawer and pulled out a photo. He passed it to the doctor.

It was a photo of Lizzie and the kids.

"Because of them," said Jack.

"But I thought your wife passed away."

Jack shook his head. "Doesn't matter."

"What?"

"When you love someone, you love them forever."

12

Two days later, Jack was in his room eating a full meal. He'd put on three more pounds. The doctor walked in and perched on the edge of the bed.

"Okay, I officially believe in miracles. Your blood work came back negative. No trace of the disease. It's like something came along and chased it away. Never seen anything like it. There's no way to explain it medically."

Jack swallowed a mouthful of mashed potatoes and smiled. "I'm glad you finally came around."

He saw his kids that night on the computer. He believed he actually made Jackie understand that he was getting better. At least his son's last words had been, "Daddy's boo-boo's gone."

Cory had blurted out, "When are you coming to see me?"

"I hope soon, big guy. I'll let you know. I've still got a ways to go. But I'm getting there."

Mikki's reaction surprised him, and not in a good way.

"Is this some kind of trick?" she asked.

Jack slowly sat up in his chair as he stared at her. "Trick?"

"When we left you, Dad, you were dying. That's what hospice is for. You said good-bye to all of us. You made me go live with Gramps and *her*!"

"Honey, it's no trick. I'm getting better."

She suddenly dissolved into tears. "Well then, will you be coming to take us home? Because I hate it here."

"I'm doing my best, sweetie. With a little more time I think—"

But Mikki hit a key and the computer screen went black.

Jack slowly sat back. He never heard the squeak of the gurney as the woman across the hall made her final journey from this place.

Day turned to night, and Jack hadn't moved. No food, no liquids, no words spoken to anyone who came to see him.

Finally, at around two a.m., he stirred. He rose from his bed and walked up and down the hall before persuading a nurse to scavenge in the kitchen for some food. He ate and watched his reflection in the window.

I'm coming, Mikki. Dad's coming for you.

A week later he weighed over one-sixty and was walking the halls for an hour at a time. Like an infant, he was relearning how to use his arms and legs. He would flex his fingers and toes, curl and uncurl his arms, bend his legs. The nursing staff watched him carefully, unaccustomed to this sort of thing. Families of other hospice patients observed him curiously. At first Jack was afraid they would be devastated by his progress when their loved ones still lay dying. At least he thought that, until one woman approached him. She was in her sixties and was here every day. Jack knew that her husband had terminal cancer. He'd passed by the man's door and seen the shriveled body under the sheets. He was waiting to die, like everyone else here.

Everyone except me.

She slipped her arm through his and said, "God bless you."

He looked at her questioningly.

"You give us all hope."

Jack felt slightly panicked. "I don't know why this is happening to me," he said frankly. "But it's an awfully long shot."

"That's not what I meant. I know my husband is going to die. But you still give us all hope, honey."

Jack went back to his room and stared at himself in the mirror. He looked more like himself now. The jawline was firming, the hair fuller. He walked slowly to the window and looked outside at a landscape that was still more in the grips of winter than spring, though that season was not too far off. He'd spent several winters apart from his family while he carried a rifle for his country. Lying in his quarters outside of Baghdad or Kabul he had closed his eyes and visualized Christmas with his family. The laughter of Mikki and Cory as they opened presents on Christmas morning.

And then there was the memory of Lizzie's smile as she looked at the small gifts that Jack had bought her before he was deployed for the first time. It had been the summer, so he had gotten her sunblock, a bikini, and a book on grilling. She'd later sent him a photo by e-mail of her wearing the bikini while cooking hot dogs on the Hibachi with mounds of snow behind her. That image had carried him through one hellish battle after another. His wife. Her smile. Wanting so badly to come back to her. That all seemed so long ago, and in some important ways it was.

He went to his nightstand and pulled out the bundle of letters. Each had a number on the envelope. He selected the envelope with the number one on it and slid the paper out. The letter was dated December eighteenth and represented the first one he'd written to Lizzie. He gazed down at the handwriting that was his but that also wasn't because the disease had made him so weak. Sometimes while writing he'd had to put down the pen because he just couldn't hold it any longer. But still it was readable. It said what he had wanted to say. It was the accomplishment of a man who was doing this as his final act in life.

Dear Lizzie,

There are things I want to say to you that I just don't have the breath for anymore. That's why I've decided to write you these letters. I want you to have them after I'm gone. They're not meant to be sad, just my chance to talk to you one more time. When I was healthy you made me happier than any person has a right to be. When I was half a world away, I knew that I was looking at the same sky you were, thinking of the same things you were, wanting to be with you and looking forward to when I could be. You gave me three beautiful children, which is a greater gift than I deserved. I tell you this, though you already know it, because sometimes people don't talk about these things enough. I want you to know that if I could've stayed with you I would have. I fought as hard as I could. I will never understand why I had to be taken from you so soon, but I have accepted it. Yet I want you to know that there is nothing more important to me than you. I loved you from the moment I saw you. And the happiest day of my life was when you agreed to share your life with mine. I promised that I would always be there for you. And my love for you is so strong that even though I won't be there physically, I will be there in every other way. I will watch over you. I will be there if you need to talk. I will never stop loving you. Not even death is powerful enough to overcome my feelings for you. My love for you, Lizzie, is stronger than anything.

*Love,
Jack*

He put the letter back in the envelope and replaced the packet in the drawer. He slipped the photo from the pocket of his robe and looked at it. From the depths of the color print, his family smiled back at him. He thought of all the others in this place who would never leave it alive. He had been spared.

Why me?

Jack had no ready answer. But he did know one thing. He was not going to waste a second chance at living.

13

A few days later, Jack Armstrong was discharged from hospice and sent to a rehab facility. He rode over in a shuttle van. The driver was an older guy with a soft felt cap and a trim white beard. Jack was his only passenger.

As they drove along, Jack stared out in childlike wonder at things he never thought he would experience again. Seeing a bird in flight. A mailman delivering letters and packages. A kid running for the school bus. He promised himself he would never again take anything for granted.

As they pulled up in front of the rehab building, the man said, "Never brought anybody from that place to this place."

"I guess not," said Jack. He held his small duffel. Inside were a few clothes, a pair of tennis shoes, and the letters he'd written to Lizzie. When he got to his room, he looked around at the simple furnishings and single window that had a view of the interior outdoor courtyard, which was covered in snow. Jack sat on the bed after putting his few belongings away.

He looked up when a familiar person walked into the room.

"Sammy? What are you doing here?"

Sammy Duvall was dressed in gray sweats and had on a checkered bandanna. "Why the hell do you think I'm here? To get your sorry butt in shape. Look at you; you've obviously been dogging it. And they told me you were getting better. You look like crap."

"I don't understand. You didn't come by the hospice. And I left you phone messages."

The mirth left Sammy's eyes, and he sat down next to Jack on the bed. "I let you down."

"What are you talking about? You've done everything for me."

"No, I haven't. I told you at the cemetery that I'd always be there for you, but I wasn't." He paused. Jack had never seen Sammy nervous before. That emotion just never squared with a man like him. Nothing rattled Sammy Duvall.

Sammy's voice trembled as he said, "I should've come to visit you. But...seeing you in that place, just waiting to..."

Jack put a hand on the older man's shoulder. "It's okay, Sammy. I understand."

Sammy wiped his eyes and said, "Anyway, I'm here now. And you're probably gonna wish I wasn't."

"Why?"

"I'm your drill instructor."

"What?"

"Worked a deal with the folks here."

"How'd you do that?"

"Told 'em you were a special case. And you need special treatment. And if you're okay with it, so are they."

"I'm definitely okay with it. That was one reason I called you. To have you help me get back in shape."

"Famous last words, boy, because I'm gonna kick your butt."

The weeks went by swiftly. And with pain. Much pain.

The sweat streaming off him during one particularly arduous workout, Jack told Sammy, "I can't do one more damn push-up. I can't!"

"Can't or won't? 'Cause that's all the difference in the world, son."

Jack did one more push-up and then another and then a third, until he could no longer feel his arms. Jack had gone on to pump thousands of pounds of weights, run on the treadmill until he couldn't stand the stink of his own sweat, perform more push-ups until his arms nearly fell off, jump rope until his knees failed.

He cursed at Sammy, who laughed at him and goaded him into doing more, and more.

"You call yourself an army ranger? Sam Jr. can work harder than you, and he's a big, fat baby."

And Sammy didn't just instruct. He got down on the floor and did the exercises with Jack. "If an old man like me can do this, you sure as hell can," was his usual taunt.

On and on it went. Sammy screaming in his face and Jack gnashing his teeth, furrowing his brow, and doing one more pull-up, one more push-up, one more mile on the treadmill, one more set of curls, a hundred more pounds on the squat bar. But the thing was, Jack was growing stronger with every rep.

He talked to his kids every day. They knew he was in rehab. They knew he was getting stronger.

On one joint Skype session, Jack showed Cory and Jackie his muscles.

"You're ripped, Dad," said Cory.

"Whipped," crowed Jackie.

Later that night he saw Mikki. She hadn't agreed to do a Skype session with him in a while, but repeated phone calls from him and finally Sammy had convinced her.

"You look great, Dad," she said slowly. "You really do."

"You look thin," he replied.

"Yeah, well, Grandma is watching her weight, which means we all eat like birds."

"Cheeseburger's on me."

"When?" she said quickly.

"Sooner than you think, sweetie. I know I probably should have come out to see you before now. And I miss you more than anything. But...but I want to do this right. When I was in the army and we'd go on patrol, I always analyzed everything that might come up. Some of the other guys liked to wing it. Just turn on the fly. And sometimes in combat you have to do that. But being prepared for everything because you've done your homework is the best way to survive, Mikki. I hope you understand. I want to do this right. For all of you."

"I get it, Dad." She added playfully, "And Skype will get you ready for when I go to college and you really miss me."

Finally, the day came on a surprisingly warm spring morning. Jack's bag was packed and he was sitting on his bed when Sammy came into the room. "It's time."

"I know it is," said Sammy.

"I couldn't have done this without you."

"Sure you could, but it wouldn't have been nearly as much fun."

While his discharge papers were being finalized, Jack sat in a chair outside the rehab office. The months had been a blur. He drew a long, measured breath, trying to collect his thoughts. He looked out the window, where winter had passed and spring had arrived. Crocuses were pushing through the earth and trees were starting to bud out. *The world is waking up from a long winter's nap, and so am I.* He opened his duffel and pulled out an envelope with the number two on it. He slid out the letter.

Dear Lizzie,

Christmas will be here in five days, and I promise that I will make it. I've never broken a promise to you, and I never will. It's hard to say good-bye, but sometimes you have to do things you don't want to. Jackie came to see me a little while ago, and we talked. Well, he talked in Jackie language and I listened. I like to listen to him because I know one day very soon I won't be able to. He's growing up so fast, and I know he probably won't remember his dad, but I know I will live on in your memories. Tell him his dad loved him and wanted the best for him. And I wish I could have thrown the football to him and watched him play baseball. I know he will have a great life.

Cory is a special little boy. He has your sensitivity, your compassion. I know what's happening to me is probably affecting him the most of all the kids. He came and got into bed with me last night. He asked me if it hurt very much. I told him it didn't. He told me to say hello to God when I saw him. And I promised that I would.

And Mikki.

At this point Jack's hand trembled a bit. He remembered stopping at this point too as he was writing the letter. There was an old teardrop that had made the ink blotch. He started to read again.

> *Mikki is the most complicated of all. Not a little girl anymore but not yet an adult either. She is a good kid, though I know you've had your moments with her. She is smart and caring and she loves her brothers. She loves you, though she sometimes doesn't like to show it. My greatest regret with my daughter is letting her grow away from me. It was my fault, not hers. I see that clearly now. I only wish I had seen it that clearly while I still had a chance to do something about it. After I'm gone, please tell her the first time I ever saw her, when I got back from Afghanistan and was still in uniform, there was no prouder father who ever lived. Looking down at her tiny face, I felt the purest joy a human could possibly feel. And I wanted to protect her and never let anything bad ever happen to her. Life doesn't work that way, of course. But tell her that her dad was her biggest fan. And that whatever she does in life, I will always be her biggest fan.*
>
> *Love,*
> *Jack*

14

After being discharged, Jack rode with Sammy to his house. Along the way, he asked his friend to pass by his old home. Jack was surprised to see his pickup truck in the carport.

Sammy explained, "Went with the house sale, so I heard."

"Bonnie and the Realtor handled all that. Is that my tool bin in the back?"

"Yep. Guess that went too. All happened pretty fast." He eyed Jack. "Knew you'd beat that damn thing. Still got the tickets to Disney World?"

"Yeah," said Jack, staring glumly out the window.

Five of them.

Later, Jack drove to his bank. They had kept the account open to pay for expenses. It had a few thousand dollars left in it. That was a starting point. He had his wallet, and his credit cards were still valid. Driver's license was still good. Contractor's license intact. He drove to his old house and offered the owner eight hundred bucks on the spot for the truck and tools. After some negotiation back and forth, he got them for eight-fifty, the owner apparently glad to get the heap out of his driveway. Jack raced to the bank and got a cashier's check; the title was signed over, and he drove off in his old ride the same day.

He called the kids and told them he was out of rehab and getting a place for them all to live in. He next talked to Bonnie and explained things to her.

"That's wonderful, Jack," she'd said. But her words rang hollow. She asked him what his next step would be.

"Like I said, getting my family back. I'll be coming out there really soon."

"Do you think that's wise?"

"Bonnie, I'm their father. They belong with me."

That night he treated Sammy to dinner. While Sammy had a medium-rare burger, fries, and black coffee, Jack made three trips to the salad bar before settling down to devour his heaping plate of surf and turf.

"So what's the plan, chief?"

"Get my kids back pronto. But I need a place for us to stay."

"You're welcome to stay at my place, long as you want."

Sammy's place had one bedroom and a bathroom attached to the back with only an outside entrance; Sammy's massive Harley was parked in what he referred to as "the parlor." Besides that, his "puppy," Sam Jr., had the bulk of a Honda.

"That's fine for me, but with three kids, I'll need something a little bigger."

Late that night he slowly pulled his truck down the narrow roads of the cemetery. He'd been here only once, on a bitterly cold day, the ground flash-wrapped in ice and snow. And yet even though he'd been sick, he'd memorized every detail of the place. He could never forget where his wife was buried any more than he could ever fail to recall his own name.

He walked between the plots until he reached hers, represented by a simple bronze plate in the grass. He knelt down, brushed a couple of dead leaves off it. There was a skinny metal vase bolted to the plate where one could put flowers. There were roses in there, but they were brown. Jack cleaned them all out and placed in the vase a bunch of fresh flowers he'd brought with him. He sat down on his haunches and read the writing on the plate.

"Elizabeth 'Lizzie' Armstrong, loving wife, mother, and daughter. You will always be missed. You will always be loved."

He traced the letters with his fingers, even as his eyes filled with tears.

"I'm going to get the kids, Lizzie. I'm going to bring them home, and we're going to be a family again." He choked back a sob and tried to ignore the dull pain in his chest. "I wish you could be here with me, Lizzie. More than anything I wish that. But you were there for me in the hospital when I needed you. And I promise I will take good care of the children. I will make them proud. And I will raise them right. Just like you did."

The words finally failed him, and he lay down in the soft grass and wept. He finally became so exhausted, he fell asleep. When he woke he didn't know where he was for a few seconds, before he looked over and saw the grave. The dawn was breaking, the air chilly. As he looked overhead, he could see flocks of birds arriving for the start of spring.

Jack's clothes were damp from the dew. He coughed to clear his throat. His eyes and face were raw. In the distance he could hear the sounds of early morning traffic on the roads that fronted the cemetery. He walked silently back to his truck and drove off without the one person he needed more than anyone else.

15

One day later, Jack found it, a house owned by an elderly couple who had moved to an assisted-living facility. They couldn't sell their home because it needed a lot of repairs. And with dozens of homes in default on their street, it was difficult to sell anyway. Jack called the Realtor and offered his labor for free to fix up the place in exchange for staying there at no cost. Since the couple wasn't making any money off the house anyway, they quickly agreed. It wasn't perfect, but he didn't need perfect. He just needed his kids under the same roof as him. Jack moved his few possessions in the next day, after signing a one-page agreement. He made some quick cosmetic changes and bought some secondhand furniture.

Now it was time.

Using his credit card, he booked his plane tickets, packed his bag, and left for the airport. He went to collect Mikki first, because he knew if he went to the sisters' homes first, they would be on the phone to their mother before he'd even left their driveways.

He landed in Phoenix, rented a car, and drove to Tempe. He reached Fred and Bonnie's house but then drove past it. He parked a little down from the house and waited. An hour later a car pulled into the driveway, and Fred and Mikki got out. She was carrying her schoolbag. His heart ached when he saw her. She'd grown even taller, Jack noted, and her face had changed too. She was wearing a school uniform, white polo shirt and checked skirt. Her hair was in a ponytail and had nary a strand of pink or purple in it. She looked utterly miserable.

They went into the house. Jack parked in their driveway, took a deep breath, climbed out of the car, and walked up to the door.

"Dad?"

Mikki stared at him openmouthed. When he held out his arms for a hug, she tentatively reached out to him. He stroked her hair and kissed the top of her head.

"Dad, is it really you?"

"It's me, sweetie. It's really me."

Bonnie and Fred came around the corner, saw him, and stopped.

"Jack?" said Fred. "My God."

Bonnie just stood there, disbelief on her features.

Jack moved into the house with Mikki. He held out his hand, and Fred shook it. He looked at Bonnie. She still seemed in a daze.

"My God," she said, echoing her husband's words. "It's true. It's really true. Even with all the phone calls and seeing you on that computer. It's not the same."

"What is all the commotion?" Cecilia came into the room, skimming along on her walker, her oxygen line trailing behind her. When she saw Jack, she didn't freeze like Fred and Bonnie had done.

She cackled. "I knew it." She came forward as fast as she could and gave him a prolonged squeeze. "I knew it, Jack, honey," she said again, staring up at him and blinking back tears of joy.

They all sat at the kitchen table sipping glasses of iced tea. Jack eyed Bonnie. "Docs gave me a clean bill of health."

Bonnie just kept shaking her head, but Fred clapped him on the shoulder. "Jack, we're so happy for you, son."

Later, when they were alone, Bonnie asked, "How long will you be staying?"

"From here I'm heading to LA and then on to Portland."

"To see the kids?"

"No, to take them back with me, Bonnie. I've already told Mikki to start packing her things."

"But the school year will be done in less than two months."

"She can go to school in Cleveland as easily as she can here."

"But the house was sold."

"I'm renting another one."

"How will you support them?"

"I've started my business back up."

"Okay, but who will watch them when you're working?"

"Mikki and Cory are in school the whole day. And they're old enough now to come home and be okay by themselves for a few hours. Jackie will be in extended day care. And if unexpected things come up, we'll deal with them. Just like every other family does."

Bonnie pursed her lips. "Michelle has settled into her new life here."

Jack said nothing about how miserable the girl had been here. He simply said, "I don't think she'll mind."

"You could have called before you came."

"Yeah, I could have. And maybe I should have. But I don't see what harm it did."

"What harm? You just expect us to give her back to you, with no notice, no preparation? After all we've done."

"I've been in constant contact over the last few months. I kept you updated on my progress. Hell, you've *seen* me on the computer getting better. And I told you I would be coming to take the kids back. Soon. So this shouldn't come as a shock to you. And it's not like you're never going to see them again." He paused, and his tone changed. "Even though you did leave me by myself."

"You said it was all right. You told us to do it. And we thought you were dying."

"Come on, Bonnie, what else could I tell you under the circumstances? But for the record, dying alone is a real bitch."

As soon as Jack finished speaking, he regretted it. Bonnie stood, her face red with anger. "Don't you dare talk to me about dying alone. My Lizzie is lying dead and buried. There was no one with her at the end. No one! Certainly not you."

Jack eyed her. "Why don't you just say it, Bonnie, because I know you want to."

"*You* should be dead, not her." Bonnie seemed stunned by her own words. "I'm sorry, I didn't mean that." Her face flushed. "I'm very sorry."

"I *would* give my life to have Lizzie back. But I can't. I've got three kids who need me. Nothing takes priority over that. I hope you can understand."

"What I understand is that you're taking your children from a safe, healthy environment into something totally unknown."

"I'm their father," said Jack heatedly.

"You're a single parent. Lizzie isn't here to take care of the kids."

"I can take care of them."

"Can you? Because I don't think you have any idea what's in store for you."

Jack started to say something but stopped.

Could she be right?

16

"Mr. Armstrong?"

Jack stared down from the ladder he was standing on while repairing some siding on a job site. The sun was high overhead, the air warm, and the sweat on his skin thick. He had on a white tank top, dirty dark blue cargo shorts, white crew socks, and worn steel-toed work boots. The woman down below was pretty, with light brown curly hair cut short, and she wore a pair of black slacks and a white blouse; her heels were sunk in the wet grass.

"What can I do for you, ma'am?"

"I'm Janice Kaplan. I'm a newspaper reporter. I'd like to talk to you."

Jack clambered down the ladder and rubbed his hands off on the back of his shorts. "Talk to me about what?"

"Being the miracle man."

Jack squinted at her. "Come again?"

"You are the Jack Armstrong who was diagnosed with a terminal illness?"

"Well, yeah, I was."

"You don't look terminal anymore."

"I'm not. I got better."

"So a miracle. At least that's what the doctor I talked to said."

Jack looked annoyed. "You talked to my doctor? I thought that was private."

"Actually, he's a friend of mine. He mentioned your case in passing. It was all very positive. I became interested, did a little digging, and here I am."

"Here for what?" Jack said, puzzled.

"To do a story on you. People with death sentences rarely get a second chance. I'd like to talk to you about the experience. And I know my readers would want to know."

Jack and the kids had been back for nearly four weeks now. With parenting and financial support resting solely on his shoulders, Jack barely had time to eat or sleep. Bonnie had been right in her prediction. He didn't have any idea what was in store for him. Mikki had really stepped up and had taken the laboring oar with the cooking and cleaning, the shopping, and looking after the boys. He had never had greater appreciation for Lizzie. She'd done it all, from school to meals to laundry to shopping to keeping the house clean. Jack had worked hard, but he realized now that he hadn't come close to working as hard as his wife had, because she did all that and worked full-time too. At midnight he lay in his bed, numb and exhausted—and humbled by the knowledge that Lizzie would have still been going strong.

"A story?" Jack shook his head as he dug a hole in the mulch bed with the toe of his boot. "Look, it's really not that special."

"Don't be modest. And I also understand that you turned your life around, built your business back, got a house, and went to retrieve your children, who'd been placed with family after your wife tragically died." She added, "I was very sorry to hear about that. On Christmas Eve too, of all days."

Jack's annoyance turned to anger. "You didn't learn all that from my doctor. That really is an invasion of privacy."

"Please don't be upset, Mr. Armstrong. I'm a reporter; it's my job to find out these things. And I'm probably not explaining myself very well." She drew a deep breath while Jack stared at her, his hands clenching into fists with his anxiety. "It's strictly a feel-good piece. One man's triumph against the odds, a family reunited. These are hard times for folks, especially around here. All we hear is bad news. War, crime, people losing their jobs and their homes. I write about that stuff all the time, and while it is news, it's also very, very depressing. But this is different. This is a great story that will make people smile. That's all I'm shooting for. To make people feel good, for once."

His anger quickly disappearing, Jack looked around while he considered her request. He saw Sammy up on another ladder watching him intently. He waved to show him things were okay. Jack turned back to the woman.

"So what exactly do I have to do?"

"Just sit down with me and tell your story. I'll take notes, do a draft, get back to you, polish it, and then it'll be published in the paper and on our Web site."

"And that's it?"

"That's all. I really believe it will be positive for lots of people. There are many folks out there with what seem like insurmountable obstacles in front of them. Reading about how you overcame yours could do a lot of good. It really could."

"I think I just got lucky."

"Maybe, but maybe not. From the research I've done on

your condition, the odds were zero that you would recover. No one else ever has."

"Well, I'm just happy I was the first. How about tomorrow after dinner?"

"Great. About eight?"

Jack gave her his address. She glanced at his exposed upper right arm and then his scarred calves. "I understand you were in the military. Is that where you got those?" She indicated the ragged bullet wound on his arm and the network of scars on his legs.

"Arm in Afghanistan and legs in Iraq."

"Two Purples then?"

"Yeah. Were you in the military?"

"My son just got back from the Middle East in one piece, thank God."

"I guess we both have a lot to be thankful for."

"I'll see you tomorrow."

The story ran, and a few days later Janice Kaplan called.

"The AP picked up my article, Jack."

Jack had just finished cleaning up after dinner.

"What does that mean?" he asked.

"AP. Associated Press. That means my story about you and your family is running in newspapers across the country. My editor still can't believe it."

"Congratulations, Janice."

"No, thank *you*. It wasn't the writing; it was the story. And it was a great picture of you and the kids. And I think lots of families will be inspired by your struggle and triumph. I just thought I'd give you a heads-up. You're famous now. So be prepared."

17

Janice Kaplan's words proved prophetic. Letters came pouring in, including offers to appear on TV and to tell his story to major magazines; one publisher even wanted Jack to write a book. Overwhelmed by the blitzkrieg and wanting a normal life with his kids, he declined them all. He figured with the passage of time other stories would emerge and take the focus away from him. His fifteen minutes of fame couldn't be over soon enough for him. He was no miracle man, he knew, but simply a guy who got lucky.

A week after Kaplan's call, Jack was lying in bed when he heard voices downstairs. He slipped on his pants and crept down to the main level.

"Stop it, Chris!"

Jack took the last three steps in one bound. Mikki was at the door, and a teenage boy had his hands all over her as she struggled against him. It took only two seconds for Jack to lift the young man off his feet and slam him against the wall. Jack said, "What part of *no* don't you get, jerk?" He looked over at Mikki. "What the hell is going on?"

"We...he just came over to work on some...Dad, just let him down."

Jack snapped, "Get upstairs."

"Dad!"

"Now."

"I can handle this. I'm not a child."

"Yeah, I can see that. Upstairs."

She stalked up to her room. Jack turned back to the young man.

"I ever catch you with one finger on her again, they won't be able to find all the pieces to put you back together, got it?"

The terrified teen merely nodded.

Jack threw him outside and slammed the door. He stood there, letting his anger cool. Then he marched up the stairs and knocked on his daughter's door.

"Leave me alone."

Instead he threw open the door and went in. Mikki was sitting on the floor, her guitar across her lap.

"We need to get a few rules straight around here," Jack said.

She stared up at him icily. "Which rules? The ones where you're ruining my life?"

"What was I supposed to do, let that little creep paw you?"

"I told you I could handle it."

"You can't handle everything. That's why there are people called parents."

"Oh, is that what you're pretending to be?"

Jack looked stunned. "Pretend? I brought all of you back

home so we could be together. Do you think I did that just for the hell of it?"

"I don't have a clue why you did it. And you didn't even ask me if I wanted to come back. You just told me to pack, like I was a child."

"I thought you hated it out there. You told me that a dozen times."

"Well, I hate it here too."

"What do you want from me? I'm doing the best I can."

"You were gone a long time."

"I explained that. Remember? I told you that story about being in the army? About taking your time and being prepared for every eventuality."

"That's crap!"

"What?"

"In case you hadn't figured it out, this isn't the army, Dad. This is about family."

"I did all that to make sure we *could* be a family," he shot back.

"A family? You don't have a clue what to do with us. Admit it. You're not Mom."

"I know I'm not, believe me. But you two were always arguing."

"That doesn't mean I didn't appreciate what she did for us. Now I do most of the cooking and cleaning and the laundry, and looking after Jackie. And your grocery-shopping skills are a joke."

Jack felt his anger continue to rise. "Look, I know I'm not in your mom's league, but I'm trying to make this work. I love you guys."

"Really? Well, Cory's being bullied at school. Did you

know that? His grades are going down even though he's a really smart kid. The teachers have sent home tons of notes in his bag, but you never check that, do you? And Jackie's birthday is in two weeks. Have you planned anything? Bought him a present? Planned a party for his friends or even thought about a cake?"

Jack's face grew pale. "Two weeks?"

"Two weeks, *Dad*. So you might want to try harder."

"Mik, I—"

"Can you please just leave me alone?"

When he left her room, Cory was standing in the hall in his underwear.

Jack looked embarrassed. "Cor, *are* you being bullied at school?"

Cory closed the door, leaving his dad alone in the hall.

18

Jack and Sammy were unloading Jack's truck in his driveway after a long day at work. Jack nearly dropped a sledgehammer on his foot. Sammy looked over at him.

"You okay? Haven't been yourself the last couple of days."

Jack slowly picked up the tool and threw it back in the truck bed. "What do you think Jackie would like for his birthday? It's just around the corner, and I wanted to get him something nice."

Sammy shrugged. "Uh, toy gun?"

Jack looked doubtful. "I don't think Lizzie liked to encourage that. And where can I get a cake and some birthday things? You know like hats and...stuff?"

"The grocery store up the street has a bakery."

"How do you know that?"

"It's right across from the beer aisle."

Jack drove to the store and got some items for Jackie's birthday. He was standing at the checkout aisle when he saw it. He had never been more stunned in his life. He was looking at *his* photo on the cover of one of the tabloid magazines that were kept as impulse buys at the checkout. He slowly reached out his hand and picked up a copy.

The headline ran, "Miracle Man Muddied."

What the hell?

Jack turned to the next page and read the story. With each word he read, his anger increased. Now he could understand the headline. The writer had twisted everything. He'd made it seem that Jack had forced Lizzie to go out on an icy, treacherous night to get his pain meds. And then, even worse, the writer had suggested that Jack thought his wife was having an affair with a neighbor. An obviously distraught Lizzie had run a red light and been killed. None of it was true, but now probably millions of people thought he was some kind of monster.

He left his items on the conveyor belt and rushed home.

On the drive there, it didn't take him long to figure out what had happened.

Bonnie had been the writer's source. But how could she have known? Then it struck him. Lizzie must've called her on the drive over to the pharmacy and told her what she was doing. Maybe she mentioned something about Bill Miller, and Bonnie had misconstrued what Jack's reaction had been, although it would have been pretty difficult to do that. More likely, Bonnie might've just altered what Lizzie had told her to suit her own purposes.

Jack could imagine Bonnie seething. Here he was getting all this notoriety, adulation, and sympathy, and Lizzie was in a grave because of him. At least Bonnie probably believed that. A part of Jack couldn't blame her for feeling that way. But now she had opened a Pandora's box that Jack would find difficult to close. And what worried him the most was what would happen when his kids found out. He wanted to be the first to talk to them about it, especially Mikki. He gunned the truck.

Unfortunately, he was too late.

19

Mikki was waiting for him on the front porch with a copy of another gossip paper with a similar headline. She was trembling and attacked him as soon as he got out of the truck. "This is all over school. How could you make Mom go out that night? And how could you even think that she would cheat on you?"

Jack exploded, "That story is full of lies. I never accused your mom of anything. I saw her slap Bill Miller. She and I had a laugh about it because he was drunk. And I didn't insist she go out that night. In fact, I told her not to."

"I don't believe you."

"Mikki, it's the truth. I swear. Tabloids make stuff up all the time. You know that."

"This never would have happened if you hadn't agreed to do that stupid Miracle Man story in the first place. That *was* your fault."

"Okay, you're right about that. I wish I hadn't but—"

"So now everybody thinks Mom was a slut and you're a

jerk. And I'll spend the rest of the school year having people talking behind my back."

"Will you just listen to me for a sec—"

Before he could finish, she'd fled inside, slamming the door behind her. When he started to go in the house after her, he heard the lock click. Staring through the side window at him was Cory. He gave his father a furious scowl and ran off.

Jack ended up taking Cory and Jackie to Chuck E. Cheese's for Jackie's third birthday. Jack wore a ball cap and glasses so people wouldn't recognize him during his fifteen minutes of "infamy." On the table in front of him were a half-eaten cheese pizza and a mass-produced birthday cake. While Jackie jumped into mounds of balls along with a zillion other kids, Cory sat slumped in a corner looking like he would rather be attacked by sharks than be here. Jack didn't even know where Mikki was. The only moment in his life worse than this was when the cop told him Lizzie was dead.

Later, after they returned home, Jackie played with the monster truck that Jack had rushed out to buy him the night before. Cory had escaped into the backyard.

"You like the truck?" Jack asked quietly.

Jackie made guttural truck noises and rolled it across his dad's shoulder.

At least I've still got one kid who doesn't hate me.

Carrying his youngest son, Jack walked up the stairs and peered inside Mikki's bedroom. It was small, lighted by a single overhead fixture that gave out meager illumination, and her clothes were all over the floor. A half-empty jar of Nutella sat on a storage box. Her guitar and keyboard were in one corner. A device to mix musical tracks was on the floor. Sheet music was stacked everywhere. There was an old beat-up microphone on a metal fold-up table that she used as a desk.

Jack put his son down and then walked over and picked up some of the music. It was actually blank sheets with pencil notes written in, obviously by his daughter. Jack couldn't read music and didn't know what the markings represented, but they looked complicated. She could create this but couldn't even manage a B in math or science? Then again, he hadn't been a great student either, except in the subjects that interested him.

He took Jackie's hand and walked into the bedroom the boys shared. It was far more cluttered than Mikki's because it was smaller and housed two people instead of one. The beds were nearly touching. There was a small built-in shelf crammed with toys, books, and junk that boys tended to collect. Cory had stacked his clothes neatly in the small bureau Jack had gotten thirdhand. Jackie's clothes were on top of the bureau.

Jack noticed a box crammed with papers on the floor next to Cory's bed. He looked inside. When he saw the top page, he started going through the rest. It was printed information about his disease. He saw, in Cory's handwriting, notes on the pages.

"He thought maybe he could find a cure."

Jack spun around to see Mikki standing there.

She came forward. "He wanted to save you. Dumb, huh? He's only a kid. But he meant well."

Jack slowly rose. "I didn't know."

"Well, to be fair, you were pretty out of it at the time." She sat down on one of the beds, while Jackie rushed toward her and held out his truck for her to see. "That's really cool, Jackie." She hugged her brother and said, "Happy birthday, big guy."

"Big guy," repeated Jackie with a huge smile.

She glanced at her dad. "It's a nice gift."

"Thanks." He stared back at her. "So where does that leave us?"

"This is not where we say stupid stuff and hug and then bawl our eyes out and everything is okay, cue the dumb music. It's one day at a time. That's life. Some days will be good and some days will suck. Some days I'll look at you and feel mad; some days I'll feel crappy about being mad at you. Some days I'll feel nothing. But you're still my dad."

"The thing is, I was supposed to be gone, not your mom. I'd accepted that. But then your mother was gone. And somehow I got better. It just wasn't supposed to happen that way."

"But it did happen exactly that way. You *are* here. Mom isn't."

"So where do we all go from here?"

"You're really asking me?"

"You obviously know a lot more about this family than I do."

His cell phone rang. He looked at the caller ID. It was Bonnie's number. Now what? Hadn't she done enough damage?

"Hello?" he said, bracing for a fight.

It was Fred. He sounded tired, and there was something else in his voice that made Jack stiffen.

He said, "Fred, is everything okay?"

"Not really, Jack, no."

"What is it? Not Bonnie?"

"No." He paused. "It's Cecilia. She died about two hours ago."

20

Though she'd lived the last ten years in Ohio with her daughter and son-in-law, except for her short stint in Arizona, Cecilia Pinckney was a southerner through and through. She'd requested to be buried in Charleston, South Carolina, in the family crypt. So Jack bundled the kids into a pale blue 1964 VW van with white top that Sammy had lovingly restored, and headed south. A large crowd gathered under a very hot sun and high humidity for the funeral. Bonnie looked older by ten years, shrunken and bowed. Seeing this, Jack couldn't bring himself to offer anything other than brief condolences. As she looked up at him, Jack thought he could see some affection for him underneath all the sorrow.

"Thank you for coming," she said.
"Cecilia was a great lady."
"Yes, she was."
"When some time has passed, we need to talk."
She slowly nodded. "All right. We probably should."
After the service was over, Jack and the kids drove back to

the hotel, where they were crammed into one room. Jack had just taken off his tie and jacket when the hotel phone rang. He answered, thinking it might be Fred, but it was a strange voice.

"Mr. Armstrong, I'm Royce Baxter."

"Okay, what can I do for you?"

"I had the pleasure of being Mrs. Cecilia Pinckney's attorney for the past twenty years."

"Her attorney?"

"That's right. I was wondering if I could meet with you for a little bit. My office is only a block over from your hotel. Fred O'Toole told me where you were staying. I assumed you'd be heading back to Ohio soon, and I thought I would catch you before you left. I know the timing is bad, but it is important and it won't take long."

Jack looked around at the kids. Jackie was passed out in a chair, and Cory and Mikki were watching TV.

"Give me the address."

Five minutes later he was sitting across from the very prim and proper Royce Baxter, who was dressed in a dark suit. He was in his sixties, about five-ten, with a bit of a paunch and a good-natured face.

"Let me get down to business." Baxter drew a document out of a file. "This is Ms. Cecilia's last will and testament."

"Look, if she left me anything, I really don't feel that I should accept it."

Baxter peered at him over the document. "And why is that?"

"It's sort of complicated."

"Well, she made this change to her will very recently. She told me that even if you never used it, it would always be there for you."

"Well, what is it exactly?" Jack said curiously.

"The old Pinckney house on the South Carolina coast in a town called Channing."

"The Palace, you mean?"

"That's right. So you know about it?"

"Lizzie told me about it. But I've never been there. Once she moved to Ohio she never went back."

"Now, let me warn you that while it's right on the beach, it's not in good condition. It's a big, old, rambling place that has never been truly modernized. But it's in a lovely location. The coastal low country is uniquely beautiful. And I say that with all the bias of a proud South Carolinian. Ms. Cecilia told me that you're very good with your hands. I believe she thought you were the perfect person to take care of it."

"Beachfront? I couldn't afford the real estate taxes."

"There are none. Years ago Ms. Cecilia placed the property into a conservancy so it could never be sold and developed. She and her descendants can use the property but can never sell it. In return the taxes were basically waived."

"But we've got a home in Cleveland. The kids are in school."

"Ms. Cecilia thought that you might have some trepidation. But since most of the summer is still ahead of us, the issue of school does not come into play."

Jack sat back. "Okay. I see that. But I still don't think—"

Baxter interrupted. "And Cecilia said that you told her that Lizzie was thinking of taking the kids there this summer."

"That's right, Lizzie was. She told me that. I thought it was a good idea but..." Jack's voice trailed off. He'd made Lizzie promise him that she would take the kids to the Palace. Now she couldn't.

Baxter fingered the will and studied him. "Would you like to see it before you make up your mind?"

"Yes, I would," Jack said quickly.

21

Less than two hours after leaving Royce Baxter's office, Jack and the kids pulled down a sandy drive between overgrown bushes after following the directions the lawyer had given him. He surveyed the landscape. There were marshes nearby, and the smell of the salt water was strong, intoxicating.

"Wow!" said Cory as the old house finally came into view.

Jack pulled the VW to a stop, and they all climbed out. Jack took Jackie's hand as they walked up to the front of the house, which was shaded by two large palmetto trees. It was an elongated rambling wood-sided structure, with a broad, covered front porch that ran down three-quarters of the home's face. A double door of solid wood invited visitors to the entrance. The wood siding was faded and weathered but looked strong and reliable to Jack's expert eye. The hurricane shutters were painted black, but most of the paint was gone, leaving the underlying wood exposed to the elements. Five partially rotted steps carried them up to the front entrance.

The furniture on the porch was covered. When Jack and the

kids looked underneath, they found quite the mess, along with animal nests. One squirrel jumped out and raced up a support post and onto the roof, which had many missing shingles, Jack had already noted. A snake slid out from under a pile of wood, causing the older kids to scream and run. Jackie approached the serpent and attempted to pick it up before Jack snatched him away. He looked at the other kids, who were cowering by the VW.

"It's a black snake. Not poisonous, but it will bite, so stay clear of it." He watched as the snake slowly made its way down the steps and into the underbrush around the house.

"They don't have giant snakes in Cleveland," said a breathless Cory.

"It was only a three-footer, son. And there *are* snakes in Ohio."

That information did not seem to make Cory feel any better.

"Come on," said Jack. "Let's at least check it out while we're here."

Using the key Baxter had given him, he opened the front door and went inside with Jackie. He turned to check on the other two kids. They hadn't budged from next to the VW. "Remember, guys, that snake is out there with *you*, not in here with us."

A moment later, the two kids flew up the front steps and past their dad into the house, with Cory screaming and looking behind him for the "giant freaking snake."

Jackie and his father exchanged a glance.

Jackie pointed at his brother and said, "Corwee funny."

"Yeah, he's a riot," said Jack, shaking his head.

Inside, the spaces were open and large, with high, sloped ceilings where old fans hung motionless. The kitchen was spacious but poorly lighted by tiny windows, and the bathrooms were few in number and small. There was an enormous stone fireplace that reached to the ceiling in the main living area, a big table for dining that showed a lot of wear and tear, and several other rooms that served various purposes, including a laundry room and a small library. On the lower level were an old billiards table, its green felt surface worn smooth with use, and a Ping-Pong table with a tattered net. Water toys, flippers, flattened beach balls, and the like were stacked in a storage room.

The furniture was old but mostly in good shape. The floors were random-width plank, the walls solid plaster. Jack knocked on one section and came away impressed with the craftsmanship. Yet when he stepped toward the back of the house, he drew in a breath. The rear of the house was mostly windows and glass doors; there was also a second-floor screened-in porch with stairs leading down to the ground. The view out was of the wide breadth of the Atlantic, maybe two hundred feet away, the sandy beach less than half that distance.

Jack breathed in the sea air and pointed out to the ocean. "There's really not a drop of land between here and Europe or Africa," he said. "Just water."

As the kids stared out at the views, Jack looked down at the backyard. It was sandy, with dunes covered in vegetation. He stepped back inside and smelled the burned wood of fires from long ago.

They clumped upstairs and looked through the shotgun line of bedrooms there, none of them remarkable, but all functional. Where others might have seen limitations, builder Jack saw potential. All the bedrooms had views of the ocean, and the largest one had a small outdoor balcony as well.

"What do you think is up there?" This came from Mikki, who was pointing to a set of stairs at the end of the hall going up another half flight.

"Attic, I suppose," he said.

Jack eased open the door and fumbled for a light switch. Nothing happened when he flicked it, and it occurred to him that the power had been turned off when the place became uninhabited. The room was under the eaves of the house, and the ceiling slanted upward to a peak. It was large, with two windows that threw in good morning light, though now the sun had passed over the house and was going down. There was a bed, an old wrought-iron four-poster, a large wooden desk, a shelf filled with books, and an old trunk set in one corner. A door led to a closet that was empty. Jack stepped cautiously over the floor planks to test their safety.

"Okay," he said after his inspection was complete. "Explore."

Cory made a beeline for the trunk, while Jack led his youngest over to the desk and helped him open drawers. He glanced back at Mikki, who hadn't budged from the doorway.

"You going to look around?"

"Why? You're not thinking about moving here, are you?"

"Maybe."

Her face flushed with anger. "I already had to move to Arizona. And all my friends are in Cleveland. My band, everything."

"I'm just looking around, okay?" But in his mind, Jack was already drawing up plans for repairs and improvements.

In his mind's eye, there was Lizzie seated next to him on the bed, on what would turn out to be her last day of life.

You never know, Jack, you might enjoy it too. You could really fix the place up. Even make the lighthouse work again.

"So Grand left you this place?" asked Mikki.

Jack broke free from his thoughts. "Yeah, she did."

"Well, why don't you sell it, then? We could certainly use the money."

"I can't. It's a legal thing. And I wouldn't have felt right selling it even if I could."

Mikki shrugged and leaned against the doorway, adopting a clearly bored look.

Jack glanced over at Cory, who'd nearly tumbled into the large trunk he'd opened in his eagerness. He came up wearing on old-fashioned top hat, black cloak, and a half mask covering the upper part of his face.

"Moo-ha-ha-ha," he said in a dramatically deep voice.

"That Corwee?" said Jackie, uncertainly, hugging his father tighter.

"That's Cory acting funny," said Jack encouragingly as he gently pried his youngest son's frantic fingers from around a patch of his hair.

Jack picked up a book and opened it, and his jaw dropped.

"What is it?" asked Cory, who had seen his reaction.

Jack held up the book. There was a bookplate on the inside cover.

"Property of Lizzie O'Toole," read Jack. "This was your mother's book," he said. "Maybe they all were." He looked excitedly around. "I bet this was your mom's room growing up."

Now Mikki stepped into the room and joined them. "Mom's room?"

Jack nodded and pointed eagerly to the desktop. "Look at that."

Carved into the wood were the initials *EPO*. Mikki looked at her dad questioningly.

He said animatedly, "Elizabeth Pinckney O'Toole. That was you mom's full name. Pinckney was Grand's maiden name. She kept her last name even after she married."

"Why did Mom leave her books behind?" she asked.

"Maybe she thought she would come back," replied Jack uncertainly.

"I remember her telling me about a beach house she grew up in, but she never really said anything else about it. Did you know much about it?"

"She told me about it. But I'd never been here before."

"Why'd she never bring us here?" Mikki asked.

"I know that she wanted to. In fact, she was planning to bring all of you here this summer after I...Anyway, that was her plan."

"Is that why we're here, then? Fulfilling Mom's wishes?"

"Maybe that's part of it."

Jackie tugged on his dad's ear.

"Corwee?" asked Jackie.

Jackie was pointing at his brother, who was now wearing a pink boa, long white gloves, and a tiara.

"Still Cory," said Jack, smiling broadly. "And obviously completely secure in his masculinity."

He glanced at Mikki, who was running her fingers over her mom's initials.

Jack looked out the window. "Hey, guys. Check this out."

The kids hurried to the window and stared up in awe at the lighthouse that rose into the air out on a rocky point next to the house.

"It's really close to the house," said Mikki.

Cory added, "Do you think it belongs to us too?"

Jack said, "I know it does. Your mom told me about it. It was one of her favorite places to go."

They rushed outside and over to the rocky point. The lighthouse was painted with black and white stripes and was about forty feet tall. He tried the door. It was locked, but he peered through the glass in the upper part of the door. He saw a spiral wooden staircase. There were boxes stacked against one wall, and everything was covered in dust.

"What a mess," said Mikki, who was looking through another pane of glass.

On the exterior wall of the lighthouse was an old, weathered sign. He scraped off some of the gunk and read, "Lizzie's Lighthouse." Jack stepped back and stared up at the tall structure with reverence.

Cory looked at the hand-painted sign. "How could this be Mom's lighthouse?"

"Well, it was one of her favorite places, like I said," answered his father, who was now circling the structure to see if there was another way to get in. "Isn't it cool?"

"It's just an old lighthouse, Dad," Mikki said.

He turned to look at her. "No, it was your *mom's* lighthouse. She loved it."

Jackie pulled on his dad's pants leg again. He pointed at the lighthouse.

"What dat?"

Cory said, "It's a lighthouse, Jackie. Big light."

"Big wight," repeated Jackie.

Jack gazed around at the property. "I'm sold."

"What?" exclaimed Mikki.

"This will be a great place to spend the summer."

"But, Dad," protested Mikki. "It's a dump. And my friends—"

"It's *not* a dump. This is where your mother grew up," he snapped. "And we're moving here." He paused and added in a calmer tone, "At least for one summer."

22

Back in Cleveland, they moved out of the rental and parked their few pieces of furniture at Sammy's place, because he'd decided to come with them to South Carolina.

"What am I gonna do by myself all summer?" he'd said when told of the family's plans. "And Sam Jr. expects the kids to be around now. Whines all the time when they're not here. I mean, I can get by without you folks, but it's the damn dog that troubles me."

They closed up Sammy's garage house and pushed Sam Jr.'s big butt into the VW, and off they went. Sammy drove the VW, and Jack followed in his pickup truck with Sammy's Harley tied down in the cargo bed. They made one stop, though, to Lizzie's grave. Jack knew it would be hard on everyone, but he also didn't want the kids to leave without going there to visit their mom.

They put fresh flowers in the vase, and each of the kids said something to their mother, though Mikki's remarks were inaudible. Jack stood behind them, trying to hold the tears back. When Jackie wanted to know where his mom was, Mikki told him that she was sleeping. Jackie lay down next to his mom's grave and started whispering things as though he didn't want to wake her. At that point Jack disappeared behind some bushes and cried into his hands.

They split the trip up into two days, spending the night in adjoining rooms at a motel outside of Winston-Salem, North Carolina. They left Sam Jr. in the van with the windows down and a big pan of water; he was too big to climb through the opening. But around midnight he started howling so mournfully that Jack and Sammy had to run out and bundle him into their room before anyone could see them. That night, Sam Jr. slept curled up around Jackie on a blanket on the floor.

Jack woke up early in the morning and went outside to get some fresh air. He found Mikki already fully dressed and leaning against the VW.

"What's up?" he asked, stretching out his back.

"Why are we doing this?" she said in a surly tone.

"Doing what?"

"You know what!"

He walked over to her. "What is your problem?"

"I don't have a problem. Do you?"

"What's that supposed to mean?"

"We just settled back in Cleveland, Dad. And now you're moving us down to South Carolina."

"Yeah, to the home where your mom grew up."

"Okay, Dad, but in case you didn't realize it, Mom's not there."

She turned and walked back to her room.

Jack stared after her, shook his head, and headed off to get ready for the rest of the trip.

They got an early start and arrived in Channing, South Carolina, before lunch. Jack had had the electricity and water turned back on at the beach house before they got there. He'd also found a cable TV provider, so when they hooked up the TV they'd brought it actually worked. Huge TV watchers Jackie and Cory were immensely relieved by this development.

It didn't take them long to unload. They put the Harley under a side deck. As they were carrying things in, Jack found an envelope on the knotty pine kitchen table. It was addressed to him with a Post-it note on the outside from the lawyer, Royce Baxter. It read,

> *This is a letter that Ms. Cecilia left for you, with instructions to deliver it to you when you moved into the beach house.*

"Man," said Sammy, dumping his old army duffel bag on the floor and looking around. "This place is something else."

"This 'something else' needs a lot of work," said Jack. "But it's got great bones. I made a list when I was down here before. We'll need materials and a lot of sweat. There's a hardware store the lawyer recommended that's not too far from here."

Sammy looked at him curiously. "Fixing it up? You said you couldn't sell it."

"That's right, I can't."

"So why are you planning to fix it up?"

"Because Lizzie—I mean, because we might be staying down here."

"Staying down here? For how long?"

Jack didn't answer but pointed out the window.

Sammy exclaimed, "Is that a lighthouse?"

"Yep."

"Does it work?"

"No. But it used to. That's Lizzie's Lighthouse."

"Lizzie's Lighthouse?"

"Yeah. It was kind of her place."

Sammy eyed the letter that Jack was holding. "What's that?"

"Just something from Cecilia's lawyer." Jack stuffed the letter into his pocket, and they all spent the next several hours putting things away, cleaning up, and exploring. After that they changed into bathing suits. The kids sprinted toward the water, with Mikki in the lead, Cory second, and Jackie bringing up the rear. Sam Jr. stayed back with him, keeping pace with the chubby-legged three-year-old, who ran on his tiptoes. Sammy and Jack carried towels, a cooler, beach chairs, and an umbrella to stick into the sand. They'd found the chairs and umbrella in the lower level of the Palace.

After playing in the water for a while, Cory went up to the house and returned with a tattered old football.

"Hey, Dad," he called out. "Can you throw with me?"

Jack didn't look thrilled by the request; he was tired. However, right before he was about to decline, a memory struck him.

It had been a basketball, not a football. In his driveway. His father had driven up after work, and six-year-old Jack was bouncing his new ball. He'd asked his dad to play with him. He wasn't sure if his dad had even answered. All he'd remembered was the side door closing with a thud. And if that memory had stuck with him all these years?

He got up from his chair. "You're on, Cor."

Sammy said, "Okay, big guy, show your old man some moves."

They threw for more than an hour. Jack hadn't lost his touch from high school. And Cory, after a few dropped balls, started catching everything that came his way. Jack could see the athleticism showing through his son's chubby, prepubescent frame. Jackie, and even Mikki, finally joined them, and Jack ran them through some old high school football plays he remembered.

After everyone was sufficiently exhausted, Cory said, "Thanks, Dad, that was great."

Jack rubbed his son's head. "Nice soft pair of hands you got. Wish I had you on my football team in high school."

Cory beamed and Jackie squealed, "Me too?"

Jack snatched Jackie up, held him upside down, and ran to the water. "You too."

Hours later, the sun started to set while the kids were still running around in knee-deep water, building castles, chasing wide-butted Sam Jr., and throwing a Frisbee that they'd also found in the house. Sammy and Jack sat back in the tattered beach chairs, Jack with a Coke and Sammy with a Corona.

Sammy finally tipped his baseball cap over his eyes and leaned back, settling himself so deeply in the chair that his butt touched the sand. Jack drew the letter out of his pocket and opened it. In spidery handwriting, Cecilia sent her love and hope that Jack and the kids would find as much fun and contentment from the house as she and Lizzie had. As Jack read the letter it was as though Cecilia was talking to him in her richly soothing, southern cadence.

She wrote:

My life on earth is over of course, or else you wouldn't be reading this letter. But I had a fine, old run, did everything I wanted to do, and, hell, the things that might've got left out I didn't need anyway.

I'd never seen a little girl who loved the ocean and sand more than Lizzie. And she loved this old house, even though, as you know, it carries some bad memories. And Lizzie's Lighthouse, as she called it. That child was always up there. I think Mikki, Cory, and dear Jackie will love this place too; at least that's my hope. And I feel sure that you, Jack, will find some comfort and peace in the place where Lizzie grew up.

I know it has been a most difficult and heartbreaking time for you. I know that you loved Lizzie more than anyone could. And she loved you just as much back. Fate dealt you a terrible hand by separating you two long before you should have been. But remember that every day you wake up to those three darling children, you are waking up to the most precious things that you and Lizzie ever made together. Because of that, you will never be apart from the woman you love. That may not seem like nearly enough right now, when you want to be with her so badly. But as time goes by, you will realize that it will actually make all the difference in the world. It's not so much that time heals all wounds, honey, as it is that the passage of the years lets us make peace with our grief in our way.

I know they called you the miracle man after you got better. But just so you know, I considered you a miracle from the moment you came into Lizzie's life. And I know she felt the same way. You got a second chance of sorts, son, so you live your life good and well. And Lizzie will *be waiting for you when your time has run too. And I'll probably come by for a cup of coffee myself. Until then, keep hugging those precious children and take care of yourself.*

*Love,
Cecilia*

Jack slid the letter back in his pocket, drew a long breath, and wiped his eyes. Even though he had never been to this place before, he felt like he'd just come home. He rose, took off his shoes, and jogged out toward the water to be with his kids. When they were tired out and headed inside for a late dinner, Jack stayed behind, walking along the beach as the sun dropped into the horizon, burning the sky down to fat mounds of pinks and reds. The warm waters of the Atlantic washed over his feet. He stared out to sea, one of his hands absently feeling for the letter in his pocket. It had been a good first day.

"Hey, Dad!"

He turned to see Cory frantically waving to him from the rear screen porch.

He waved back. "Yeah, bud?"

"Jackie turned the hose on."

"Uhhh...okay?"

"After he dragged the other end in the house."

Jack started to walk fast to the Palace. "In the house? Where's Sammy?"

"In the bathroom with a magazine."

Jack started to jog. "Where's Mikki?"

Cory shook his head helplessly. "Dunno."

Jack started to run faster as he yelled, "Well, can't you turn the hose off or pull it out of the house?"

"I would, but the little knobby thing came off in my hand and Jackie won't let go of the end of the hose. He's a lot stronger than he looks." Cory's eyes grew a little wider. "Is it bad that stuff's starting to float, Dad?"

Oh, crap.

Jack started to sprint, rooster tails of sand thrown up behind him. "Jackie!"

My three precious children. This one's for you, Cecilia.

23

The next day, while Sammy stayed with the other kids, Jack and Mikki drove in the pickup truck to the hardware store in downtown Channing, about three miles from the beach house. Along the way, they reached a stretch of oceanfront that was lined with magnificent homes, estates really, thought Jack. There was serious money down here. If he could catch some work from some of these wealthy folks, it might really be good.

Mikki said, "Are those like condo buildings?"

"They're mansions. This is prime beachfront property here. Those places are worth millions each."

"What a waste. I mean, who needs that much room?" she said derisively.

He glanced at her. "Are you feeling better about things?"

"No."

As they passed one house that was even larger than the others, a teenage girl came out into the cobblestone driveway dressed in a bikini top and tiny shorts with the words

HUG 'EM printed on the backside. She was blond and tanned and had the elegant bone structure of a model. She climbed into a Mercedes convertible about the same time a tall, lean, tousled-haired young man came hustling up the drive. He had on wakeboard shorts and a tank top. He hopped in the passenger seat, and the car roared off, pulling in front of their old truck and causing Jack to nearly run off the road.

Mikki rolled down the window and yelled, "Jerks!"

The girl made an obscene gesture.

"Catch up to them, Dad; I want to kick her butt."

"Since when did you develop such anger issues, my little miss sunshine?"

"What are—" She stopped when she saw him smiling.

She muttered, "Shut up."

They reached Channing and climbed out of the truck. Jack had on jeans and a white T-shirt and sneakers. Mikki was dressed in knee-length cotton shorts and a black T-shirt. Her skin was pale, and her hair was now partially green and purple. His daughter's supply of hair colors seemed endless.

Mikki looked around as Jack checked his list of supplies.

"Looks like something right out of Nick at Nite," she said. "Pretty old-fashioned place."

Jack looked around and had to admit, it was a little like stepping back in time. The streets were wide and clean and the storefronts well maintained. The shops were mostly mom-and-pops. No big-box retailers here, it seemed. A bank, grocery, large hardware store, barber's shop with a striped pole, restaurants, an ice cream parlor, and a sheriff's station with one police cruiser parked in front were all in his line of sight. They also saw a public library with a sign out front that advertised free Wi-Fi service inside.

Mikki said, "Well, at least we can get online here."

People walked by in shorts and sandals; some of the older ladies had scarves around their heads. One elderly gent had on seersucker shorts, white socks, and white sandals. Others rode bikes with wicker baskets attached to the fronts. A few people had dogs on leashes, and some kids ran up and down the street. Everyone was very tanned. There was also a sense of prosperity here. Most of the cars parked along the street were late-model luxury sedans or high-dollar convertibles. Some had out-of-state license plates, but most were from South Carolina. But then Jack noted dented and dirty pickup trucks and old Fords and Dodges rolling down the street. The people in those vehicles looked more like he did, Jack thought. Working stiffs.

They passed a shabby-looking building with a marquee out front that read, CHANNING PLAY HOUSE. An old man was sweeping the pavement in front of the double-door entrance. Next to the entrance was a glass ticket window. The man stopped sweeping and greeted them.

"What's the Channing Play House?" Jack asked.

"Back in its day it was one of the finest regional theater houses in the low country," said the man, who introduced himself as Ned Parker.

"Regional theater?" said Jack.

Parker nodded. "We had shows come all the way down from New York City to perform. Singers, dancers, actors; we had it all."

"And now?" Jack said.

"Well, we still have the occasional performance, but it's nowhere near what it used to be. Too many video games and big-budget movies." He pointed at Mikki. "From your generation, missy."

Mikki pointed to the marquee, which read, CHANNING TALENT COMPETITION. "What's that?"

"Hold it every year in August. Folks compete. Any age and any act. Baton, dancing, fiddling, singing. Lot of fun. It's a hundred-dollar prize and your picture in the *Channing Gazette*."

They continued on, and Jack and Mikki went to the local, well-stocked hardware store and purchased what they needed. A young man who worked at the store helped Jack load the items. Jack noticed that the boy was giving Mikki far more attention than he was Jack. He stepped between the young man and his daughter. "Some of this stuff won't fit in my truck bed," Jack pointed out.

Before the helper could answer, a stocky man in his seventies with snow-white hair strolled out. He was dressed in pleated khaki pants and a dark blue polo shirt with the hardware store's name and logo on it.

He said, "That's no problem; we deliver. Can have it out there today. You're in the Pinckney place, right?"

Jack studied him. "That's right; how'd you know?"

He put out his hand and smiled. "You beat me to it. I was coming out to see you later today and formally introduce myself. I'm Charles Pinckney, Cecilia's 'little' brother." He turned to Mikki and extended his hand. "And this must be the celebrated Mikki. Cee wrote me often about you. Let me see, she said you could play a guitar better than anyone she'd ever heard and were as pretty as your mother. I haven't heard you play, but Cee was spot-on with her assessment of your beauty."

In spite of herself, Mikki blushed. "Thanks," she mumbled.

Pinckney looked at the young helper. "Billy, take the rest of these materials and set it up for delivery."

"Yes, sir, Mr. Pinckney." He hurried off.

Jack said, "Now I remember. You were at the funeral, but we didn't get a chance to talk."

Pinckney nodded slowly. "I'm the only one left now. Thought for sure Cee would outlive me, even though she was a lot older."

"There were ten kids? At least that's what Lizzie told me."

"That's right. Mother and Dad certainly did their duty. I was the closest with Cee. We talked just about every day. Feel like I lost my best friend."

"She was a fine lady. Really helped me out."

"She was one of a kind," agreed Pinckney. "She was duly proud of her heritage. Not many ladies of her generation kept their maiden name, but it wasn't a question for her. In fact, she told her husband he could change his surname to Pinckney if he wanted, but she wasn't switching." He chuckled at the memory.

"Sounds like Cecilia."

"She thought a lot of you. I suppose that's why she left you the Palace. She loved that place. Wouldn't have left it to just anyone."

"I appreciate that. But it came as a total shock. I knew about the place and all, but I'd never been here."

"Cee actually talked to me about it. I know she wanted you to have it, and I was all for it. Especially after Lizzie died. She loved the place too, maybe more even than Cee."

Mikki, who'd been listening closely, added, "If she loved the place so much, why did they move to Cleveland?"

Pinckney said, "I think it had to do with Fred's work."

"People don't buy cars down here?"

"Mikki, knock it off," said her father.

"So why do you call it the Palace?" asked Mikki.

Pinckney grinned. "It was our mother's doing. Her mother and father, my grandparents, were quite the Bible thumpers, but she wasn't. Naming it the Palace made it seem like it was a casino or a saloon or something. It worked. Her parents never visited there, far as I know," he added with a smile.

"Sounds like my kind of woman," Mikki said tartly.

Pinckney looked at the materials in Jack's truck. "So, fixing the place up?"

"Yeah."

"Cee said you were great with your hands."

"If you hear of anyone who needs work done, let me know. I'm not in a position where I can just take the summer off. I've got a lot of mouths to feed."

"I'll put the word out. Good luck with the Palace. Love to see the old place like it used to be."

"Thanks," Jack said. "It has great bones, just needs some TLC."

"Don't we all," said Pinckney. "Don't we all."

24

"Friendly people," remarked Mikki grudgingly as they continued down the street.

"Southern hospitality, they call it. Hey, how about some lunch before we head back?"

"Dad, you don't have to—"

"It's just lunch, Mik. Work with me here, will you?"

"Fine," she said dully.

As they rounded the corner, the Mercedes sports car that had almost caused them to wreck earlier flew around the same corner. The girl's head was swaying to the music blasting from the car's radio. The same young man was in the front seat next to her.

Mikki yelled, "Hey!"

"Mik," said her dad warningly.

But she was already in the street flagging the car down. The girl hit her brakes and snapped, "What the hell do you think you're doing?"

"First, turn off that crap you think is music," said Mikki.

The girl made an ugly face, but the guy hit the button and the sounds died.

"*You* cut us off earlier and almost made my dad roll his truck."

The girl laughed. "Is your hair naturally that color, or did someone throw up on it?"

The guy grimaced. "Tiff, knock it off."

The girl gave Mikki a condescending look and then laughed derisively. "Okay, whatever. Hey, sweetie-pie, now, why don't you go on off and play somewhere." She hit the gas, and they sped off.

"Creeps," Mikki screamed after them. She glared over at her dad. "Wow. So much for Southern hospitality."

When she saw the sign a few moments later, her face brightened. "Okay, *that* is the place for lunch."

Jack looked where she was pointing.

"Little Bit of Love Bar and Grill?" Jack read. "Why is that the place?"

"Come on, Dad, I have to see if this is what I think it is."

She hurried inside, and Jack followed. There were twenty retro tables with red vinyl covers on them and chairs with yellow vinyl covers. The floor was a crazy pattern of black-and-white square tiles. The walls were covered with posters of famous rock-and-roll bands. Behind the bar, which took up one entire wall, were acoustic, bass, and electric guitars along with various costumes actually worn by band members, all behind Plexiglas. Stenciled on another wall were lyrics from famous rock songs.

Mikki looked like she'd just discovered gold in a tiny coastal town in South Carolina. "I knew it. So cool."

Most of the tables were occupied, and the bar was doing a brisk business. Waiters and waitresses dressed in jeans and T-shirts were moving trays of food and drink from the kitchen to the patrons. Along another wall were old-fashioned pinball machines, all with a musical theme.

A woman about Jack's age headed toward them.

"Two for lunch?" the woman said.

Jack caught himself staring at her. She was tall and slim and had dark hair that curved around her long neck. Her eyes were a light blue, and when she smiled Jack felt his own mouth tug upward in response.

"Um, yeah," said Jack quickly. "Thanks."

They followed her to a table, and she handed them menus.

"I can take your drink order."

They told her what they wanted. She wrote it down and said, "Haven't seen you before."

Jack introduced himself and Mikki.

"I'm Jenna Fontaine," she said. "I own this pile of bricks."

"As soon as I saw the name, I just knew," said Mikki.

Jack looked at her. "What do you mean?"

Jenna and Mikki exchanged smiles. Mikki said, "Def Leppard, am I right?"

"You know your rock-and-roll lyrics." When Jack still looked puzzled, Jenna said, "'Little Bit of Love' is a Def Leppard song."

"So you're into music?" said Jack.

"Yes, but not nearly as much as that guy."

She pointed to a tall, lanky teenager with long black hair who was setting plates full of food down at the next table.

"That's Liam, my son. Now, he's the musical madman in

the family. When I decided to chuck the life of a big-city lawyer and move here and open a restaurant, the theme and décor were his idea."

Mikki eyed Liam and then turned back to her. "Does he play?"

"Just about any instrument there is. But drums are his specialty."

Mikki's eyes glittered with excitement for the first time since stepping foot in South Carolina.

"I take it you're into music too," said Jenna.

"You could say that," said Mikki modestly.

"So where y'all staying?"

"My great-grandma left us a house."

"Wow. That's pretty impressive. Well, enjoy your lunch."

She walked off, and Jack looked down at the menu but wasn't really seeing it.

Mikki finally touched his hand, and he jumped.

"Dad?"

"Yeah?"

"She's really pretty."

"Is she? I didn't notice."

"Dad, it's—"

"Mik, let's just get something to eat and get back, okay? I've got a lot of work to do."

After Mikki took refuge behind her menu, Jack snatched a glance at Jenna as she seated another party. Then he looked away.

25

It took several days of backbreaking work to thoroughly clean the house, and all the kids pitched in, although Mikki did so grudgingly and with a good deal of complaining. "Is this how the summer's going to go?" she said to her dad as she scrubbed down the kitchen sinks. "Me being a slave laborer?"

"If you think this is tough, join the army. There you clean the floor with a toothbrush, and it only takes about twelve hours, until they tell you to do it again," Jack told her. She glared at him darkly as he walked off with a load of trash.

They next attacked the outside, cleaning out flower beds, pruning bushes, clearing away dead plants, and power washing the decks and the outdoor furniture. The rest of the acreage was beyond their capability—and Jack's wallet.

With much tugging and cursing, Jack and Sammy were finally able to get the door to the lighthouse open. As Jack stepped into the small foyer, dust and disturbed spiderwebs floated through the air. He coughed and looked around.

The rickety steps looked in jeopardy of falling down. He

looked through some of the boxes stacked against the wall. There was mostly junk in them, though he did find a pair of tiny pink sneakers that had the name "Lizzie" written on the sides in faded Magic Marker. He held them reverently and imagined his wife as a little girl prancing around in them on the beach. He looked through some other boxes and found a few things of interest. He carried them up to his bedroom.

They all trooped down to the beach that afternoon and ate lunch, letting the sun and wind wash over them. After the meal was over, Jack looked at Mikki, grinned, and said, "Let me show you something."

"What?"

"Stand up."

She did so.

"Okay, grab me."

"What?"

"Just come at me and grab me."

Mikki looked around, embarrassed, at the others. "Dad, what are you doing?"

"Just grab me."

"Fine." She rushed forward and grabbed him, or tried to. The next instant she was facedown on the sand.

She lay there for a second, stunned, then rolled over and scowled up at him. "Gee, Dad, thanks. That was really a great closer after a picnic on the beach."

He helped her up. "Let's do it again, and I'll show you exactly what I did."

"Why?" she asked. "Is this like National Kick Your Daughter's Butt Day and nobody told me?"

Sammy interjected. "He's showing you some basic self-defense maneuvers, Mik."

Mikki looked up at her dad. He said, "So you can handle yourself in certain situations. Without me helping," he added.

"Oh," she said, a look of understanding appearing on her face.

They went through the moves a dozen more times, until Mikki had first her dad, then Sammy, and even Cory lying facedown in the sand. Jackie begged until she did it to him too, and then started crying because he got sand in his eyes.

"Hello!"

They all turned to see Jenna Fontaine walking down the beach. She had on shorts and a tank top and a broad-brimmed sun hat. She was waving and holding up a picnic basket. "I brought you some things from the café."

Jack came forward. "There was no need to do that."

"No trouble. I know how it is coming to a new place." She showed him what was in the basket, and then Jack introduced her to Cory, Sammy, and Jackie. His youngest son hid behind his dad. She smiled and squatted down. "Well, hello, little man. You look just like your daddy."

"Daddy," said Jackie shyly, hiding his face.

Mikki asked, "So where do you live, Jenna?"

Jenna pointed to the south. "About a half mile that way. We have a rocky point too. So when you hit the rocks, our house is the pile of blue shingles with the vibrating roof."

"Vibrating roof?" said Mikki curiously.

Jenna looked at Jack. "It's another reason I stopped by. Charles Pinckney said you were a whiz at building things. He was the one who told me you were staying here. What I really need—to stop myself from either killing my son or committing myself to a mental institution—is a soundproof room for his music studio."

"He has a music studio?" exclaimed Mikki.

"Well, he calls it that. Most of the equipment is secondhand, but he's got a lot of stuff. I don't understand most of what it does, but what I do know is it's killing my ears." She looked at Jack again. "Want to come by and give me an estimate?"

Jack looked uncertain for a moment but then said, "Sure, I'd be glad to."

"You want to stop by tomorrow evening? Liam will be there, and he can sort of tell you what he needs."

"It might be a little expensive," said Jack. "But we've done soundproofing before. You'll notice a big difference."

"I think saving my hearing and my sanity is worth any price. Say about eight?"

"That'll be fine," said Jack.

Jenna told them her address, waved, and headed off.

Jack watched her go. When he turned back, he saw Mikki and Sammy staring at him. Jack said nervously, "Uh, I've got some stuff to do."

He handed the picnic basket to Mikki and trudged back to the Palace.

Sammy looked at Mikki. "Is he okay?"

Mikki glanced in Jenna's direction, then up to her dad, who was just entering the house. "I don't know," she said.

Jack fell asleep that night with the tiny pair of pink sneakers on his chest.

26

Mikki had insisted on coming along with Jack to the Fontaines' house, so Sammy stayed behind to watch the boys. They drove there in Jack's pickup truck.

Jenna met them at the door and ushered them in. The house was old but well maintained, and the interior was surprising. Instead of a typical beach look, it was decorated in a Southwestern style, with solid, dark, and what looked to be handcrafted furniture. There were textured walls faux painted in salmon and burnt orange, oil paintings depicting both snowcapped mountains and smooth deserts, and brightly colored woven rugs with geometric patterns.

Jenna sat across from him. Jack ran his gaze over her and then looked away. She was wearing white capri pants and a pale blue pullover, and her feet were bare.

"Nice place," said Jack.

"Thanks. We tried to make it feel like home."

"Where's that?" asked Mikki as she looked around. "Arizona? I was just there recently."

Jenna laughed. "I've never been to Arizona or the Southwest in general. That's why I decorated the house this way. Probably as close as I'll ever get, and I love the look and feel of it. We originally came from Virginia. I went to college and law school up there. Ended up in D.C., though."

"You look pretty young to have a teenager," said Mikki.

"Mik!" her father began crossly, but Jenna laughed.

"I'll take that as a huge compliment. Truth is, I had Liam while I was in high school." She pursed her lips but then smiled. "The best thing that came out of that marriage was Liam."

"So how did you end up down here?" asked Jack.

"Got tired of the rat race in D.C. I'd made really good money and invested it well. We came down to Charleston one summer, took a drive, happened on Channing, and fell in love with it." She glanced keenly at Jack. "When I talked to Charles Pinckney, he told me about his sister leaving you the Palace. It's a great old place. Never been inside, but I've always loved that lighthouse."

"Yeah, it's pretty cool," said Mikki, looking at her dad.

"My wife grew up in that house," said Jack.

"Charles told me about that too." She paused and added solemnly, "And I'm very sorry for your loss."

"Thanks," said Jack quietly.

Jenna stood and reassumed a cheery air. "Well, do you want to see the mad musician's space?"

Mikki jumped up. "Absolutely."

Mikki could see at a glance that it was set up as a recording studio, albeit on a tight budget. To her expert eye, the soundboard, mixing devices, mikes, and the like were old and looked jury-rigged. She knew because she and her band had done the very same thing. New equipment was far too expensive.

A piano keyboard was against one wall; a bass guitar sat in a stand in a corner. A banjo and a fiddle hung on hooks on the wall.

And yet there were no sheets of music. No songbooks.

"Where's Liam?" Mikki asked. "I thought you said he'd be here."

"He's on his way. He was taking some inventory at the restaurant. What will you be next year, a junior?"

"Yeah."

"Liam too. He goes to Channing High. Only high school in town."

"He's a big kid," said Jack. "Does he play ball?"

Jenna smiled and shook her head. "He's a good athlete, but this"—she pointed at the room—"this is where his heart is."

Mikki slid over to the bass guitar. "Do you think he'd mind?"

"Go for it."

Mikki strapped the guitar on, placed her fingers, and started to play.

"Wow," said Jenna. "That's really good."

She started to take off the guitar, but a voice said, "Play those last two chords again."

They all turned to see Liam standing in the doorway. He had on wire-rimmed glasses and a T-shirt that said SAVE THE PLANET, CUZ I STILL LIVE HERE.

"Liam, I didn't hear you come in," said his mother. "Everything okay at the Little Bit?"

"A place for everything, and everything in its place." He looked at Mikki again. "So knock those last two chords out."

Surprised, but pleased at his request, she did so. The sound rocked the room again.

He walked over to her and placed her index finger on the

guitar neck in a slightly different spot. "Try that; it'll give the sound more depth," he said.

Her grin disappeared, and she flushed angrily. "I know how to place my fingers. I've been playing since I was eight."

He seemed unfazed by her hostility. "So let me hear it now."

"Fine, whatever." She checked the new position of her index finger and played the chord. Her eyes displayed her amazement. The sound was far richer. She looked at him with new respect. "How did you figure that one out?"

He held up his hand. His fingers were amazingly long and the tips heavily calloused. "Anatomical."

"What?"

"The fingertip has different strength points on the surface. Once you understand where they are and place your fingers accordingly, the tightness on the strings is increased. Gives a fuller sound because there's less vibration coming off the neck."

"You worked that out on your own?"

"Nope. I'm not that smart. Read about it in a article in *Rolling Stone*," he said. "So what's your name?"

"Mikki Armstrong. That's my dad."

Jack and Liam shook hands.

"Mr. Armstrong is here to see if he can save my hearing," said Jenna.

Jack said, "Just call me Jack."

Liam grinned. "Think you can help Mom out? I don't want her going deaf on me. But then again, that might have its advantages."

Jenna smacked him lightly on the arm. "Don't make me put you over my knee at your age."

Jack surveyed the room and then went around the space knocking on the walls. "Drywall on two-by-four studs set at standard width." He reached up and tapped the low ceiling at regular intervals. "Same here. Yeah, I can handle it if the hardware store has what I need."

Jenna looked impressed. "When can you start?"

"Soon as I get materials. I'll work up an estimate so you know how big a hit your pocketbook will take."

Mikki blurted out, "My dad is great at this stuff. He can build anything."

Jenna smiled. "I believe it."

Mikki eyed the room. "Liam, where's your music?"

He tapped his head. "All up here."

"But what about new pieces? You need sheet music to learn them."

"I can't read music. I play by ear."

"Are you kidding?"

He grinned. "Want to test me?"

She looked down at the bass guitar she was still holding. When she saw what it was, she exclaimed, "This is a Gibson EB-3 from the late sixties. Jack Bruce from Cream played one. It's vintage. How'd you score it?"

"EBay. Saved up two summers for it. Got a great deal. It's box is so smooth, and the sound is so pure. I think it's the best four-string ever made."

Jenna looked at Jack. "I don't know about you, but I don't speak this language. You want some coffee while our kids talk shop?"

Jack hesitated, but after a pleading look from Mikki he said, "Sure."

After they left, Mikki said, "Okay, Mr. Play-by-Ear, here's

your test." She played a minute-long piece of a song she'd recently composed. She handed him the Gibson.

"Okay, go for it."

He strapped on the bass, set his fingers, and played back her song, note for perfect note.

Mikki exclaimed, "You're like Mozart only on percussion and bass. Ever been in a band?"

He scoffed. "There are no bands in Channing."

"Who're your favs?"

"Hendrix, AC/DC, Zeppelin, Plant, Aerosmith, to name a few."

"Omigod, they're like my top five of all time."

Liam picked up his drumsticks. "Want to score a few sets?"

She strapped the bass back on. "I'm dying to try out my new fingertip strength points."

27

Jenna and Jack were sitting out on her rear deck with their mugs of coffee when the music started up. The deck flooring really did appear to vibrate.

"Now do you see why I need the soundproofing?" she asked, covering her ears.

Jack nodded and laughed. "Yeah. I get it. We finally had to get Mikki to start practicing at another kid's house back in Cleveland. Even with that I'm not sure I can hear out of my right ear."

"The long-suffering parents of musical prodigies. Want to carry our coffee down to the beach? My head is already hurting."

They strolled along the sand together. It was well after eight but still light outside. A jogger passed them heading in the opposite direction, and an elderly couple were throwing tennis balls to a chubby black Lab. As the dog ran after a ball, the man and woman held hands and walked along.

Jenna eyed them and said, "That's how it's supposed to turn out."

Jack glanced at her. "What?"

She pointed at the couple. "Life. Marriage. Growing old together. Someone to hold hands with." She smiled. "A fat dog to throw balls to."

Jack watched the old couple. "You're right, it is supposed to turn out that way."

"So your wife grew up here?"

"Yeah."

"Is that why you came down here? Memories?"

"I guess so," Jack said slowly. He stopped and turned to her. "And my wife planned to bring the kids down here this summer. So I thought I'd do it for her. And I wanted to see the place too."

"You'd never been here before?"

Jack shook his head. "My wife had a twin sister who died of meningitis. They lived here for a while longer. But then I guess it just wasn't that...um...good," he finished, a bit awkwardly.

"I'm so sorry."

They started walking again. She said, "So how're the kids dealing with the move and all?"

"With three kids, they all sort of handle things differently."

"Makes my job seem simple. I've only got one."

"Well, Mikki is pretty independent. Just like her mom."

"She seems fantastic. Liam is not easily impressed when it comes to music."

"She and I butt heads a lot. Teenage girls. They need... stuff that dads just aren't good at."

"I feel that deficiency with Liam too, just on the flip side."

"He looks like he's doing fine."

"Maybe in spite of me."

"So you're divorced now?"

"Long time. Right after Liam was born. My ex moved to Seattle and has nothing to do with him. I just have to put it down to my poor choice in men."

"How'd you manage college and law school with a kid?"

"My parents were a huge help. But sometimes I'd take Liam to class with me. You do what you have to do."

Jack stopped, picked up a pebble off the beach, and threw it into the oncoming breakers. "Yeah, you do."

Jenna sipped her coffee and watched him. "So are y'all just down here for the summer?"

"That's the plan. Look, I'll write up that estimate and get it to you tomorrow."

"I tell you what. Why don't I just give you a check tonight to help cover the materials and you can get started."

"You don't want an estimate?" he said in surprise.

"No."

"Why not?"

"I trust you."

"But you don't know me."

"I know enough."

"Okay, thanks for the coffee." He smiled. "And the trust."

"Stop by the Little Bit again. Have to try the killer onion rings."

As they walked back, she said, "I really am sorry about your wife."

"Me too." Jack glanced back at the old couple still walking slowly hand in hand. "Me too."

28

Mikki awoke the next morning in her attic bedroom. She stretched, yawned, and sat back, bunching her pillows around her. Then she rose, picked up her guitar, and started playing a new song she'd been working on, using the new technique Liam had taught her. The long fingers of her left hand worked the neck of the instrument, while her right hand did the strumming. She put down the guitar, went to her desk, picked up some blank music sheets, and started making notations and jotting down some lyrics. Then she started singing while she played the guitar.

A minute later, someone knocked on her door.

Startled, she stopped singing and said, "Yeah?"

"Are you decent?" Jack called through the door.

"Yes."

He opened the door and came in. He had a breakfast tray in hand. Bacon, eggs, an English muffin smeared with Nutella, and a glass of milk. He set it down in front of her. Mikki put the guitar aside.

"How'd you know I like Nutella?"

"Did some good old-fashioned reconnaissance." He pulled a rickety ladder-back chair up next to the bed.

"What?"

"Okay, I looked in your room back in Cleveland. Dig in before it gets cold."

Mikki began to eat. "Where's everybody else?" she asked.

"Still sleeping. It's early yet. Did you have fun last night with Liam?"

Mikki swallowed a piece of bacon and exclaimed, "Omigod, Dad, he is, like, so awesome. That thing he showed me with the fingers, the pressure points? It works. We played some sets together, and he likes the bands I like, and he's funny, and—"

"So is that a yes?"

"What?"

"You did have a good time last night?"

She grinned sheepishly. "Yeah, I did. How did things go with Jenna?"

"I agreed to do the job. She gave me a check to start. Sammy and I will get the materials and go from there."

"She seems really cool. Don't you think?"

"She's very nice." Jack slipped something from his pocket and handed it to her. "I found this in a box in the lighthouse this morning."

"The lighthouse? Pretty early to have already been out there."

"Look at the picture."

Mikki held it tightly by the edges, her brow furrowing. "Is this Mom?"

"Yep. There's a date on back. Your mom was right about your age in that photo. It was taken down here at the beach.

It must've been the summer before she moved to Cleveland. The lighthouse is in the background." He paused. "You see, don't you?"

"See what?"

"That you look just like her."

Mikki squinted at the image of her mom. "I do?"

"Absolutely you do. Well, except for the weird hair color and goth clothes. Your mom was more into ponytails and pastels."

"Ha-ha, real funny. And my clothes are not goth, which is, like, so last century anyway."

"Sorry. Why don't you finish your breakfast and we can go for a walk on the beach before things get going."

"Is this part of you being a dad thing?" she asked bluntly.

"Partly, yeah."

"And the other part?"

"I had a long time to be alone after you guys left, and I hated it. I never want to be alone again."

As they hit the sand, the sun was slowly coming up and the sky was a sheet of pink and rose with the darkened mass of the ocean just below it. There was a wind that had dispelled most of the night's heat. Gulls swooped and soared over the water before diving, hitting the surface and sometimes coming away with breakfast in the form of a wriggling fish.

"It's really different down here," said Mikki, finally breaking the silence.

"Ocean, sand, hotter."

"Not just that."

"I guess no matter where we'd be right now, it would be different," he replied.

"I wake up sometimes and think she's still here."

Jack stopped walking and looked out to the ocean. "I wake

up every morning expecting to see her. It's only when she's not there that I realize..." He started to walk again. "But down here, it's different. I feel...I feel closer to her somehow."

Mikki gazed worriedly at her dad but said nothing.

They threw pebbles into the water and let the fingers of the tides chase them up and down the sand. Mikki found a shell that she pocketed to later show her brothers.

"You've got a great voice," he said. "I was listening outside the door this morning."

"It's okay," she said modestly, although it was clear his praise had pleased her.

"Do you want to study music in college?"

"I'm not sure I want to go to college. You didn't."

"That's true."

"I'm not sure the sort of stuff I want to play would be popular in college curriculums or in the mainstream music industry."

"What kind is it?"

"Are you asking just to be polite, or do you really want to know?"

"Look, do you have to make everything so complicated? I just want to know."

"Okay, okay. It's very alternative, edgy beats, nontraditional mix of instrumentals. No blow-you-out-of-the-house cheap synthesizer tricks. And no lollipop lyrics. Words that actually mean something."

Jack was impressed. "Sounds like you've given this a lot of thought."

"It's a big part of my life, Dad; of course I've thought about it."

"It's nice to have something you're so passionate about."

"Were you ever passionate about anything?"

"Not until I met your mother; then she sort of took up all the passion I had."

Mikki made a face. "That is, like, so gross to tell your own daughter."

"I didn't mean it like that. Before your mom came along, I was just drifting. I had my sports and all that. But not much else. And my dad was dying of cancer."

"But you still had your mom."

"Yeah, but we had our issues."

"Didn't get along? Like you and me?" she added, poking him in the side.

"Let's just say I spent a lot more time at the O'Tooles' instead of my house."

"What was the issue?"

His expression turned serious. "I've never really talked about this with anyone, except your mother. There were no secrets between us."

"Fine, I was just curious. You don't have to tell me."

Jack stopped walking, and she pulled up too.

"Okay, full confessional. It got to the point where I really wondered if my mom actually loved me."

Mikki looked shocked. "She had to love you. She was your mother."

"You'd think so, wouldn't you?"

"Why did you think she didn't?"

"Probably because she left when I was seventeen. Right after my dad died."

"What? Nobody ever told me that."

"Well, it's not the sort of thing you announce to the world."

"What happened?"

"She met some guy and moved to Florida. She kept the house in Cleveland, and I lived there until I married your mom and enlisted. She died in a boating accident when you were still a baby and I was still in the army."

Mikki looked at him in amazement. "You lived there, what, by yourself?"

"Didn't have any other relatives, so yeah."

"But you weren't even out of high school yet."

"But I was over sixteen. It wasn't like foster care was an option. I got part-time jobs to pay for expenses."

"My God, Dad. I mean, you were all by yourself."

"*You* like to spend time alone."

"Yeah, but I could come downstairs and everybody would be there."

"Well, I had your mom. She was my best friend. She helped me through some really tough times."

When they got back to the Palace, Mikki said, "Thanks for the walk and talk."

"Hope it's one of many this summer."

As she ran up the deck steps ahead of her father, Sammy appeared from around the side of the house. "You got an early start." He glanced at Mikki as she went into the house. "Little father-daughter time?"

"She's a pretty amazing kid, Sammy. Half her life I was carrying a gun for my country. The other half I was driving nails. I've got a lot to learn about her."

"Probably why I never got married," said Sammy. "Too complicated."

"You ever regret it? No kids, no wife?"

"I didn't, until I started hanging out with you Armstrongs."

29

Later that week, before her dad left for work and she had to watch the kids, Mikki pulled on some shorts, tennis shoes, and a tank top, stretched her legs, and headed to the beach to run. She was naturally athletic, taking after her dad, but she'd never gone out for any school sports teams. The jocks at her school were obnoxious, she thought. And she disliked the competitiveness of sports. She simply liked to run, not try to beat someone running next to her.

She headed down the beach, listening to tunes on her iTouch. She'd put on lots of sunblock because her skin was still pale from the bleak Ohio winter and cold spring. The sun felt great; the views were breathtaking. Her arms pumped, and her long legs ate up ground at a rapid pace. People were fishing from the shore; kids were playing in the sand; teenagers were body surfing in the rough breakers. Though it was still early, a few people were already lying out on beach blankets, reading and talking.

"What the—" she gasped.

The guy had run right up beside her.

"Hey," he said, grinning.

Mikki saw that it was the boy from the Mercedes convertible. He had on board shorts, no shirt. He was lean and muscled. Up close he looked like a Ralph Lauren model, which meant she instantly despised him.

She took out her earbuds, though she kept running.

"The beach is pretty wide," she said back, trying to look indifferent, "so pick another spot."

"I'm Blake Saunders." As they ran, he put out his hand to shake.

She ignored it. "Good for you."

"Can we stop running for a sec?"

"Why?"

"It's important."

She stopped, and he did too.

"Okay, what?" she demanded.

"I wanted to apologize for what happened the other day. Tiff can be a real piece of work."

"Tiff?"

"Tiffany, Tiffany Murdoch."

Mikki snorted. "She looks like a Tiffany."

"Yeah, she's pretty spoiled. Her dad was some big-shot investment guy in New York before they moved down here and built the biggest house on the beach."

"So why do you hang out with her?"

"She can be fun."

Mikki gave him a scathing look. "Oh yeah, I'm sure she can be fun." She slapped her behind. *"Hug 'em?"*

"No, I didn't mean it that way."

Mikki said, "I'm going to finish my run."

"Mind if I jog along with you? I'm the quarterback on the high school football team and I'm trying to keep in shape."

"Suit yourself, QB."

"And your name?"

She hesitated but then said, "Mikki. Mikki Armstrong."

They ran on.

"So what grade are you in?"

"Junior next year."

"I'll be a senior. So you guys just moved down here?" said Blake.

"Yeah, from Cleveland."

"Wow, Cleveland."

She looked to see if he was making fun of her. "Yeah, Cleveland. Got a problem with that?"

"No, I meant that was cool. You have a pro football team. Although no more LeBron James."

"Yeah, but we have the Rock and Roll Hall of Fame."

"That's cool. You play music?"

"Some, yeah. Mostly guitar. And bass."

"I'd like to hear it sometime."

"Why?"

"You're hard to get to know."

"Yes, I am."

"Maybe we can hang out sometime."

"Again, why? If Tiffany is your type, it would be a waste of time. Because I'm not a *Tiffany* by any stretch of the imagination."

"Because it's nice to meet some people who aren't from around here. Small towns can be pretty boring."

"Well, I plan to run on the beach about this time every day."

"Great. Maybe next time I won't get the evil eye as much."

He playfully punched her in the arm, and Mikki let slip a tiny smile.

"Finally, a crack in the armor," he kidded.

"Do you know Liam Fontaine?" she asked.

"Yeah, he's cool but a little odd."

"Odd? Why?"

"No sports, though I know he's a good athlete."

"Well, he works at the restaurant and he has his music. Not much time for anything else."

"Sounds like you already know him."

"I met him. He's an amazing musician."

Blake grinned. "Maybe you should ask him out."

"Please. I don't really know him."

"That's all I'm asking for. A chance to get to know you."

Later, they finished their run. Blake said, "See you tomorrow?"

"Okay."

"You're a good runner."

"So are you," she conceded.

"Have a good one."

He took off at a full sprint, and she caught herself admiring his tanned, muscled back and legs. Then she headed on to the Palace.

30

At the Channing hardware store, Jack and Sammy loaded up the truck with the materials for the work at Jenna Fontaine's house. Charles Pinckney came outside to see them, and Jack introduced him to Sammy.

"Appreciate the referral, Charles," said Jack, as he hoisted another box into the truck bed. "And thanks for putting a rush on these materials for me. I know it's not stuff you'd normally keep in stock."

"Glad to do it. And Jenna is a fine person. She runs the most popular restaurant in town, so she can be a great lead for other work."

"And gorgeous to boot," said Sammy.

Both men were wearing cargo shorts, tank tops, and work boots. It was still morning, but the temperature was already in the eighties.

"Charles, I had a question," said Jack. "I was wondering about the lighthouse. Its history."

"My father built it along with the house. It was originally

listed on the official navigational charts. But one day it just stopped working."

"Anybody ever try to get it running again?"

Pinckney looked surprised. "Why, no. What would be the point? By the time it broke, they didn't use it for a navigational aid anymore."

"Just asking," said Jack.

He and Sammy left Pinckney and drove on to Jenna's house. She'd already left for the restaurant, but she'd pinned a note to the front door telling them that the entrance on the lower level was unlocked. They hauled the materials in, and after covering all of Liam's musical instruments and the furniture with drop cloths, they began to tear out the existing drywall. The plan was to backfill the wall and ceiling spaces with soundproofing materials and then replace the original drywall with specialized denser material that would also act as a sound block.

Around one o'clock they heard someone upstairs.

"Hello?" It was Jenna's voice.

"Down here," called out Jack.

She came down the steps carrying a large white bag.

She held up the bag. "Well, I hope you boys haven't eaten yet."

"You didn't have to do that," said Jack.

"Well, I'm glad you did. I'm hungry," exclaimed Sammy.

Jenna smiled and unpacked two large turkey and cheese sandwiches, chips, pickles, cookies, and sodas on a table against a wall. While she did this, she gazed around the room. "Boy, you two have been busy."

Jack nodded. "It's going better than I thought it would. That means it'll be less expensive for you."

Sammy put down his tools, wiped off his hands on a clean

rag, walked over, and examined the food she'd brought. He bowed formally and said, "You are a goddess sent from above for two weary travelers."

Jenna laughed. "It's so nice to meet a real gentleman."

Jack rinsed off his hands using a bottle of water and a rag and sat down across from Sammy. He looked at Jenna. "You didn't bring yourself anything?"

"I always eat early before the lunch crowd gets in. Place is packed. Always is during the summer."

"Looks like you have a gold mine there," Jack noted.

She sat on a small hassock, crossed her legs, and said, "We do fine. But the profit margins are small and the hours are long."

"Buddy of mine ran a restaurant," said Sammy after he swallowed a bite of his sandwich. "Said it was the hardest work he'd ever done."

Jack munched on a chip and said, "So why do you do it, then, Jenna?"

Jenna had on a black skirt and a white blouse. She'd slipped her heels off and was rubbing her feet. Jack's gaze dipped to her long legs before quickly retreating. If she noticed, she didn't react.

"I'm my own boss. I'm a people person. I admit I get a kick out of walking into the Little Bit and knowing it's mine. And it's something I can leave for Liam, if he wants it, that is. He'll probably be off touring with a band. But it'll be there for him."

"Nice legacy for your kid," said Sammy.

"I know about Jack, but do you have any children, Sammy?"

"No, ma'am. Uncle Sam was my family. That was enough."

"Uncle Sam? You mean?"

Jack answered. "Sammy was in the army. 'Nam. After that, Delta Force."

Jenna looked at Sammy in awe. "That's pretty impressive."

Sammy wiped his mouth with a napkin. "Well, Jack won't tell you about himself because he's too damn modest. So I'll do the honors."

"Sammy," Jack said in a warning tone. "Don't."

"Two Purple Hearts and a Bronze Star," Sammy said, giving Jack a defiant look. He pointed to Jack's bullet wound on his arm. "Purple for that." He pointed to Jack's scarred calves. "And a Purple for that. And the Bronze for saving a bunch of his buddies from an ambush that almost cost him his life."

Jenna gazed at Jack, her lips slightly parted, her eyes wide. "That's amazing."

"What it was, was a long time ago." Jack finished his meal and balled up the paper, putting it in the white bag she'd brought. "Really appreciate the lunch, Jenna." He rose. "We need to get back to work, Sammy."

Jack started cutting out more of the walls.

Jenna eyed Sammy.

In a low voice, he said, "He's a complicated guy."

As Jenna watched Jack attack the walls, she said, "I'm beginning to see that."

31

Later that night, after the kids were asleep, Jack grabbed a flashlight and headed out to the lighthouse. He opened the door and shone his light around. He'd already gone through the boxes lining the walls, but now he walked up the rickety stairs carefully, testing each step before continuing on.

He heard scurrying feet and flashed his light in time to see a mouse rush past his foot. He kept going as the old wooden stairs creaked under his weight. He finally reached the top platform, directly under the access door that led into the space where the light mechanism was located.

As Jack moved his light around, it picked out things in the darkness; the images flew by like a reel of black-and-white film on an old projector. He stopped at one point and drew closer. It was an old mattress. He knelt down and touched it. Sitting on the mattress with its back against the wall of the lighthouse was an old doll. Jack reached down and picked it up. The doll's hair was grimy and moldy, its face stained with dirt and water. Still, he looked at it as though it were a bar of gold. He *knew* this had been Lizzie's. He'd seen her holding it in an old photo of her as a child.

He stood and moved the light around some more. His beam froze on a picture that had been drawn with what looked to be black Magic Marker on the wall. It was a little girl with pigtails and a huge smile. Under the figure was the name "Lizzie." Next to the picture of the girl was a drawing of the lighthouse with the beam on. Above that was written the word "Heaven." Jack noted that the lighthouse beam had been extended out to encompass the word.

He was about to move on when his light caught on something else. He knelt down and held the flashlight close to the wall. The image had been partially rubbed out, but Jack could still tell what it was. It was another drawing of a little girl, with pigtails. At first Jack thought it was merely a second drawing of Lizzie. But as he eyed the faded image more closely, he saw there was a major difference. In the drawing the little girl wasn't smiling. Her mouth pointed downward.

"Not a happy girl," whispered Jack. His gaze shot lower. He edged closer to read what was written there on the wall. Three letters: "T-i-l."

It had to refer to Tillie, Lizzie's twin sister, who'd died of meningitis. He sat back on his haunches and viewed the drawing in its entirety. The remaining letters had faded too badly to be read.

The drawing of the beam of light from the lighthouse extended outward but fell short of encompassing the image of Tillie. She remained firmly in the dark.

"You never found Heaven, Lizzie. And you never found Tillie."

Jack felt tears creep to his eyes, and his lungs suddenly couldn't get enough air.

Holding the doll under one arm, he pushed open the door that led to the catwalk encircling the top exterior of the lighthouse. Jack stared up at the dark sky. Heaven *was* up there somewhere. And, of course, so was Tillie.

And now Lizzie too.

He held up his hand and waved to her. And then, feeling slightly foolish, he let his hand drop but continued to stare up. Right this minute his wife seemed so close to him. He shut his eyes and conjured her face. It couldn't possibly be more than six months since he'd heard her voice and her laugh, felt her skin or watched her smile.

It can't possibly be that long, Lizzie.

He reached up. His finger covered a star that was probably a trillion light-years away and the size of the sun. But his finger covered it all. How close Lizzie must be to him, if he could cover up an entire star with his finger.

Heaven must be right up there.

He carefully set the doll down and slipped the envelope from his pocket. It had the number three written on the outside. The letter was dated December twentieth. He already knew what it said. He'd memorized every word of every letter. But if Lizzie could not read them, he would do it for her.

Dear Lizzie,

Christmas is five days away and it's a good time to reflect on life. Your life. This will be hard. Hard for me to write and hard for you to read, but it needs to be said. You're young and you have many years ahead of you. Cory and Jackie will be with you for many more years. And even Mikki will benefit. I'm talking about you finding someone else, Lizzie.

One Summer

I know you won't want to at first. You'll even feel guilty about thinking about another man in your life, but, Lizzie, it has to be that way. I cannot allow you to go through the rest of your life alone. It's not fair to you, and it has nothing to do with the love we have for each other. It will not change that at all. It can't. Our love is too strong. It will last forever. But there are many kinds of love, and people have the capacity to love many different people. You are a wonderful person, Lizzie, and you can make someone else's life wonderful. Love is to be shared, not hidden, not hoarded.

Jack paused for a moment as a solitary tear plunked down on the paper.

And you have much love to share. It doesn't mean you love me any less. And I certainly could never love you more than I already do. But in your heart you will find more love for someone else. And you will make him happy. And he will make you happy. And Jackie especially will have a father to help him grow into a good man. Our son deserves that. Believe me, Lizzie, if it could be any other way, I would make it so. But you have to deal with life as it comes. And I'm trying my best to do just that. I love you too much to accept anything less than your complete and total happiness.

Love,
Jack

Jack slipped the letter into the envelope and put it back in his pocket. He picked up the doll and stared out over the ocean for a long time. He finally walked back down the stairs and out into the humid night air. He stared up at the lighthouse.

Lizzie's Lighthouse.

He walked back to the house, his heart full of thoughts of what should have been.

32

Mikki rolled over in her bed. Outside she could hear the breakers. The physics of waves crashing on sand had been completely foreign to her a short while ago. Now she'd grown so accustomed to their presence that she wasn't sure she ever wanted to be without the sound.

She yawned, sat up, and did a prolonged cat stretch. Glancing at her clock, she saw it was six thirty a.m. She liked to take her run around now so she could get back before her dad and Sammy left for work.

She slipped off the long-sleeve T-shirt she normally slept in and pulled on running shorts, a tank shirt, ankle socks, and sneakers. She made a pit stop at the bathroom and tied her hair back in a ponytail. On the way out she looked in on both her brothers, who shared a room at the end of the hall next to her dad's bedroom. They were both still asleep. Cory was sprawled on his stomach, while Jackie was on his back, but with both legs bent so his covers made a tent.

She smiled as she listened to her brothers' gentle snores.

As Mikki passed her dad's room, she could hear him stirring.

She rapped on the door. "Dad, I'm going running. I'll put the coffee on. Be back in about an hour."

"Okay. Thanks," came his sleepy response.

She put on the coffee and laid out two mugs for her dad and Sammy. The men got their own breakfast, but Mikki had been making her brothers' meals. Sometimes it was just cereal. But other times she'd pull out the black skillet and whip up eggs, bacon, and something called grits, apparently a Southern thing, which her brothers had instantly loved but she couldn't stand.

She bounced down the steps and passed through the dunes to the flat beach. She did a more thorough stretch and started her run. She kept to the hard, compacted sand, and her long strides carried her down the beach at a rapid clip. About a half mile into her run, Blake joined her. They talked as they ran. All normal subjects that teens gabbed about. She found herself liking him more, in spite of his association with someone like Tiffany Murdoch. He made her laugh.

He said his good-byes a few miles later and jogged back up to the street.

Mikki made her turn to head back toward the Palace when she saw someone out in the surf.

"Liam?"

She jogged down closer to the edge of the water as he stood up and waved.

"Early-morning swim?" she asked.

He high-stepped through the surf to stand next to her.

"Musicians and short-order cooks come here to keep in shape. And I'm not into running."

She smiled and looked out at the water.

"My mom taught me to swim in a wading pool in our backyard," she said.

"Always a good skill to have." He brushed sand out of his hair. "You look like you're working out. Don't let me interrupt you."

"Just a few more miles to go."

"Miles! I'd be puking."

"Come on! You look like you're in awesome shape."

"If I keep eating at the Little Bit, they'll have to start wheeling me out of the kitchen."

"My dad says the soundproofing is coming along."

"Then we can really jam. And my mom won't kill me."

"Looking forward to it."

Back at the Palace, Mikki showered and changed her clothes. Her dad had surprised her by making breakfast for everyone. Pancakes and ham.

"I help," announced Jackie. He proceeded to pour about a gallon of syrup on his dad's pancakes.

Before her dad and Sammy left, Mikki ran back up to her closet to get some things to take down to the beach later with the boys. Her bag spilled over, though, and when she started crawling around the floor picking things up, she noticed a loose floorboard near the rear of the closet. When she pressed the board up, she saw the edge of the photo. She pulled it out and studied the images. She went downstairs and showed her dad, who was finishing up his breakfast.

Jack looked at the picture of Lizzie as a young girl. She was surrounded by her family. A much younger Fred and Bonnie. And her siblings.

"See, Dad," said Mikki. She pointed to one of the people in the photo.

"Yeah, honey, I see."

"That was mom's twin, right? The one who died?"

"Yes. Her name was Tillie."

"Is that why they left here? Not because of Gramps' job? But because it was so sad with her dying and all?"

"Yeah," admitted Jack. "I guess that was part of it."

"I don't know what I'd do if something happened to Cory or Jackie. And to lose a twin. It's like you lost a part of yourself in a way."

"I think you're right."

He held out his hand for the photo, but Mikki drew it back.

"Do you mind if I keep this?"

"No, sweetie, I don't mind at all."

33

"Bonnie?"

When Jack had opened the door in answer to the knock, his mother-in-law was the last person he expected to see.

She was dressed casually in slacks and a turquoise blouse, with sandals on her feet. She slid off her sunglasses and said, "Can I come in?"

"Of course." He moved aside and looked behind her.

"Fred didn't come with me," she said.

"When did you get in?"

"A couple of days ago. We're renting a house on the marsh."

"Here?"

"Yes. This *is* my hometown."

"Of course. I was just surprised."

They sat on the couch in the front room.

"I have to say, I was surprised that Mother left the place to you," she began.

"No more than I was."

"Yes," she said absently. "I suppose not."

Jack hesitated and then just decided to say it. "I heard Lizzie tell you she wanted to bring the kids here after I died."

Bonnie shot him a glance but said nothing.

"That stunned you, didn't it? Her wanting to come back here?"

"Where are the kids?" she asked, ignoring his question.

"On the beach. I can call them up."

"No, let's talk first." She looked around. "I noticed the new boards on the porch and steps, and the yard looks good."

"Sammy and I have been doing a little work to it. Electrical, plumbing, roofing, some landscaping."

"Probably more than a little." She stared at him. "I suppose that's why she left you the place. You could fix it up."

"Like I said, it came as a total shock."

"She left me a letter that explained things."

"She left me one too."

"Mother always did think of everything," Bonnie noted dryly.

"I've been thinking about fixing up the lighthouse too. Lizzie's Lighthouse."

"Please don't do that. Do you know she became obsessed with that damn thing?"

"She told me about it," said Jack. "But she was a little kid."

"No, it lasted for years. She would go up in that lighthouse every night. She would make us turn on the light and shine it over the sky looking for Tillie."

"Heaven," said Jack.

"What?"

"Lizzie said she was looking for Tillie in Heaven."

"Yes, well, it was very stressful for all of us. And then the light stopped working and she became very depressed. When

Fred got the job offer in Cleveland, we jumped at it to get away from here. And to answer your question, I *was* stunned when she told me she was thinking of coming back here."

"But she was a grown woman with three kids. She wasn't going to be searching the sky for Heaven and her dead sister."

"Can you be sure of that?"

"Yeah, I can."

"How?"

"Because I know Lizzie."

Bonnie looked away but did not appear to be convinced.

Jack decided to change the subject. "You and Fred are welcome to use the place anytime you want. It's certainly more your home than mine."

"That's very nice of you, but I really couldn't. It took everything I had just to come here today." She stood and went over to one doorjamb that had horizontal cuts in the wood. "I measured the kids' heights here. Lizzie grew faster than her older sisters. Drove them crazy."

"We saw that," said Jack. "I was going to start doing that for Cory and Jackie."

Bonnie went over to the window and gazed up at the lighthouse, and then shuddered again. "I can't believe the damn thing is still standing."

She sat back down. "I'd like to see the kids while Fred and I are here."

"Of course. Anytime you want."

Jack started to say something else but then caught himself. They were having such an unusually pleasant time together that he didn't want to shatter it. However, Bonnie seemed to sense his conflict.

"What is it?"

"The tabloid story about the Miracle Man?" he said.

"Disgusting. If I could have found that reporter I would have strangled him."

Jack looked confused. "If you could have found him?"

She stared at him, and then what he was thinking apparently dawned on her. Her face flushed angrily. "Do you really think I would have spoken to a trashy gossip paper about my own daughter?"

"But the things in the story. Who else would have known about them?"

"I don't know. But I can assure you it wasn't me. They made Lizzie out to be...well, someone she very clearly wasn't."

"But you never called about it."

"Why would I? I knew none of it was true. Lizzie cheating on you? As preposterous as you cheating on her. I knew you never would have suspected that about her."

"And her going back out that night for the meds? You brought me the bag of pills. You seemed really angry about it."

Bonnie looked embarrassed. "I *was* angry about it. But I knew it wasn't your doing. I called Lizzie thinking she was home. She was at the pharmacy. She told me you hadn't wanted her to go out, that you could do without them. I only acted that way toward you because...well, I'd just buried my daughter, and I was hardly thinking clearly. I'm sorry."

"Okay, I completely understand that."

"I care about the children. I want the best for them."

"I know; so do I."

She drew an elongated breath. "Jack, this is hard, but hear me out."

Okay, here it comes, thought Jack. *The real reason she's here.*

"I've spoken with numerous doctors since your recovery."

"Why would you do that?" he said sharply.

"Because they are only one parent from becoming orphans; that's why."

"I'm alive, Bonnie, in case you hadn't noticed."

"Every doctor I talked to said it's not possible. The disease you have is fatal, without exception. I'm sorry, but that's just what they said."

"Had. I *had* the disease. I don't have it any longer. I was given a clean bill of health."

"Which these same doctors—and one of them was from the Mayo Clinic—said was also impossible. It does not go away. It may go dormant, but it always comes back. And when it does, the consensus is that you won't have more than a few weeks."

"Bonnie, why are we having this discussion? Look at me. I'm not sick anymore."

"Those three children have been through so much. You on your deathbed. Lizzie dying. Having to be uprooted and moved around the country."

"That was your doing, not mine."

"And what choice did I have exactly? Tell me that."

Jack looked away. "Okay, maybe you didn't have a choice. But I don't see your point now."

"What if you get sick again? What if it comes back? And you die? Do you have any idea what it will do to them? A person can only take so much misery, so much sorrow. They're only children; it will destroy them."

"What do you want me to do? Give them back to you? Go crawl off in a corner and wait and see if I get sick again?"

"No, but you could come and live with us in Arizona. You and the kids. That way they can get into a stable routine. And if something does happen to you, we'll be there to help you, and the kids will be used to living with us."

Jack looked askance at her. "Are you telling me that you're willing to take me and all three kids?"

"Yes. Even though Mother left you the Palace, she also left me quite a bit of money. We're in a position to purchase a larger house and have the resources to support all of you."

"I appreciate that, but I can support my own family," he said firmly.

"I didn't mean it that way."

"Okay."

"I'm just looking to help you."

"I appreciate that."

"So you won't consider my offer?"

"No, I'm afraid not."

Bonnie stood. "Well, I guess that's that. Can I go and see the children now?"

"Absolutely. I can take you down there. And I want you involved in the kids' lives."

"I want that too."

34

On Sunday, while Sammy took his motorcycle for a spin, Jack piled all the kids into the VW and drove into Channing. He'd been working hard at Jenna's house and a few other jobs, and the kids needed a break from the Palace. Jack had gotten hold of Ned Parker, and he'd agreed to give the family a behind-the-scenes tour of the playhouse.

Parker met them outside the theater, and over the next hour he took them through the darkened spaces. He showed Cory how to manipulate the house lights, lift and lower scenery, move equipment on stage dollies, and work the trapdoor in the middle of the stage that would allow people to seem to vanish. Jackie in particular thought that was very cool.

They left the theater and walked along, looking at various restaurants. Someone called out to Jack from across the street. He looked over and saw Charles Pinckney hurrying over to them. He was dressed casually in khaki shorts and a short-sleeve button-down oxford shirt with a T-shirt underneath it; leather sandals were on his feet.

"Taking the Sabbath off to enjoy some sunshine and the pleasures of Channing?"

Jack nodded. "Get away from the house for a bit. See the town."

"You hungry?"

Jack said, "We're deciding where to go."

Charles's eyes twinkled. "Then there's only one real option."

"A Little Bit of Love," said Mikki immediately.

Jack said, "We've already been there. How about another place? There're three right here on this block."

"But Jackie and Cory haven't seen it." She turned to her brothers. "It's full of musical stuff; it's so cool."

"Cool," chimed in Jackie.

She smiled. "You want a bit of love, Jackie, huh?"

He jumped up and down. "Bitalove. Bitalove." He grabbed his dad's leg. "Bitalove. Bitalove."

Cory said, "That was, like, such a cheap trick, Mikki."

"Jenna does the best Sunday brunch in town, actually," advised Charles. "I was just heading there myself."

"Okay," Jack said in a resigned tone.

Jenna smiled when she saw them come in. The place was crowded, but she said, "I've got a nice window table. Catch some of the breeze from outside. Follow me."

She seated them at the table, handed out menus, and took their drink orders.

"Is Liam around today?" asked Mikki.

"In the kitchen, grilling. He's turned into quite the short-order cook."

"We'd arranged that I could come by tonight to do a few sets."

Jack looked at her. "You did?"

She stared back at him and said sharply, "Yeah, I did. Sitting home all day watching Cory and Jackie isn't exactly how I planned to spend my summer."

"You don't need to watch me," said Cory.

"Yeah," said Jackie. "Not me."

Jenna looked at Jack and, sensing his distress, said, "Well, your dad is working really hard on the soundproofing, but it's not done yet. And while you guys sound great together, I do like a little peace and quiet in the evening. But I tell you what: Come by around eight. Liam will be home by then, and that's when I take my walk on the beach. I'll be gone about an hour or so. Does that work?"

"That's cool, Jenna, thanks."

Jenna looked at Jack. "And is that cool with Dad?"

"Yeah," Jack said slowly.

"So where's your Delta buddy?" she asked.

"Out riding his Harley," answered Cory.

"Ah. Well he better watch himself. I know a few single ladies of a certain age in this town who will snap him up."

"Snap!" cried out Jackie.

After Jenna left, Jack leaned over and whispered to his daughter, "This is strictly music between you and Liam, right?"

"Dad, please."

"Just asking." He turned to Charles. "Bonnie came by to see me."

"She told me she was."

"Did she tell you what about?"

"Yes. I saw her afterward too. She told me what you two talked about. She told me what you said. And I told her I agreed with you. I don't think that's what she wanted to hear, but so be it."

Mikki, who'd been listening, said, "What didn't she want to hear?"

"Another time, Mik; not now," said her father, shooting a glance at the boys. Then he added, "Did you have a good visit with her, Mik?"

"She was more laid-back than in Arizona," Mikki replied. "There she was like a control freak. Drove me nuts."

Jack turned to Charles. "I checked out the lighthouse the other night."

"Did you? And how is it looking?"

"Not great, actually."

"It really was something in its day."

"I bet it was," said Jack. "I bet it was."

35

After lunch they were walking back to the van when Charles pointed across the street and said, "Speak of the devil."

Jack saw where he was pointing. Bonnie and Fred were just entering a gift shop. Mikki walked up beside him and said in a low voice, "Okay, Dad, what is going on with Grandma? Why is she really here?"

"She just came by to make an offer." Mikki waited expectantly. "For us all to go and live with her in Arizona."

"No way. You're not thinking of doing that, are you?"

"No, I'm not."

Mikki was about to say something else when she saw Blake Saunders coming down the street with two beefy young men. They were all wearing mesh football jerseys with CHANNING HIGH printed on the front.

"Hi," said Mikki. Jack looked at her questioningly. "Blake and I met on the beach when I was going for a run," she explained. "And we've run a few more times together since then."

"Thanks for telling me." He eyed Blake. "You look familiar."

Blake looked embarrassed. "I was in the car that almost ran you off the road that day."

"The girl's name is Tiffany," said Mikki. "And she's super-rich. What a shock."

Blake said, "I told her to slow down, but she doesn't listen to anyone."

"Yeah, I bet," said Mikki.

Blake turned to her. "Hey, we're having a little party on the beach next Saturday. I was wondering if you'd like to come out and hang with us. There's food, a bonfire, and we play some tunes."

"And no alcohol, of course," interjected Jack.

"No, sir," said Blake right away, though his friends gave goofy grins.

"*Right*. She'll have to get back to you on that, sport," said Jack, while Mikki scowled at her father.

"Nine o'clock. About the midpoint of our run, near where the big yellow house is," he added.

"Right."

"Okay, hope to see you there."

The young men walked off.

"What was that all about?" demanded Jack.

"Do you have a boyfriend?" a grinning Cory wanted to know. "I thought you liked this Liam guy."

Mikki's face reddened. "Will you two just knock it off?"

"That guy doesn't even have an earring, and his hair is perfectly normal," said Jack. "He's not your type. He's a football player, for God's sake. You hate football players."

"Who told you that?"

"Your mom. She made a big joke out of it because she *married* a football player."

"I think I can decide for myself what my type is," Mikki said hotly.

"Well, I'm still your dad and I don't like the idea of—"

"Hey, Miracle Man!"

Jack jerked around to see where the voice had come from.

"Over here, Miracle."

Jack turned to see two large men sitting in the cab of a pickup truck staring at him. One man stuck his head out of the truck. "I need me a miracle. You want'a come over here and sprinkle some water on my head?" He waved a five-dollar bill. "I ain't expecting miracles for free. I'll pay good money for it." Both men burst out laughing. They got out of the truck and leaned against it, their big arms folded over their thick chests. They were dressed in jeans and dirty T-shirts, with greasy ball caps on their heads. Their bare arms were covered in tattoos.

Cory said fearfully, "Dad?"

"It's okay, son. We'll just keep on walking."

They passed by the men.

One of them said, "Hey, Miracle, you too good to stop for us poor folk?"

Mikki whirled around and said, "Grow up, you creeps!"

"Mikki," Jack snapped. "Just keep walking."

"Yeah, Mikki," mimicked one of the men. "Just keep walking, sugah."

Jack stiffened at this remark. He almost turned around, but his kids were with him, and he knew nothing good would come out of a confrontation. Jack said to the kids, "We'll go on down to the beach when we get back, and—"

"Hey, Miracle, was it true your slutty wife was cheating on you with your best bud?"

Jack moved so quickly, Cory's hand was still up in the air

where it had been clutching his dad's. When Jack rushed at them, the first man threw a punch. Jack ducked it, grabbed the man's hand, ripped it back and then over his shoulder, swung him around, and slammed him headfirst into the truck. When the bloodied man turned back around and charged at Jack, he sidestepped the attack and leveled the guy with a crushing blow to the jaw. The second man slammed into Jack's back, propelling him forward and face-first into a lamppost. In the next instant he'd spun out of the man's grasp, laid a fist into his diaphragm, doubling him over, and then kicked his legs out from under him. Jack's elbow strike to the back of the man's neck sent him down to the pavement, where he stayed, groaning loudly.

Jack was bent over, his breaths coming in gasps and blood pouring down his face from where he'd hit the post. As he straightened up and looked around, it seemed like the entire town of Channing was staring back at him. No one moved; no one seemed even to be breathing. As he glanced across the street, he saw Jenna and Liam staring at him from the door to the Little Bit. When he looked to his left, he saw Bonnie and Fred gawping at him in shock from the entrance to the gift shop. Bonnie looked at Jack, then to the unconscious men, and then back at her bleeding son-in-law.

"Daddy!"

Jack looked over his shoulder. Jackie was standing on the sidewalk bawling. Cory stood there looking in amazement at his dad, while Mikki glowered contemptuously at the two men lying on the pavement. "Idiots," she said.

Jack quickly piled his kids into the VW and drove off.

36

Jack sat at the kitchen table with ice wrapped in a paper towel and held over his left cheek. Dried blood was stuck to his forehead from the impact with the street lamp. When someone knocked on the door, Jack half expected it to be the police.

"Old man and wady," squealed Jackie after he managed to open the door.

Jenna and Charles strode in. She was carrying a small bag and sat down next to Jack. She started pulling things out: sterilized wipes, Band-Aids, an ice pack, and antibiotic cream.

"What are you two doing here?" asked Jack.

Jenna moved Jack's hand away from his battered face and cleaned up the cuts, applied the ointment, and covered it all with a large Band-Aid.

Charles said, "We thought you might need a little assistance."

"Those two idiots," said Jenna. "Going off half-cocked like that. Probably drunk."

"You know them?" asked Jack.

"They come into the bar every once in a while. But I can't really say I know them."

"They're from Sweat Town," added Charles.

Jenna frowned. "I despise that term."

"Well, it's not very nice, but I think the residents actually coined it," said Charles.

"What exactly is Sweat Town?" asked Mikki.

"Other side of the tracks," replied Charles. "Poor side of town. Every coastal area has them. Most of the people who do the actual work around here live there."

Jenna said, "Here's an ice pack. It'll work faster on that swelling."

"Thanks."

She closed up her bag, sat back, and studied Jack's face. "Okay, you should be good to go."

"You're pretty slick at that," said Mikki.

"Just your mom-standard-procedure stuff."

Jackie jumped up and down trying to get to her bag of medical supplies. Jenna finally placed a Band-Aid on his finger and kissed it. "Now your boo-boo is all gone too." She straightened back up and gazed steadily at Jack. "Looks like you didn't forget your army training. Those weren't small guys, and you put 'em down pretty fast."

Jack grimaced. "It was stupid. Never should've happened."

The door opened, and Sammy walked in carrying his motorcycle helmet. "Had a nice little ride—" When he saw Jack, he exclaimed, "What the hell happened? You fall off a ladder?"

Jackie yelled, "Daddy pighting." The little boy did a kick and then swung his fist so hard he fell over.

"Fighting? Who with?" demanded Sammy.

Mikki and Cory both started telling Sammy what had happened. The older man's features turned dark as he listened to them. When they got to the slur that the one man had called Lizzie, Sammy went over to his toolbox and pulled out a crowbar. "You tell me what they look like and where I can find these maggots."

"No, Sammy," said Jack.

"I'm not letting them get away with this crap," barked Sammy.

"I'll handle it."

"What, you think I'm too old to take care of myself?"

"That's not the point. You beat them up, your butt will land right in jail."

Charles said, "He's right, Sammy. That's not the way to go about it."

"Uh-oh," said Jackie. He was peering out the window into the front yard.

"What is it, Jackie?" asked his sister.

Jackie pointed to the door, his eyes so big they appeared to touch. *"Cop dude,"* he said in a very un-Jackie-like whisper. Then he sped into the next room to hide.

Jack looked sternly at his older kids. "Cop dude? Where did he learn that?"

Mikki looked uncomfortably at the floor. Cory studied the ceiling, his teeth clenched over his bottom lip.

"Great," said Jack stiffly as he rose to answer the door.

The sheriff identified himself as Nathan Tammie. He was a big man with a bluff, serious face and dark curly hair. He took Jack's statement and scratched his chin. "That pretty much matches up with what other people said happened. But you *did* go after them."

"He was provoked. They were saying nasty things about our mom," exclaimed Mikki. "What did you expect him to do?"

Jenna said, "Sheriff, Charles and I saw the whole thing. It's exactly as Mikki said. He was provoked. Anybody would've done what Jack did."

"I'm not saying I wouldn't have done the same thing, Jenna, but I also can't let things like this happen in town without consequences. I've already told those two boys to back off. And I expect you to hold on to your temper, Mr. Armstrong. If something happens again, you come tell me, and I'll handle it. Do we understand each other? 'Cause if there's a next time, people are gonna end up in jail."

"I understand."

After the sheriff left, Charles said, "He's a good man, but he also means what he says." He looked at Jenna. "I can drive you back to town."

"Can you give me a minute, Charles?"

A sulking Sammy had gone into another room, and the kids had disappeared.

Jenna said to Jack, "Miracle Man?"

Jack stared at her, the ice pack held to his face. "It's a long story."

"I'm a good listener."

"I appreciate that, Jenna. It's just that..."

"I can tell you're the sort of man who doesn't open up easily. Keeps it all inside."

"Maybe we can talk about it. Just not right now."

"Well, you need anything else, just let me know." She rose to go.

"Jenna?"

She turned back to see him watching her. "Yes?"

He touched the Band-Aid on his face. "Thanks for coming over. Means a lot."

She smiled. "Only next time I hope I don't have to bring my first-aid kit."

37

The sound woke all of them. Lights burst on. Jack and Sammy made sure the kids were okay before checking the rest of the house.

"Sounded like a bomb going off," said Sammy. "Or a building collapsed."

Jack looked at him quizzically and then said, "Oh, damn!"

He ran toward the rear of the house.

"Jack! What is it?"

Sammy raced after him.

Jack sprinted across the backyard and over to the rocks. He ripped open the door of the lighthouse and stopped. The stairs had collapsed. He shone his light upward. Forty vertical feet of wood had tumbled down.

Sammy ran up next to him and saw what he was looking at. "Hell. Weren't you just up there?"

Jack nodded, his gaze still on the fallen structure. Now he couldn't get to the top.

"Close call, boy."

Jack turned to him. "I need to rebuild the stairs."

"What?"

"We can go get the materials tomorrow."

"But we still have to finish some other jobs. And Charles has got some more referrals for us. Lady named Anne Bethune has a big house on the beach. She wants a screen porch enclosed and some other stuff done. Good money."

"I'll do this on my own time."

"Yeah, all your spare time."

"I *have* to do it, Sammy."

Sammy looked at the jumble of splintered wood. "Gonna be expensive."

"Take it out of my share. And I don't expect you to help."

Sammy frowned. "Since when do we have shares and don't help each other?"

"But this is different, Sammy. I can't expect you to do this too."

Sammy looked at the hand-painted sign next to the door and said quietly, "We'll take some measurements in the morning. Get the materials. We'll do the paying stuff during the day and this after hours. Okay?"

"Okay," said Jack. As Sammy turned to go back in the house, he added, "Thanks, Sammy."

He turned around. "Never been married, Jack. But I understand losing somebody. Especially someone like Lizzie."

He continued on into the house, and Jack turned to look back at the lighthouse he was now going to rebuild.

"What's all this for?" Charles asked as Jack and Sammy finished loading the truck to capacity. He eyed the items in the truck bed. "Scaffolding, and you've ordered enough wood to build another Noah's ark?"

"Had a little accident at the Palace," said Sammy when it appeared Jack was not going to answer the man's question.

Charles looked alarmed. "Accident? Was anyone hurt?"

"Stairs in the lighthouse fell down," said Jack. "No one was hurt."

"So you're going to rebuild the stairs?" he asked, looking perplexed.

"Yes," said Jack tersely.

Sammy eyed Charles and shrugged.

"But the light doesn't even work."

"He plans on fixing that too," replied Sammy.

"But why? It's not registered as a navigational aid anymore."

Jack finished strapping everything down before he looked at Charles and pulled out a sheet of paper and handed it to him. "I found a schematic on the lighting system. I'd appreciate it if you could see if these pieces of equipment could be ordered."

Charles glanced down at the list. "Might take some time. And it won't be cheap."

Jack started to climb into the truck. "Thanks."

Sammy gave Charles a helpless look and got in the truck.

As they were driving out of town, Sammy said, "Isn't that Bonnie?"

Jack looked where he was pointing. It was indeed Bonnie. And she was sitting in a car with a younger man dressed in a suit.

"Who's the guy?" asked Sammy.

"Never seen him before."

"She's a strange bird."

"Yeah." Jack glanced back at the woman and then drove on.

They unloaded the materials at the Palace. Then Sammy took the VW and drove off to meet with Anne Bethune about what she needed done, while Jack continued on to Jenna's house in the truck.

Jenna met him at the door. She was still dressed in a robe and slippers.

"Sorry about my appearance. The restaurant business isn't nine to five; it's more like ten a.m. to midnight. You want some coffee?"

Jack hesitated.

"No extra charge," she said, smiling.

"Okay, thanks."

She poured out a cup and brought it down to him in the music room. She watched him work hanging new drywall.

"You really know what you're doing," she said.

"It's just drywall. Once you know what to do, it's pretty easy."

"Right. I can't even hang a picture."

"I doubt being a lawyer in D.C. was easy."

"Just a bunch of words, legal gobbledygook."

"If you say so."

Jenna sipped her coffee and continued to watch. "Our kids have really hit it off playing music together."

"Yeah, Mikki told me."

"First time I've seen Liam really take an interest in anyone down here."

"He seems like a fine young man. And Mikki's mood is a lot better. That's worth its weight in gold."

He put down his tool and took a sip of coffee. "Mind if I ask you a personal question?"

She eyed him with mock caution. "Should I be scared?"

"No."

"Then shoot."

"Ever think about getting married again?"

"I've thought about it, sure."

"I mean, from what you've said, you've been divorced a while. You're young, well-off, smart, and educated. And... really pretty."

"Can I hire you as my publicist?"

"I'm serious, Jenna."

She put her cup down, sat, and covered her bare knees with her robe. "There have been some men interested in a permanent relationship with me. Some right here in Channing."

"But?"

"But they weren't the right ones. And I'm a woman who's willing to wait for the real Mr. Right. Especially considering how *wrong* I got it the first time."

Jack picked up his tool again. "Lizzie and I met in high school. We would've celebrated our seventeenth wedding anniversary this year."

"Sounds like you found Mrs. Right on your first try."

"I did," he said frankly.

"I suppose that makes the loss that much harder."

"It does. But I've got our kids to raise. And I have to do it right. For Lizzie."

"And you, Jack. You're part of the equation too."

"And me," he said. "I hope you find Mr. Right."

"Me too," said Jenna wistfully, as she stared at him.

38

Sammy turned to Jack and said, "I think it's time to knock off. It's almost midnight."

"You go on. I'm just going to finish up a few things."

They were in the lighthouse. After working most of the last three days at Anne Bethune's house, Sammy and Jack had eaten a hasty dinner and worked another four hours on the lighthouse. They had cleared out all the wood from the collapsed stairs and assembled the scaffolding up to the top platform, which also needed repair. Fresh lumber delivered from Charles Pinckney's hardware store was neatly stacked outside in preparation for the rebuilding process.

"Jack, you've put in sixteen hours today. You need to get some rest."

"I will, Sammy. Just another thirty minutes."

Sammy shook his head, dropped his tool belt on the lower level of the scaffolding, stretched out his aching back, and walked slowly to the Palace.

Jack tightened down some of the scaffolding supports and

then climbed up to the top and stepped out onto the catwalk. What he was trying to imagine was how Lizzie the little girl would have thought of the view from up here.

"Were you scared at first, Lizzie? Did you think you might fall? Or did you love it the first time you saw it?" He stared out at the dark ocean and let the breeze wash over his face. He eyed the sky, looking for the exact spot where little Lizzie had imagined Heaven to be perched. And also where her twin sister had gone.

And now where you are, Lizzie.

Farther out to sea he could see ship lights as they slowly made their way across the water. He closed his eyes, and his thoughts carried back to that frozen cemetery four days after Christmas, when they'd laid Lizzie into the ground. She was there right now, alone, in the dark.

"Don't, Jack," he said. "Don't. Nothing good will come from dwelling on that. Remember Lizzie in life. Not like that."

He looked to his right and was surprised to see someone walking along the beach. As the person drew closer, Jack could see that it was Jenna. She was holding her sandals in one hand, slowly swinging them as she walked close to the waterline. He looked at his watch. It was nearly one in the morning. What was she doing out here?

She suddenly looked up and under the arc of moonlight saw him. She waved and started toward the rocks.

She called up to him. "Working late?"

He said, "Just finishing up a few things. Surprised to see you out."

"I sometimes take a walk on the beach after closing down the Little Bit. Helps to relax me." She gazed at the lighthouse. "Heard you were fixing it up."

"Trying." He added, "Guess it seems pretty crazy."

"I think it's a good idea," she said, surprising him.

"Why?"

"I just think it's a good idea. That's all." He didn't say anything. "By the way, you did a great job on the soundproofing. Can't hear a thing. It's raised the quality of my life a thousand percent. And I won't have to kill my only child."

"I'm glad I could help."

"Well, I guess I better head back."

Jack looked down the dark beach from where she had come. "Do you want me to walk back with you? It's pretty dark out there."

"No, I'll be fine. It's a safe place. And you look like you have some thinking to do still."

Before he could say anything, she'd turned and walked off. He slowly climbed back down the scaffolding. When he touched bottom, he passed through the doorway and then turned and looked at the hand-painted sign.

"I'm going to get it working," he said. "Lizzie, I promise that this light will work again. And then you can look down from Heaven and see it."

And maybe see me.

39

"Oh, great," said Mikki. It was Saturday night and she was at the beach party Blake Saunders had invited her to. There were lots of people already there, and one of them was Tiffany Murdoch, holding court by the large bonfire that spewed streams of embers skyward. There were quite a few large young men in football jerseys and teenage girls in short shorts, tight skirts, and tighter tops. A catering truck was parked on the road near the beach. Mikki, who'd brought a blanket and a bag of marshmallows, looked on in shock as men and women in white jackets carried trays of food and drinks around to the teens partying on the sand.

Blake spotted her and strolled over, a bottle in his hand.

"Hey, glad you could make it."

"Never been to a beach party that was catered before," she said in a disapproving tone.

"I know. But Tiffany's dad is a big football booster, and he pays for the party every year."

"So I guess that's why Tiff's here?"

"Oh, yeah. The center of attention as always. A real queen bee."

"Bees sting," Mikki shot back.

"What's in the bag?" he said.

"Nothing," she said quickly, hiding the bag of marshmallows behind her.

He held up the bottle. "Want a taste?"

"Thanks, but I'll pass."

"It's not alcohol."

"I'll take your word for it."

A little put off, he said, "Well, there's plenty of food and drink. Help yourself and then come join us."

He left, and Mikki went to the tables manned by other adults in white jackets. She asked for a Coke. The woman, weathered looking with stringy gray hair, poured it out for her.

"Thank you," said Mikki.

The woman looked surprised.

"What?" asked Mikki. She looked down at her jeans and T-shirt. "Something wrong?"

"You're not with that group, are you?" said the woman quietly.

"No, we just came down from Ohio for the summer. Why?"

"You said thank you."

"And that's, like, unusual?"

The woman eyed the partygoers. "With some folks it's apparently impossible. Ohio? Are you Cee Pinckney's folks?"

"She was my great-grandmother. I'm Mikki."

"Nice to meet you, Mikki. Ms. Pinckney was a fine lady. Sorry she's gone."

"I take it you live in Channing?"

"All my life, but just not the postcard part."

"What?"

"You know the part you see on postcards? I live in the area tourists never see. We can't afford the pretty ocean views."

"Would that be Sweat Town?"

"So you've heard of it?"

"Somebody told me. Sounds like where we lived in Cleveland. What's your name?"

"Folks call me Fran."

"It was nice talking to you, Fran."

"Same here, honey."

She turned away to serve someone else.

Troubled by what Fran had told her, Mikki strolled around the pockets of people, many of whom were already wasted. The boys looked at her with lust, the girls with hostility.

Why did I come?

"Well, look who we have here."

Inwardly groaning, Mikki closed her eyes and then opened them. Things were about to get worse.

Tiffany stood in front of her, swaying slightly, plastic cup filled with beer in hand. She had on a string-bikini bottom with a mesh cutoff jersey that barely covered her chest. "What's your name again?"

Between gritted teeth she said, "Mikki."

"Oh, like Mickey Mouse." Tiffany giggled and looked around at the others and made an exaggerated bow. "Mickey Mouse, people." Laughter swept through the ranks of the partiers. A nervous-looking Blake ran up and put his arm around Tiffany's bare waist. "Hey, Tiff, let's go get something to eat."

"Not hungry," said Tiffany with a pout. Mikki could sense

this was her method of getting what she wanted. Putting her thick lips together and acting like a two-year-old.

Mikki looked at the beer and then eyed Tiffany's red convertible parked by the catering truck. "Hope you're not the designated driver."

"I can be anything I want," Tiffany replied, a coy smile on her face.

Blake pulled on her arm. "Come on, Tiff, let's get some food. You don't want to piss off your dad again, remember?"

"Shut up!" snapped Tiffany. She looked at Mikki. "I hear you and Blake have been running together on the beach."

"Yeah, so?"

"I was just surprised."

"Why's that?" Mikki asked, a hard edge to her voice.

"I didn't think he liked hanging out with freaks."

Mikki eyed the other girl's scant clothing. "You know, next time you might want to consider something that actually comes close to covering your big butt."

"Shut up!"

"Okay, I'm leaving now." Mikki turned to walk away.

"Hey, I'm talking to you."

Tiffany grabbed her shoulder. Mikki's arms and legs seemed to move of their own accord. Her hand clamped like a vise on the other girl's wrist. Mikki spun the arm behind Tiffany's back, jerked upward, angled one of her feet in front of Tiffany's legs, and gave a hard shove from behind. The next moment Tiffany was lying facedown in the sand, her mesh top up around her head.

Blake looked at her in amazement. "How'd you do that?" he asked Mikki.

Mikki looked down at her hands as if they belonged to someone else. "My...my dad taught me."

They both looked down at Tiffany, who was spitting out sand and crying. Other people were walking toward them.

"I'm outta here," said a panicked Mikki.

She turned, pushed past some folks, and raced off. As she passed by Fran, the woman winked at Mikki and raised a serving spoon in silent salute.

40

Hurrying down the beach, Mikki collided with someone who appeared, ghostlike, out of the darkness.

"Liam?"

The tall, gangly Liam had on a hoodie and sweatpants.

"What are you doing here?" she asked breathlessly.

"Walking. What about you?" He looked over her shoulder in the direction of the party Mikki had just left. "Tiffany's party? Don't tell me you've gone over to the dark side?" he said with a grin.

"It was stupid," admitted Mikki.

"Well, if you want to come with me, I'll show you a much better party."

"What?"

"But I have to warn you, they don't have caterers."

"How'd you know Tiffany's party was catered?"

"Because my mom did it for a couple years until little Tiffany demanded alcohol be served. Then my mom told old man Murdoch where to stick it."

"Good for her."

"Yeah, funny, for some reason, after that, I never got invited to her little shindig. Well, enough about the rich and the spoiled. Let's get going."

He started to walk off, and Mikki hurried after him. "Where to?"

"Like I said, a better party."

The breakers crashed on the beach, providing a slow, melodious chorus to their footsteps slapping against the hard, wet sand. The sounds and the lights reached them about a quarter of a mile down the beach.

"Is that the better party?" she asked.

"Yep."

As they drew closer, the scene became clearer. The bonfire was full and the flames high. Girls and guys sat around the fire holding out sticks with hot dogs and marshmallows riding on their points. Mikki could hear a guitar strumming and sticks popping on a drum pad. Laughter and whoops amid the crash of waves. There were a few couples making out, but most were just hanging out, talking and dancing.

"Hey, Liam," said one guy as he approached them. "Everyone was hoping you'd make it." He handed them each a long stick. "Dogs are cooking." They joined the crowd. Mikki could see a few football jerseys, but most were dressed in jeans and T-shirts. There were no designer labels in sight. Everyone greeted Liam with high fives, chest bumps, and knuckle smacks.

"Pretty popular guy," Mikki remarked.

"Nah, the guys think my mom is hot, and the girls want jobs at the Little Bit. They're just looking to use me."

Mikki laughed. "So do all of you go to high school together?"

"Yeah. But most of these kids are from Sweat Town, which I find a lot more palatable than Tiffany's mansion crowd." Liam eyed the two guys playing the guitar and the drum pad. He looked at Mikki. "Want to really get this party cooking?"

She instantly got his meaning. "Oh, let's *so* do it."

They played for nearly thirty minutes while the crowd whooped and cheered.

Mikki sang parts of a song she was working on and that the crowd really got into, even chanting back parts of the lyrics. Then Mikki grabbed the drumsticks and showed herself to be nearly as adept at drums as she was at guitar. Even Liam looked at her in amazement when she finished her set. She explained, "When I formed my band, I learned every instrument. I'm sort of a control freak."

Afterward they roasted some hot dogs. When someone started playing tunes off a portable CD player, Liam said, "Hey, you want to do some sand dancing?"

"What's that?"

"Uh, it's really complicated. It's dancing in the sand in your bare feet."

She smiled. "I think I can manage that."

He put both arms around her waist, and she put her hands on his shoulders. They moved slowly over the beach.

"Feels sort of cool," Mikki said. "On the feet," she added quickly.

"Me too," he said, grinning. "Okay, now it's time for the old tradition of sand angels. Now, that's—"

"Let me guess." She plopped down on her back in the sand and moved her arms and legs up and down.

Liam joined her. "Wow, brains and beauty."

As the music played on, they danced and grew closer.

"This is really nice, Liam."

"Yeah, it is."

She cupped his chin with her hand.

"Mikki?" he said questioningly.

She kissed him and then stepped back. "I had a great time, Liam. Thanks for bringing me."

"Any time. I'm working the late shift this coming week at the Little Bit. Come on down, and I can get you anything you want for free."

"How can you do that?"

"I'm the cook. Ain't nothing happening without me."

Mikki laughed.

"You need a way home?" he asked.

"I actually rode a bike I found at the house. Left it up on the street. It's not that far."

"I've got a bike too. I'll ride with you. It's on my way."

"You don't have to do that."

"I know. I want to." He paused, looking embarrassed. "I mean…"

"I know what you mean," she said softly.

He saw her safely to her house, waved, and rode off.

When she walked in the house, her dad called out to her from the darkened front room.

"So?" he said.

She came forward, squinting in the poor light to see him. He was on the couch looking at her.

"So what?"

"Have fun?"

"Yeah, just at a different party."

She told her dad about the evening.

"Sounds like you made the right choice."

She sat down next to him. "So how's the lighthouse coming? You've really been spending a lot of time on it."

He looked down. "I know it must seem strange."

"Dad, it doesn't seem strange. Okay, maybe a little," she amended with a smile. "But you said the reason we came down here was so you could spend more time with us. Remember? But you and Sammy work all the time, and I'm stuck watching Cory and Jackie."

Jack's head dropped lower with this comment. "It's just... I don't know. It's complicated, Mikki. Really complicated."

Mikki rose. In a disappointed tone she said, "Yeah, I guess it is."

"But I'll try to get better. Maybe we can do something next weekend?"

She brightened. "Like what?"

Jack said lamely, "Um, I haven't thought of it yet."

Her face fell. "Right. Sure. Good night."

As she headed up the stairs to bed, Jack started to call after her, but then he stopped and just sat there in the dark.

Neither one of them noticed Sammy standing at his bedroom door listening to their exchange. The former Delta Force member went into his room, picked up his cell phone, and made a call.

41

As Mikki was running on the beach a few days later, Blake joined her.

He said immediately, "Look, I'm sorry about what happened at the party. Tiff was wasted."

"Gee, really?"

"She's usually not that obnoxious."

"Give me a break. She's a fricking nightmare in a G-string."

"Okay, maybe she is. Where'd you end up?"

"Another party on the beach."

"What party?"

"One Liam Fontaine took me to. And most of the people there were from Sweat Town. Heard of it?"

"Mikki, I live in Sweat Town."

This stunned her so much she stopped running. "What?"

"My mom works as the housekeeper for the Murdochs."

"Then why do you hang out with Tiffany?"

"Like I said, my mom works for them."

"And what, that obligates you to do her bidding?"

Blake laughed nervously. "I don't do her bidding. I just hang out with her sometimes."

They started running again. "Well, good for you. Who you hang out with says a lot about a person."

"Hey, what's wrong with me being friends with her? Are you saying poor people can only hang out with other poor people?"

"No, of course I'm not saying that."

"I have a lot of friends in Sweat Town. I play football with a bunch of them. And I go to Tiffany's and she has cool stuff and I have fun with her. So what?"

"Look, do what you want."

"Well, what I want is to go out with you." This time Blake stopped running, forcing Mikki to do the same. "So how about it? Will you go out with me?"

"Why?"

"Why? Because I like you."

"You don't really know me."

"Which is a perfect reason to go out. To get to know each other better. But hey, if you're not interested, forget it. Have a good one, and I'm sorry I don't fit your idea of a perfect person. Maybe Liam does." He started to jog off in the other direction.

"Wait a minute."

He stopped as she walked over to him. "What exactly do you want to do on this date?"

"What?"

"The plan, Blake. I need to know the parameters of what you're talking about. I'm not looking to run into a crowd of rich people again and have to kick somebody's butt." She added, "Unless it's Tiffany's. I actually enjoyed that."

"It's nothing like that. There's a coffee bar in town. They play music at night. Nothing live, but they have a DJ who's really good. I thought we could go and listen to some tunes, dance, and chill out. That's all."

She considered this. "That sounds okay. But just dancing and listening to tunes."

He eyed her closely. "Why? You got something else going?"

"No, I just—"

"Liam?"

"That's none of your business," she said hotly.

"Okay, okay. You're right. Look, I've got my license. I can pick you up tomorrow night around seven?"

"I'll check with my dad, but I think that'll be okay."

"Good," said Blake. "Glad we got that settled. Want to finish the run?"

She grinned and pushed him backward over a bump in the sand. He fell sprawling on his backside. "Catch me if you can," she called out as she sprinted off laughing.

He jumped up and raced after her.

42

"I'm hungry, Jack, so let's go."

They were parked on the street in Channing. Sammy was eyeing Jenna's restaurant, but Jack didn't seem to want to budge.

"It's not like this is the only place to eat in town, Sammy."

Sammy opened his door. "You just need to get over it."

"Over what?"

Sammy snapped, "She's just a nice lady who's trying to be friends with you, and you won't give her the time of day because you feel guilty about Lizzie."

"I don't know what the hell you're talking about! I'm nice to her."

"Great. If that's the way you want it. I'm going to eat. Stay here if you want."

Sammy slammed the truck door and went inside A Little Bit of Love.

Jack sat there brooding, his fingers tapping against the steering wheel. Finally, he climbed out of the truck and followed Sammy inside. His friend was tucked in a corner, already studying his menu. Jenna wasn't at the hostess stand, so Jack wandered back and sat down across from Sammy. The older man handed him a menu. "Figured your empty belly would bring you to your senses."

Jack took the menu, glanced at it, and then dropped it on the table. "I don't know what you expect from me."

"I don't expect anything from you."

"Well, something's clearly bugging the crap out of you."

Sammy dropped his menu too. "Okay, man, let's hash this out. When's the last time you played with Jackie? Or Cory? Or said two words to Mikki?"

"I talked to Mikki about stuff just the other night."

"I know you did because I was there listening. But what exactly has changed? You work all day, and then you work on that damn lighthouse all night. It's not healthy, Jack. You planning on having any fun ever again?"

Jack stared hard at his friend. "What makes you think I deserve to have any fun ever again?"

"You half killed yourself clawing your way back from a death sentence. And for what? To be miserable the rest of your life?"

Jack picked up the menu. "You're making it way too simple."

"And you're making it way too complicated. You got kids, Jack. They need you."

"I'm busting my ass to support them."

"Is that all?"

"What do you mean?"

"The only reason you're busting your ass? Because of them?"

"I know I haven't exactly been the perfect father. My daughter has already reminded me of that."

"She does that because she cares about you. And, hell,

she's damn near sixteen. She probably wants to spend her time down here doing something other than watching her two kid brothers all day."

"She went to a party on the beach. She plays music with that Liam kid."

"Okay, fine, excuse me for giving a damn."

Jack's anger evaporated with this last comment. "You're right. It's not enough to support my kids. I have to be there for them."

Sammy looked surprised and relieved. "Well, hallelujah. Maybe after all that work on the lighthouse, you're finally seeing it."

"What?"

"The damn light."

But Jack wasn't listening to him anymore. He was thinking about something else Sammy had said.

She's damn near sixteen.

The date popped into Jack's head. Her birthday. Coming up fast. And it was a big one.

"You guys ready to order?"

Jack looked up to see a waitress standing next to their table. "What?"

The woman smiled and tapped the menu. "This is a restaurant. And that's a menu. I just took it on faith that you might want to order some food."

"I'll take care of these two, Sally," said a voice. Jenna walked up. "They could be trouble," she added with a coy smile.

"Okay, boss." Sally walked off.

Sammy looked at her and grinned. "So tell me the specials."

"Now, Mr. Duvall, you know that everything on the menu is special, and you've eaten most of it."

Jack looked at Sammy in surprise. "You have?"

Sammy said defensively, "I get hungry. Just because you don't eat doesn't mean I have to do the same."

"How about our famous pork barbecue sandwich with fried onion rings and slaw on top? It's hell on the arteries, but you're guaranteed to die with a smile on your face."

"Sounds good," said Sammy. He stared at Jack. "Make it two. And make sure you put a smiley face on his; might improve the man's mood." He winked at Jenna.

She said, "Well, I wanted to talk to you about something anyway, Jack. Let me put your order in, and I'll be right back."

She walked off and returned a minute later, drawing up a chair.

"I'll get to the point. Your daughter would like to waitress here. And I want to hire her."

"What?" said Jack. "She didn't tell me about it."

Sammy said testily, "She wanted to, but it's not like you've been around."

Jack ignored this and looked at Jenna. "Waitress?"

"It's an honest profession, and I pay a fair wage."

Jack glanced at Sammy. "I'll have to get someone to watch the boys."

Jenna said, "I actually thought of that. The lady you're doing work for, Anne Bethune? She runs a summer camp at her place. It's right on the beach. The boys could go there. They'd have a great time."

Sammy said, "I've gotten to know Anne, and I saw how the camp was set up. They'll love it."

"But *I* don't really know the woman."

"She's the principal at the local elementary school, Jack," said Jenna. "She has two kids of her own. In fact, when I first moved here, I put Liam in the camp and he had a blast. She has qualified people helping her too."

Sammy added, "So that way Mikki can work here during the day. Earn some money, get out of the house. Have a life."

Jenna added, "And she gets her meals free. I think it'll be good for her."

"How much does the camp cost?"

"Now, that's the interesting thing," said Sammy. "I'm doing some extra work for her on the side, and Anne agreed to let the boys come there in exchange for it."

"Sammy, you didn't have to do that."

"Like hell I didn't. They need to have some fun too."

Jack looked between Jenna and Sammy. "Why do I sense this was all planned out?"

Sammy snapped, "You got a good reason not to do it?"

"Well, no. It actually sounds like a great idea."

"Okay, then. So what's the problem?"

Jack locked gazes with Sammy for a long moment before finally looking away. "Okay, fine."

Sammy slapped the table. "There you go. That wasn't too hard, was it? Now, Jenna, can you add two beers to our order? I feel the need to celebrate."

Jenna went off to do this while Jack pretended to go to the restroom. Instead he followed Jenna. "Can I talk to you about something?"

She looked at him in surprise. "Is everything okay?"

"Yeah," he said quickly. "I just need to ask you about something."

"Look, Jack, I know it seemed like we ganged up on you about the camp and Mikki working here, but—"

He smiled. "I actually really appreciate what you're doing."

"Thank Sammy. It was his idea. You got a good friend in that man."

"You're right. I do." He looked at her. "And a good friend in you too."

This comment seemed to catch Jenna off guard.

"I'm just... It's not that..."

She stopped in midsentence and looked away, flustered.

Jack said, "I know I've been a little unfriendly with you, and I'm sorry."

She quickly looked back at him. "You don't have to apologize, Jack. In my book you've done nothing wrong. So what did you want to ask me?"

"I don't want to do it now. What time would be good later?"

"I can get away from here around nine."

"I can pick you up here. Drive you home."

"That's fine. Liam has his license. He can drive the car back."

"I'll see you then."

43

The café was crowded, and Blake and Mikki got as close to the DJ as possible. The tunes were already blasting, and people were dancing. Blake and Mikki got Cokes from the bar and settled into a corner to watch and listen.

"You look really good," Blake said.

Mikki had on jean shorts, flip-flops, a white sleeveless blouse, and a pair of earrings her mother had given her for her fourteenth birthday. Her hair was tied back in a ponytail, and she'd washed the latest color out of the strands. Her skin had tanned, and her face glowed.

Blake had on jeans and a long-sleeve shirt worn out with the sleeves rolled up. She eyed him. "You don't look so bad either."

He laughed. "Thanks a lot. Want'a dance?"

"Okay."

They hit the dance floor and spent a half hour getting sweaty and out of breath, as they jostled next to kids doing the same thing. After another couple hours of listening to the music, things started to wind down. Blake said, "How about a walk on the beach? Nice night."

"Okay, but remember what I did to Tiffany." She held up her hands in a pseudo–martial arts pose.

Blake laughed. "I'm not messing with you. Or your dad."

They strolled along the sand. Mikki took her flip-flops off and carried them in one hand. Her free hand touched Blake's, and he wrapped one of his fingers around one of hers. At first she pulled back, but a moment later they were holding hands.

They reached an isolated section of beach where tall dunes were covered with lush, tangled vegetation.

Blake said, "I guess we better head on back."

"Okay."

He turned to her. She faced him.

"This was nice," she said.

"Not just saying that?"

"No, I'm not."

"Most girls are easy to read. But not you."

"I get that a lot."

He grinned, cupped her chin with his hand. He dipped his head to hers.

She pulled back.

He looked annoyed. "What's wrong? You've kissed before, right?"

"Of course I have," she said heatedly. "I'm almost sixteen."

"So what's the problem?"

"There's no problem." She grabbed him by the neck and planted a kiss on him. When they pulled apart, he exclaimed, "Wow. Okay, that was cool."

However, from Mikki's look, the kiss had not had the same effect on her. In fact, she looked a little guilty.

"Let's get back," she said hurriedly.

They'd only walked a few feet when Blake said, "What was that?" He turned around and stared at the dunes.

"What was what?" said Mikki.

Then the sound came again. Something was moving through the dunes.

"What is it?" Mikki asked, her fingers closing around Blake's wrist.

"I don't know. But something's up there."

"Maybe a dog or a cat?"

Another sound.

Mikki said, "That's not a dog or cat. That was someone talking. Blake, let's just get out of here."

"Hold on, there's something weird going on here. I think I recognize that voice." He called out, "Dukie? Dukie, is that you?"

"Who's Dukie?"

"Left tackle on the football team. Big and dumb. I don't know what he'd be doing here." He looked around. "Look, just hang here a sec; I'll be right back."

"Blake, don't go up there."

"Just hang on; I'll be right back."

He scooted toward the mounds of sand and quickly disappeared into the darkness. Mikki stood there looking anxiously around. There was no moon tonight, and it was hard to tell where the water ended and the land began.

"Blake?" she whispered harshly, but there was no answer. She moved closer to the dunes. "Blake?"

Hands came out of nowhere and grabbed her. She tried to scream, but something clamped over her mouth. As she looked frantically around, she saw that all the people around her were wearing Halloween masks, dark, gruesome ones.

Somebody put duct tape across her mouth. Another bound her hands behind her back. She jerked and pulled and fell down. Hands held her against the sand. Something was poured over her hair. Someone covered her eyes, and she felt something being sprayed on her clothes. She kept jerking and trying to scream. Tears poured down her face.

Someone yelled, and then there was a loud grunt.

Suddenly, whoever was holding her down fell over hard. The crowd abruptly moved away from her. Mikki sat up and struggled to see what was going on. As her eyes focused, she saw Liam hitting one of the masked people, and the person crumpled. Someone jumped on Liam's back, but he whirled around and threw the attacker off. As the person hit the sand, the mask popped off and Mikki saw Tiffany Murdoch staring at her. Mikki managed to get the rope off her hands and tore the duct tape off her mouth as another, larger person in a mask hit Liam and knocked him down. Two others jumped on top of him. Then another guy roughly pulled those two off and straddled Liam. Mikki leapt up, raced across the sand, and jumped on top of the guy, pulling his head backward, her nails raking his face.

He yelled something and pushed her off as he twisted away and fell down. Then he jumped to his feet, his mask askew. Sitting on her butt in the sand, Mikki looked up in disbelief.

"Blake?"

He rubbed the scratch marks on his face, turned, and ran. Mikki saw him grab Tiffany's hand, and they raced off toward the dunes. Mikki tore her gaze away from them in time to see the remaining guy drive his foot into Liam's stomach. She scooped up some sand, jumped up, ripped off the guy's mask, and threw the sand in his eyes. He yelled and started jumping around, clawing at his eyes. She pushed him backward, and he fell, then picked himself up and staggered after the others.

Mikki raced over to Liam, who lay facedown in the sand holding his stomach.

"Oh my God, Liam, are you okay?"

He slowly sat up, breathing hard. She wiped the sand off his face and clothes.

"Wow, you really know how to party," he said, grinning weakly.

"What are you doing here?" she asked.

"Just got off work. Was taking a stroll to wind down before I drove home. Then I heard some weird stuff and saw some people behind that dune. Then you two came walking by. When they jumped you I came flying in."

"You...you were watching us? Then you saw...?"

"Hey, no big deal. I'm just glad you're okay." He rose gingerly. "Come on. I'll drive you home."

Mikki didn't move. "I'm sorry, Liam."

"Sorry for what?"

"It wasn't nearly as cool as when you and I kissed."

He looked down, his fingers clenching as though looking for the comfort of his drumsticks. "Really?"

"Absolutely, really."

She stood. "You were really brave to do that. You saved me."

"Jerks." He looked at her and drew in a quick breath. "Damn."

"What?"

"Your hair and your clothes."

She looked down at her clothes. They were spray painted red along with her exposed skin. She touched her hair; it was sticky and clumped and smelled like rotten eggs.

"Jerks," she said. She looked in the direction of the dunes. "Blake was part of it. I can't believe I was that stupid."

"So were you on a date with him? I mean, that's cool. He's the quarterback, not a bad-looking guy either."

"It was a mistake," she said, gripping his arm. "For a lot of reasons. And he set me up. I bet it had to do with me beating up Tiffany at the beach party."

Liam looked shocked. "You beat up Tiffany? You didn't tell me that."

"Well, she had it coming."

He laughed and then grabbed his ribs.

"Are you sure you're okay?" she said worriedly as she put a hand around his waist to support him.

As their bodies touched, they looked at each other.

She said, "I'm really gross right now, Liam."

"No, you're not; you're beautiful."

Mikki went up on her tiptoes even as the tall Liam bent down to her. They kissed, this time far longer than they had the first time.

As they drew apart and opened their eyes, she said, "You're my knight in"—she looked at his dark clothes and smiled—"black shining armor and hiking boots."

He touched her cheek and grinned. "And you're my fair maiden in flaming red with stinky stuff in her hair."

"Liam, we can't tell our parents. My dad will go after all of them and probably end up in jail."

"But what about your clothes and hair?"

"I'll clean up before I sneak in the house."

Liam said, "So we're not going to get back at Tiffany and her friends?"

"Oh, I didn't say that. We're going to get back at them, but we're going to do it the right way, not the stupid way they tried to do it."

"So how, then?"

"You'll see."

She plopped down in the ocean water and started to scrub.

44

Jack was waiting outside the restaurant when Jenna came out promptly at nine. She climbed in the VW van, and he pulled off.

"This looks like a vintage ride," she said.

"Sammy's. He likes to tinker with cars."

"That's not all he likes to tinker with."

He glanced at her. "Meaning what?"

"Meaning he and Anne Bethune are seeing each other."

"What? Why am I always the last to know?"

She squeezed his shoulder. "You just need to get out more, honey."

"When did it start?"

"Oh, about the time they laid eyes on each other; at least that was how Anne described it. In fact, that's where he was the day you beat up those guys. They went for a ride on his Harley." Jenna bent down and took off her shoes and started rubbing her feet. "Sorry, after ten hours these puppies are screaming." She rolled down the window and breathed in the crisp evening air. "God, I remember in college, a guy I dated had a Harley. One time when Liam was staying with my mom we rode it all over the Blue Ridge Parkway. It was so much fun."

"Were you away from Liam a lot back then?"

She rolled the window back up. "Hardly ever, actually. I went to college close to home so I could stay there. My mom was divorced and ran a business out of her house. She would watch Liam for me when I was at class or working."

"Working?"

"Only way to pay for school. No silver spoons in my neighborhood. I knew I wanted to go to college, and then law school. And then work at a big firm in a big city."

"Sounds like you had it all mapped out."

"Well, I didn't have Liam mapped out. He just happened. Two stupid teenagers." Her features grew solemn. "But I don't know what I'd do without him in my life. He's a great kid. And he and Mikki really seem to have hit it off. When I told him she was going to be working at the Little Bit, he was really psyched."

"Well, that's actually the reason I wanted to talk to you. About Liam."

"What about him?"

Jack told her his plan.

She was smiling and nodding as he finished. "Okay, that sounds terrific. In fact, I'm real proud of you, *Dad*. But in return you have to do one thing for me."

He looked at her warily. "What?"

"Can you take me for a ride on the Harley?"

Jack drove to the Palace, got Sammy's permission, and fired up the Harley. Jenna got on back, and they drove off, paralleling the ocean on the long, winding road. As the wind whipped across their faces, Jenna said, "Boy does this bring back memories."

"Having fun, then?"

"You know it." She squeezed his middle as they leaned into turn after turn. After thirty minutes he drove her home.

"Liam's not here yet. Would you like to come in for some tea or coffee, or something stronger?"

They sat out on the rear deck sipping glasses of Chardonnay Jenna had poured them. After going over the details of Jack's plan in more depth, Jenna said, "How's the lighthouse coming?"

He put down his glass. "Good. Stairs are coming along, and Charles found the parts to repair the light."

"I bet it'll be something to see it fired up again."

"Yeah, I think it will," Jack said absently.

"And why do I think that's not why you're really doing it?"

He glanced up at her. "I fix things. That's what I do."

"Some things can't be fixed with a hammer and a set of plans."

He drained the rest of his glass. "I better get going." He rose.

"Jack?"

"Yeah?" His voice seemed defensive.

"Let me know when you get the lighthouse working. I'd really love to see it."

Taken aback by her obvious sincerity, he said, "I will, Jenna."

"And thanks for the ride. Most fun I've had in a long time."

Before he realized, Jack had already said it.

"Me too."

45

The next morning at the breakfast table Jack said, "I didn't hear you come in last night, Mik."

"I actually got in early," Mikki lied as she poured out a glass of OJ.

"So how was the date?"

"It was okay. But we're just not that compatible."

"It happens."

"Yeah, it does. Hey, Dad, I'm going into town today."

"Why?"

"Just an errand to run. Liam's going with me. I won't be long. Sammy said he'd watch Jackie for me."

"When do you start working at the restaurant?"

"Tomorrow. That's when Cory and Jackie start camp."

"You know, you could have come to me with all that."

She put a hand on her hip and said, "Could I have, Dad? Really?"

He looked away. "So how are you getting to town? Want a lift?"

"Liam's picking me up."

"Look, Mikki, I want you to be able to talk to me about stuff. If we can't do that, then we've got no shot at this father-daughter thing."

"You really mean that?"

"Yeah, I do."

"Well, it would be a nice start if you didn't work all day and then go to the lighthouse all night."

"But I've almost got it finished."

"Okay, Dad, whatever. We can talk when you're done with it."

Mikki walked out to the street, where Liam was waiting for her in his car.

Liam grinned. "When you called this morning with your plan, I have to admit I was really intrigued. Now I'm downright fired up."

"Good, because so am I."

They arrived in downtown Channing and parked in front of the Play House. There were a number of cars sitting at the curb, including Tiffany's red convertible. The marquee read, CHANNING TALENT COMPETITION APPLICATIONS TODAY.

Mikki grinned. "When I saw that sign last night, I really didn't think anything of it. You know, who cares? But now—now the timing couldn't be more perfect."

"Let's do it," said Liam.

They walked inside the lobby and joined a line of people standing in front of a long table behind which sat a number of ladies with hair styled to the max and wearing clothes that probably cost more than some automobiles. One of them, an attractive blond woman in a formfitting dress, seemed to be in charge.

"Let me guess," Mikki whispered to Liam as she pointed at the woman. "Tiffany's mom?"

Liam nodded. "How'd you know?"

"I just flash-forwarded Tiffany twenty-five years."

"Chelsea Murdoch. I heard my mom once say she was even worse than her daughter."

"Wow, now, that's a lady I have got to tangle with."

When Liam and Mikki reached the table, Chelsea Murdoch looked up at them with such a haughty expression that Mikki just wanted to slap her. "Yes?"

"We'd like to enter the competition," said Mikki politely.

Murdoch glanced at Liam and looked confused. "Both of you?"

"That's right. Together."

"Liam Fontaine, right?" she said.

"The one and only."

The woman smirked, and then her gaze swiveled to Mikki. "And you are?"

"Michelle Armstrong. We're down here from Cleveland for the summer."

The woman looked amused. "Cleveland?"

"Yes, it's the largest city in Ohio. Did you know that?" Mikki said innocently.

"No, I never saw a good reason to find out," she replied dryly and then bumped elbows with the woman sitting next to her, who chuckled. Mrs. Murdoch pushed a paper toward them. "Fill this out. And there's a ten-dollar processing fee. What are you going to do for your act?"

"Music," said Mikki. "Drums, keyboard, and guitar."

Murdoch looked at her coolly. "Pretty ambitious."

"I'd like to think so," Mikki replied sweetly. "I'm sure the competition is pretty tough."

"It is. In fact, one young lady has won it three years in a row and is looking to make it four."

"Would that be Tiffany?"

"Yes. She's my daughter."

"Of course. But I already knew she'd won it three times in a row."

"How?"

Mikki pointed to the mammoth banner on the wall behind them, which had a large picture of Tiffany holding up three trophies with the words TRIPLE CROWN stenciled over her head. "That was, like, sort of the first clue."

Mikki returned Murdoch's scowl with a smile.

"Just put the form in the box over there and give your money to the lady in the blue dress," she snapped.

"Great. Thanks for all your help, Mrs. Murdoch," Mikki said in her most polite schoolgirl voice.

Mikki could feel the woman firing laser eye darts at her as they walked off. She filled out the form and gave it and their entry fee to the woman in the blue dress.

"Okay, step one is done," Liam said.

"And here comes step two."

Tiffany and some of her friends had just walked into the lobby of the theater.

When Mikki marched up to them, Tiffany stiffened.

"Hey, Tiff."

Tiffany looked puzzled, and then glanced at her friends and back at Mikki. "Hi," Tiffany said coolly.

"I wanted to thank you for the great time on the beach. It was really memorable."

Tiffany snorted, and the other girls laughed. "Uh, okay," said a grinning Tiffany.

Mikki leaned closer. "And just so we're straight, we're, like, so going to kick your ass in the talent competition."

The smile vanished from Tiffany's face, and her friends stopped laughing.

Mikki drew even closer. "Oh, one more thing. You ever lay another finger on me, they won't be able to find all the pieces to put you back together again, sweetie." She'd unconsciously used the same threat she'd overheard her dad invoke back in Cleveland.

Tiffany blinked and took a step back. "You think you're so tough?"

Mikki put her face an inch from the other girl's. "I'm from Cleveland. It's sort of a requirement."

Outside, as they passed Tiffany's red convertible, Liam glanced around to make sure no one was watching, then reached in his pocket and pulled out a white tube. Pretending to be picking up something, he squirted the clear liquid from the tube onto the convertible's driver's seat. It was invisible against the leather.

"What's that?" Mikki asked.

"After what they did to you, I think Super Glue is in order."

"Liam, I'm so liking your style, dude."

46

"Okay, so what's the conspiracy?"

Jenna had come into the kitchen at the Little Bit to find Liam and Mikki using their break to huddle in one corner.

"Nothing, Mom," Liam said a little too innocently.

"Son, you forget I was a lawyer. My lie detector is well oiled."

He looked sheepish and glanced at Mikki. "You want to tell her?"

Mikki said, "We entered the talent competition as a musical act."

"Well, that's great. Why keep it a secret?"

Liam answered. "We'll be going up against Tiffany, and I know her family is an important player in town. We beat her out of winning for the fourth year in a row, the Murdochs might mess with you."

"They can try and mess with me, but I don't think it'll do much good. The Little Bit is pretty much here to stay." She looked at both of them curiously. "So why this sudden interest in beating Tiffany Murdoch?"

The two teens looked at each other.

Sensing they were holding something significant back, Jenna said, "Okay, both of you, I happen to be the boss. And I want the truth. Right now."

Between them, Mikki and Liam told her what had happened on the beach.

When they'd finished, the look on Jenna's features was very dark. "That was a criminal assault on you, Mikki. And you too, Liam. You two could have been really hurt."

"It was no big deal, Mom," said Liam.

"It was a very big deal. Those kids need to be held accountable for what they did. Otherwise, they might do it again."

"Mom, please don't do anything. We want to handle this in our own way."

Mikki added, "And if my dad finds out, he'll beat them all up and probably end up in jail. I know my dad. He's really overprotective. They were just teenagers, and he's an ex–army ranger. You saw what he did to those two big guys. He can be like a SWAT team all by himself when he needs to be. They'd throw the book at him. So please don't say anything, Jenna. Please."

Jenna's features finally lightened. "Okay, I see your logic. But does your dad know you're entering the talent competition?"

"Not yet."

"Well, I think the sooner he knows, the better."

Mikki gazed at her. "Would you mind telling him?"

"Me? Why?"

"It might be better coming from another parent. I don't think he'll mind, but he's been a little preoccupied lately. And we've already entered. I can't pull out now."

Jenna thought about this for a few seconds. "Okay, I'll talk to him." She checked her watch and smiled. "Break time's over. We run a real sweatshop here. So get to it."

Mikki gave her a quick hug. "Thanks. You're a lifesaver. So when do you think you'll talk to him?"

"I think I know where to find him at the right time."

At a little past midnight, Jack stood on the catwalk of the lighthouse, staring out at a clear sky. After his conversation with Mikki and the disappointment so evident on her face, he had really tried to not come out here, but something made his legs move, and here he was.

He'd worked all day with Sammy on Anne Bethune's project, which had also given him time to see her camp. He had to admit that Jackie and Cory were having a wonderful time, and they were learning things too. Anne had an instructor who took the kids down to the water and showed them about marine life and other science subjects appropriate for younger kids. Cory was in his element with painting and acting out scenes that he had written in a performance art workshop the camp also offered. It was exactly the sort of experience Jack had hoped for when they came down here for the summer. However, Jack was trying not to focus on the fact that he wasn't an integral part of that experience, that it was being done through what amounted to surrogates.

If I can just finish the lighthouse.

He walked back inside the structure and gazed down at the new stairs. He'd just driven in the last nail a few minutes ago. Work still needed to be done on them, mostly finishing items, but they were safe to walk on and would last a long time. He planned to start disassembling the scaffolding tomorrow night and return it to the hardware store. He picked up Lizzie's doll and went back out on the catwalk. Sweaty from all the hard work in the confines of the lighthouse, he took off his shirt and let the cool breeze flow over him.

He looked at the doll and then gazed up at the sky. Heaven was somewhere up there. He'd been thinking about where a precocious little girl would have thought it was located. He looked at discrete grids of the sky, much like he'd compartmentalized and studied the desert in the Middle East when he was fighting in a war there. Which spot was most likely to hold an IED or a sniper?

Only now he was looking for angels and saints.

And Lizzie.

He set the doll down and took the letter from his shirt pocket. Now that he'd finished the stairs, he told himself it was time to read the next one. The envelope had the number four written on it. He slipped the letter out. It was dated December twenty-first. He leaned against the railing and read it.

Dear Lizzie,

Christmas is almost here, and I promise that I will make it. It will be a great day. Seeing the kids' faces when they open their presents will be better for me than all the medications in the world. I know this has been hard on everyone, especially you and the kids. But I know that your mom and dad have really been a tremendous help to you. I've never gotten to know them as well as I would have liked. Sometimes I feel that your mom thinks you might have married someone better suited to you, more successful. But I know deep down that she cares about me, and I know she loves you and the kids with all her heart. It is a blessing to have someone like that to support you. My father died, as you know, when I was still just a kid. And you know about my mom. But your parents have always been there for me, especially Bonnie, and in many ways, I see her as more of a mom to me than my own mother. It's action, not words, that really counts. That's what it really means to love someone. Please tell them that I always had the greatest respect for her and Fred. They are good people. And I hope that one day she will feel that I was a good father who tried to do the right thing. And that maybe I was worthy of you.

Love,
Jack

47

"Am I interrupting something?"

Jack turned to see Jenna standing there on the catwalk, a bottle of wine and two glasses in hand. She saw the letter in his hand but said nothing as he thrust it in his jeans pocket and quickly pulled his shirt on, his fingers struggling to button it up as fast as possible.

"What are you doing here?" he said a little harshly.

She took a step back. "I'm sorry if I snuck up on you."

"Well, you did."

"Look, I'll just leave."

She turned to go when he said, "No, it's okay. I'm sorry. I didn't mean to snap at you. I just wasn't expecting anyone."

She smiled. "I wonder why? It's after midnight and you're standing on your own property at the top of a lighthouse. I would've thought there'd have been hundreds of people through here by now."

His anger faded, and a grin crept across Jack's face. "Dozens maybe, but not hundreds." He eyed the wine. "Coming from a party?"

She looked around and set the glasses on an old crate while she uncorked the wine. "No, hoping I was coming *to* one."

"What?"

She poured out the wine and handed him a glass, then clinked hers against his. "Cheers." She took a sip and let it go down slowly as she gazed out over the broad view. "God, it's beautiful up here."

"Yeah, it is."

"So you finished the stairs, I see."

"Still need to do some work, but the heavy lifting's done."

"I guess you're wondering what the heck I'm doing here?"

"Honestly? Yeah, I am."

She told him about Liam and Mikki entering the talent competition but withheld the reason why.

"Hey, that's great. I bet they have a good chance to win."

"They do, actually. I'm no expert, but I'd pay money to hear them."

Jack swallowed some of his wine. "But why didn't Mikki just come and tell me?"

"I'm not really sure. She asked me to, and I agreed. Maybe you should ask her."

Jack slowly nodded. "I know I've gotten my priorities screwed up."

"Well, realizing the problem is a good first step to fixing it. And like you said, you fix things."

"Yeah, well, lighthouses are easier than relationships."

"I would imagine anything is easier than that. But that doesn't mean you can ignore it."

"I'm starting to see that."

"I know what you told me before, but why is this important to you, Jack?"

He put his wineglass down. "This feels like the place I can be closest to her," he said slowly. He glanced over to find Jenna staring at him with a concerned expression. "Look, I'm not losing touch with reality."

"I didn't think you were," she said quickly.

"But it's still crazy, right?"

"If you feel it, it's not crazy, Jack. You've been through a lot."

"The Miracle Man," he said softly.

Jenna gazed at him but said nothing, waiting for him to speak.

"I wasn't supposed to be here, Jenna. I mean living. I was just hanging on 'til Christmas, for the kids. For Lizzie."

She touched his shoulder. "I shouldn't have asked. You don't owe me an explanation about anything."

"No, it's okay. I need to get this out." He paused, drawing a long breath, seeming to marshal his thoughts. "I spent half our marriage in the army, most of it away from home." He stopped, glanced at the dark sky. "I was crazy in love with my wife. I mean, they say absence makes the heart grow fonder? I could be in the next room and miss Lizzie, much less halfway around the world."

A tear trickled from Jack's right eye, and Jenna's mouth quivered. She swallowed with difficulty.

"I always saw Lizzie and me as one person whose halves got separated somehow, but they found each other again. That's how lucky I was."

Jenna said quietly, "Most people never have that, Jack. You were truly blessed."

"The last night we were together she told me she wanted to come back here for the summer. I could tell she wanted to believe that I would be alive to come with her. She even talked about me fixing up the place. This lighthouse. I never thought I'd have the chance."

"So you're fulfilling Lizzie's last wish?"

"I guess." He turned to look back out to sea. "Because she never got the chance to come back."

Jenna said, "And then you got better?"

He glanced at her, his eyes red. "But do you know why I got better? Because Lizzie was right there with me every step of the way. She wouldn't let me die."

"Why are you telling me all this?"

"Because if I don't tell someone, I think I'm going to... to... I don't know. And you seemed like someone who would understand."

A gentle rain began to fall as they stood there. Jenna put down her glass, gripped Jack's shoulders, turned him to her, and put her arms around him.

As the rain continued to come down, they stood there in the darkness slowly swaying from side to side.

"I do understand, Jack. I really do."

48

"Jenna, you really don't have to do this," said Mikki.

They were at a women's clothing store in downtown Channing during a break from working at the restaurant.

She continued, "It's no big deal. I mean it's only dinner out with my family. Dad and Sammy and certainly Cory and Jackie aren't going to care what I have on."

"But it's also your sixteenth birthday, honey, and that only happens once in your life."

Together, they'd selected a half dozen outfits, and Mikki was trying them on. After Mikki decided on a dark sleeveless dress, Jenna helped her pick out shoes, a purse, and other accessories.

"Thanks, Jenna. I can't exactly go bra shopping with my dad."

"No, I guess you really can't." She smiled mischievously. "Though it might be kind of fun if you did. Just to see the former tough-as-nails army ranger squirm over cup sizes."

Mikki was looking down at all the items and mentally calculating the prices. Her face turned red. "Uh, I'm going to have to put some of these things back."

"Why?"

"I...I don't have enough money."

"Sure you do; I just gave you an advance on your salary."

"What?"

"I do it with all my new employees, or at least the ones turning sixteen who want something new to wear."

"I'm not looking for a freebie."

"And I'm not giving it. This will be deducted from your paycheck in equal installments over the next sixty years, young lady."

Mikki laughed. "Are you sure?"

"Absolutely. Seriously, you're a really good waitress and a hard worker. That should be rewarded."

After they left the shop, Jenna said, "How about an ice cream? I've got something I want to talk to you about."

They sat outside on a street bench with their cones.

"First things first. I spoke with your dad about the talent competition, and he's completely fine with you entering."

"Wow, that's great."

"Although he did wonder why you didn't just come and ask him directly about it."

"And what did you tell him?"

"I played dumb and basically dodged the question." She licked her cone and seemed to be choosing her next words carefully. "The lighthouse?"

Mikki sighed. "What about it?"

"Your dad spends a lot of time out there."

"How did you know that?"

"Well, aside from your miserable expression, I just know; let's leave it at that. Now, have you ever been out there with him?"

"No."

"Why?"

"I just don't; no reason."

"You resent it?"

"Resent a stupid building? That's a dumb question," she said irritably.

"Is it?"

Mikki finished her ice cream, wiped off her fingers, and threw the trash in a bin next to the bench. "Look, if he chooses to be out there instead of with his family, who am I to rock the boat?"

"I think you just answered my question. You know that was your mom's lighthouse?"

Mikki scowled. "Yeah, my mom when she was a little girl."

"So you think it's odd he seems so..."

"Obsessed? Yeah, a little. What would you think?"

"Hard to say. Now, tell me about what those jerks were yelling at your dad on the street that day. Miracle Man?"

Mikki looked uncomfortable and drew a long breath. "I don't really want to talk about that."

"Please, Mikki. I really do want to help. But I need to know."

Mikki took the next few minutes to fill her in.

Jenna looked thoughtful. "So basically the tabloid made everything up?"

"Well, that's what my dad says."

"And you believe a newspaper that makes millions selling lies over your father? How does that make sense?"

Mikki refused to look at her. She said, "Where there's smoke, there's fire."

"That makes even less sense."

"Easy for you to say. It wasn't your family getting destroyed."

"No, but let me put on my lawyer hat for a minute and analyze this." She paused, but only for a moment. "Your dad loses the woman he loves in a tragedy that was really no one's fault. Then he loses the rest of his family and is left to die alone. Instead, he somehow finds the strength to beat a certain death sentence, brings his family back together, and tries to make a go of it as a single parent. And then a bunch of gut-wrenching lies get spread all over the news and people are calling him terrible things based on those lies, and he has to just stand there and take it." She stopped. "What an evil guy your dad is."

Jenna looked over to find Mikki staring down at her feet, a stunned expression on her face.

"I guess I never looked at it that way," she said after a long silence. "I can see why you were a lawyer."

"It's the hardest thing in the world to put yourself in someone else's place, try to really feel what they feel, figure out why they do the things they do. Especially when it's easier to stick a label on something. Or someone."

"And the lighthouse?"

"Lizzie loved it at some point in her life. It was important to her. She wanted to see it work again. That's good enough for your father. He'll work himself to the bone to try and fix it."

"For her?"

"Your dad isn't crazy. He knows she's gone, Mikki. He's doing this for her memory. At least partly. This is all part of the healing process; that's all. Everyone does it differently, but this is just your father's way."

"So what do you think I should do?"

"At some point, find the courage to talk to him."

"About what?"

"I think you'll figure it out."

Mikki laid her hand on Jenna's arm. "Thanks for the ice cream. And the advice."

"You're very welcome to both, sweetie."

49

On Saturday night Jenna helped Mikki get dressed in her new clothes and did her hair. She pinned most of it back but let a few strands trickle down Mikki's long, slender neck.

Cory and Jackie were sitting on the couch together watching TV. They both stared wide-eyed at their sister when she came down the stairs followed by a proud-looking Jenna.

"Mikki bootiful," said Jackie.

Cory didn't say anything; he just kept staring, like this was the first time he'd realized his sister was a girl.

Sammy came out of the kitchen, saw her, and said, "Wow. Okay, people, heartbreaker coming through, make room. Make room."

Mikki blushed deeply and said, "Sammy, knock it off!"

"Honey, take the compliments from the men when you can," advised Jenna.

Sammy yelled, "Jack, get your butt in here. There's big trouble."

Jack walked in from the kitchen and froze when he saw her.

Mikki took in all the males staring at her and finally said, "What?"

"Nothing, sweetie," said Jack. "You look terrific."

"Jenna helped me."

Jack flashed her an appreciative look. "Good thing. I'm not really all that great with hair and makeup."

Jenna chuckled. "Gee, don't they teach that in the army?"

"So where are we going?" asked Mikki.

"Like I said, dinner with the family. To celebrate your sweet sixteen."

She looked at Cory and Jackie watching cartoons and munching on cheese curls. Jackie's face and hands were totally orange and sticky. Cory let out a loud belch. "Great," she said, trying to sound enthusiastic.

Sammy looked at Jack. "Hold on a sec. You said we had to finish that job tonight. Promised the lady. Remember?"

"Oh, damn, that's right. What was I thinking?" Jack slapped his forehead in frustration.

Mikki scowled, "Tonight? What job?"

Jack looked stricken. "A big one. I forgot, honey."

Mikki's face flushed and her eyes glistened. "Dad, it's my *sixteenth* birthday."

"I know, sweetie, I know. Thank goodness I had a backup plan."

"What?"

He opened the front door, and Mikki gasped.

Liam was standing there dressed in pressed chinos and a white button-down shirt. His face was scrubbed pink, and he'd even combed his long hair. In his hand was a bouquet of flowers.

Mikki looked from him to her dad. "Uh, what is going on?"

Jack grinned. "Like you really wanted to go out on your sixteenth birthday with your old man and two little brothers? Give me a break."

"That would've been fine," she said, trying to keep a straight face.

"Yeah, right," scoffed Sammy. He turned to Liam, who hadn't budged an inch. "Well, get in here, son, and deliver the flowers to the lady." He grabbed Liam's arm and propelled him into the room.

Liam handed the bouquet to Mikki. "You really look great," he said shyly.

"Pretty slick yourself." She eyed her dad. "How did you possibly manage this without Cory or Jackie squealing?"

"That's easy. I didn't tell them. But Jenna was a major co-conspirator."

Jenna did a mock curtsy. "Guilty as charged."

"So, what's the plan?" Mikki asked.

"Like I said, dinner. For two. Reservations have already been made."

Jenna amended, "Not the Little Bit. At the fancy restaurant in town. I know the owners really well. They've got a great table picked out for you and a special menu."

"Wow, I can't believe this is happening. I feel like Cinderella."

Jack put his arm around his daughter. "Nice to know I can still surprise you."

"Thanks, Dad. Well, I guess we better go," she said.

"Wait a sec," Jack said. "Close your eyes."

"Dad!"

"Please, just do it."

Sighing heavily, she closed her eyes. Jack slipped the necklace from his pocket and affixed it around her neck. "Okay."

She looked down and gasped. She rushed to a mirror hanging on the wall.

"This was Mom's necklace," she said in a hushed tone.

Jack nodded. "I gave it to her on our first wedding anniversary."

Mikki turned to look at him, tears glimmering in her eyes.

"Happy birthday, baby."

Father and daughter shared a lingering hug.

After Liam and Mikki had gone off on their date, Jack stood on the front porch staring at the sandy yard. Jenna joined him there. Jack's eyes were moist, and he wouldn't look at her.

"You okay, *Dad*?" she asked.

"They grow up fast, Jenna."

"Yes, they do. But growing up is okay. What we don't want them to do is grow *away* from us."

"You're pretty good at this parenting thing."

"You do something solo long enough, I guess you either get good at it or you crash."

"So there's hope for me?"

"I'd say definitely." She slid her arm through his. "She's a great kid, Jack."

"Because of Lizzie."

"Give yourself some of the credit. You did good tonight, Jack Armstrong."

"You really think so?"

"Yeah, I really do."

50

Mikki and Liam had just finished dinner when he excused himself to go to the restroom. A few seconds later, Mikki was stunned to see Blake Saunders walk up to her table.

"What are you doing here, you weasel?" she snarled.

"I work here."

"You work here?"

"Busing tables. Sweat Town, like I said."

"Gee, doesn't sweet little Tiffany give you an allowance?"

"Look, I know you're upset, and you have every right to be."

"You're wrong, Blake. If I were upset, that would mean I cared, and I don't. You had your stupid fun, but Liam could have really gotten hurt."

"I pulled those two idiots off him, in case you didn't notice. I was on top of him to protect him. Nobody was supposed to get hurt. But then you jumped on my back and basically scratched my face off."

"Hey, let's not forget that none of it would've happened if you hadn't set me up. And why exactly did you do that?"

Blake looked down. "Because of what you did to Tiff. She was upset. She wanted to get back at you."

"And you do whatever Tiff tells you to? That's beyond pathetic."

"Yeah, I guess it is," Blake admitted.

"Look, you're not going to fool me with your 'I'm all sorry' act. Okay? So just save your breath."

"Did you put the glue in her car seat?"

"Don't know what you're talking about."

"Well, in case you were wondering, she was pissed. She had to take off her pants to get out of the car. And she hadn't bothered to put on underwear. She had to run up the steps to her house. But she slipped and fell over into the bushes, scratched her rear end up good. At least that's what my mom said. Guess all the hired help got a good laugh about that later."

Hearing this, Mikki could not suppress a grin. "It's nice to know that bad things do happen to bad people."

"I heard you entered the talent competition."

"That's right. Me and Liam. I'm sure you'll be there to root on precious Tiff."

"Actually, I hope you kick her butt."

He turned and walked away.

After leaving the restaurant, Liam and Mikki drove to the beach, parked, took off their shoes, and walked along the sand.

"I never saw the ocean before coming here," said Mikki as she drew close enough to the water to let it cover her feet.

"Mom and I have always been close to the water. Well, pretty close."

"I really like it here. I didn't think I would after living in the city all my life, but I do."

"It took some adjustment on my part, but it can be cool."

"Blake Saunders came up to me at the restaurant while you were in the bathroom."

Liam did not seem annoyed by this, only curious. "Really? What did he want?"

"To apologize for helping Tiffany get the jump on me. He said he was trying to protect you, not hurt you."

"Yeah, I actually believe him."

"You do?"

"Blake is not your typical bully jock, Mikki. He's actually a nice guy. Okay, he runs around with Tiffany too much, but I've never had a problem with him. In school he's been cool with me. We even hang out and stuff sometimes."

"I didn't know that."

"Yeah."

It started to rain, and they ran toward an old lifeguard shack and took cover under the roof overhang.

"Your mom is really cool, Liam."

"I don't even remember my dad. He was gone right after I was born."

"That must've been hard."

"I guess it could've been. But my mom loves me enough for two parents," Liam said firmly.

"I really miss my mom."

Liam put an arm around her. "That's completely normal, Mikki. You should miss her. She was your mom. She helped raise you. She loved you, and you loved her."

"Pretty sensitive stuff coming from a guy."

He smiled. "I'm a musician. It's in our blood."

He put his arms around her, and they kissed as the rain and wind picked up and the breakers started to roll and crash with more intensity.

Mikki said, "Your mom talked to me the other day about my dad. It made me really start to think about things."

"What do you mean?"

"I didn't handle things really well when my dad was sick. In fact, I pretty much screwed it up."

"How?"

"When people are in trouble and they reach out, you can either reach out to them or pull back. I pulled back. I was a bitch to my mom. I was no help to my dad. In fact, I avoided him. I was rebellious, pushed the envelope, did all sorts of crap that made things harder for them." Tears trickled down her cheeks. "And do you know why I did all that?"

Liam looked at her. "Because you were scared?"

She stared back. "I was terrified watching my dad die. And instead of trying to make the time he had left pleasant, I just ran the other way. I couldn't deal with it. I didn't want to lose him, and a part of me hated him for leaving us. For leaving *me*." She let out a sob. "And it's just killing me now that my mom died and all I can think is that I made her life miserable at the end. Just *miserable*."

As she started to cry, Liam held her and then undid his cuff button and held his sleeve out for her to use as a handkerchief. When she finally stopped crying, she rubbed her eyes with his sleeve. "Thanks."

"It's okay, Mikki. This stuff is hard. No easy answers. It's not like music. The notes are all there. You just play, have a good time. Families are really hard."

"Your mom said I needed to talk to him."

"I think she's right. You do."

The rain began to let up, and they made a run for the car.

Liam drove her home. As she got out of the car, she said, "Thanks for a great sixteenth birthday."

"Hey, you made it easy."

"Right, crying on your shoulder, real easy."

"I always thought that was part of being a friend."

She leaned back in and kissed him. "It is. And you are."

51

Jack lay on his back in the room of the lighthouse that contained the lighting machinery. His hands were greasy, he was hot and sweaty, there was dust in his throat, and he was not making much progress. He'd followed the schematic detailing of the electrical and operational guts of the machinery to the letter, but still something was off. He angled his work light into a narrow gap between two metal plates.

"Dad?"

He jerked up and hit his head on a piece of metal. Rubbing the injured spot, he pulled himself out from the confined space and looked over at the opening to the area below. Mikki, her hair plastered back on her head, was staring back up at him.

"Mik, are you okay?"

"I'm fine, Dad."

He scrutinized her. "You're wet."

"It's raining."

He looked out the window. "Oh. I guess I came out here before it started."

"Can I come up?"

He gave her a hand and pulled her into the small space.

As she drew closer, he said, "It looks like you've been crying. Liam didn't—"

"No, Dad. It has nothing to do with him. Liam was great. We had an awesome date. I...I really like him. A lot."

Jack relaxed. "Okay, but then why...?"

She took her dad's hand and drew him over to a narrow ledge that ran the length of the room under the window. They sat.

"We need to talk."

"What about?" he said warily.

"What happened with Mom, you, me. Everything, basically."

"Now?"

"I think so, yeah."

Jack wiped his hands with a rag and tossed it down.

"Look, I know you guys think it's crazy what I'm doing out here. And hell, maybe it is."

She put a hand on his arm to forestall him. "No, Dad, I don't think it's crazy." She paused. "Jenna talked to me about some things."

"What things?" Jack said abruptly.

"Like how you've basically been through hell and we all need to cut you some slack and that everybody grieves in their own way."

"Oh." Jack looked over at the lighting apparatus and then back at her. "I'm trying to get through this, Mikki; I really am. It's just not easy. Some days I feel okay; some days I feel completely lost."

Mikki's face crumpled, and she began to sob as she poured her heart out. "Dad, I was just so scared when you were sick.

I didn't know how to handle it. So I just thought if I ran away from it all, I wouldn't have to deal with it. It was selfish. I'm so sorry."

He put his arm around her heaving shoulders and let her cry. When she was done, he handed her a clean rag to wipe her eyes.

"Mikki, you are one smart kid, but you're also only sixteen. You're not supposed to have all the answers. I'm thirty-five and I don't have all the answers either. I think people need to cut you some slack too."

"But I still should have known," she said, another sob hiccuping out of her.

He stroked her hair. "Let me tell you something. When my dad was dying, I did pretty much the same thing. At first I was sad, and then I was scared. I would go to bed at night scared and wake up scared. I would see him walking around in his pajamas in the middle of the day. He was just waiting to die. No hope. And this was a big strong guy I'd always looked up to. And now he was all weak and helpless. And I didn't want to remember my dad like that. So I just pushed everything inside. And I tuned everyone out. Even him. I was selfish too. I was a coward. Maybe that's why I went into the military. To prove that I actually had some courage."

She looked at him with wide, dry eyes. "You did, honest?"

"Yeah."

"Life really sucks sometimes," Mikki said, as she sat back and wiped her nose.

"Yeah, sometimes it really does. But then sometimes it's wonderful and you forget all about the bad stuff."

She looked down, nervously twisting her fingers.

"Mik, is there something else you need to tell me?"

"Will you promise not to get mad?"

Jack sighed. "Is that a condition of you telling me?"

"I guess not, but I was only hoping."

"You can tell me anything."

She turned to face him and drew a long breath. "I was the one who talked to that gossip paper."

Jack gaped at her. "You?"

Fresh tears spilled down Mikki's cheeks. "I know it was so stupid. And it got completely out of hand. Most of the junk he wrote he just made up."

"But how did you know about any of it?"

"I overheard you and Mom talking the night she died. And I saw what that jerk Bill Miller did."

"But why would you talk to a tabloid? You know what those papers do. It made your mom look…"

"I know. I'm so sorry, Dad. It was so totally stupid. I… I don't know why I did it. I was confused and angry. And I know you probably hate me. And I don't blame you. I hate myself for doing it." All of this came out in a rush that left her so out of breath she nearly gagged.

Jack put his arms around her and drew her to him. "Just calm down. It doesn't matter anymore. You messed up. And you admitted to it. That took a lot of courage."

Mikki was shaking. "I don't feel brave. I feel like a shit. I know you hate me. Don't you?"

"It's actually against the law for a dad to hate his daughter."

"I'm just really, really sorry, Dad. Now that my head's on right about things, it just seems so stupid what I did."

"I don't think either of us was thinking too clearly for a while."

"Will you ever be able to forgive me? To trust me again?"
"I do, on both counts."
"Just like that?"
He touched her cheek. "Just like that."
"Why?"
"Something called unconditional love, honey."

52

Jenna looked up from the counter at the Little Bit to see Jack standing there.

She smiled. "I heard the kids had a fabulous time."

"Yeah, Mikki's still gushing about it."

"You want something to eat? Steak sandwich is the special."

"No, I'm good. Look, I was wondering if you had time tonight for some dinner."

Jenna came from behind the counter to stand next to him.

"Dinner? Sure. What did you have in mind? Not here. Even I get sick of the menu." She smiled and then turned serious. "Hey, I can cook for you."

"I don't want you to have to do that."

"I love to cook. It's actually therapeutic. But you'll have to be my sous chef."

"What does that mean?"

"Slicing and dicing mostly."

"I can do that. But can you get away from this place?"

"For one night, yes. Practically runs itself these days, and my number one son will be here, along with your daughter. I don't think they even need me anymore. Say around seven thirty?"

"Okay, great."

"Anything in particular you want to talk about?"

"A lot of things."

When Jack got to Jenna's house that night, music was on, wine was poured, and scented candles were lit.

"Don't be freaked out by any of this," she said as she ushered him in. "I just like to be comfortable. I'm not going all *Sex and the City* on you." She eyed him. "You look nice."

He looked down at his new pair of jeans, his pressed white collared shirt, and a pair of pristine loafers that were pinching his feet. Then he looked at her. She had on a yellow sundress with a scalloped front and was barefoot.

"Not as nice as you," he replied. "And can I go barefoot too? These new shoes are killing me."

When he looked at her feet, she smiled. "You go for it. When I was a kid, my mom had to force me to wear shoes. Loved the feel of the grass on my feet. I think one reason I moved to the Deep South is because not many people wear shoes down here."

She led him into the kitchen and pointed to a cutting board and a pile of vegetables and tomatoes next to it. "Your work awaits."

Jack chopped and sliced while Jenna moved around the kitchen preparing the rest of the meal.

"So you like to cook?"

"I actually wanted to do it professionally."

"But you became a lawyer instead?"

"Yep, it was one of those crazy zigzags that life takes. When

Liam was older, I took culinary classes. Then when I was thinking about changing careers, running a restaurant seemed a nice fit. The Little Bit's menu is limited, but I've made every dish on it." She slid a pan of chicken into the oven. "And at home is where I really get to impress people."

"I'm looking forward to being impressed, then."

An hour later they sat down to eat. After a few bites, Jack raised his glass of wine in tribute to her skills in the kitchen. "I'm not exactly an expert, but this is great."

She clinked her glass against his. "I'm sure it was all due to how you sliced and diced the veggies."

"Yeah, right."

She put her glass down and eyed him. "Okay, do we talk about things now or with dessert and coffee?"

"How about *after* dessert and coffee?"

"Why?"

He looked sheepish. "Because I'm having a great time."

"And you think what you want to say will spoil that?" she said with a bit of alarm.

"No, nothing like that. But it will change it."

They walked on the beach after the cake and coffee were consumed. Jack ambled slowly, and Jenna matched his stride.

"Mikki said you and she talked."

"She's a really smart kid. She gets it, Jack. She really does."

"We talked after she came back from her date. She said you had basically told her to see things from my perspective."

"I thought that was important."

"I can understand why she was upset." He stopped and kicked at the wet sand. "After I got the kids back, I fell into my old routine. And Mikki jumped on that."

"On what?"

"That I didn't have a clue how to run a family."

"Who does? We all just wing it."

"That's nice of you to say, Jenna. But it's giving me credit I don't really deserve."

"You really put a lot pressure on yourself. Bet you did that in the army too."

"Only way you survive. You practice perfection. You have a mission, you prep the crap out of it, and you execute that prep. Same with building stuff. You have a plan, you get your materials, and you build it according to the plans."

"Okay, but did every mission and every building project go according to plan?"

"Well, no. They never do."

"Then what did you do?"

"You improvise. Fly by the seat of your pants."

"I think you just defined parenting in a nutshell."

"You really believe that?"

"Belief isn't a strong enough word. I basically *live* that."

"You'd think I'd know that by now, having three kids."

"All kids are different. It's not like one size or model fits all. I only have Liam, but I have five siblings. We drove my parents nuts, all in different ways. It's not smooth, it doesn't make sense half the time, and it's the hardest, most exasperating job you can ever have. But the payoff is also the biggest."

"Does it get easier?"

"Truthfully, some parts of it do, only to be replaced by other parts that are actually harder." Jenna gripped his shoulder. "Time, Jack. Time. And little steps. You nearly died. You lost the woman you love. You've moved to a different town. That's a lot."

"Thanks, Jenna. I needed to hear all this."

"Always ready to give advice, even if most of it is wrong."

"I think most of it is right, at least for me."

She slowly pulled her hand away. "Things get complicated, Jack, awfully fast. I'm a big believer in taking your time."

"I think I'm beginning to see that. Thanks for dinner."

She pecked him on the cheek. "Thanks for asking. But why did you think this was going to change things between you and me? I think you just wanted some assurance, maybe some comfort."

"But those are big deals for me. I don't go to people with things like that. I'm more of a loner. When Lizzie was alive, I'd go to her."

"Your soul mate?"

"And my best friend. There was nothing we couldn't talk about."

Jenna sighed resignedly. "You just described my image—no, my *dream*—of the perfect relationship."

"It wasn't all perfect. We had our problems."

"But you worked them out together?"

"Well, yeah. That's what a marriage is, right?"

"It's supposed to be that way. But more and more I don't think it is. People seem to give up on each other way too easily. Grass is greener crap."

"I'm surprised you never got married again. I'm sure it wasn't for lack of offers."

"It wasn't," she admitted. "But like I said before, I guess the right offer never came along."

As they headed back to the house, she asked, "So how's the lighthouse coming?"

"Not great," he admitted. "I guess I'll die trying to get it to work again."

As he drove off later, Jenna watched from the front porch, a worried look on her face.

53

A week later Jack turned the wrench one more time, taped over an electrical connection, spun the operating dial to the appropriate setting, and stepped back. It had been a week since he'd had dinner with Jenna. And every night he'd been out here working until the wee hours of the morning on the lighthouse. He felt like a marathoner near the end of the run. Three times he thought he had it right. Three times he turned out to be wrong. And his anger and frustration had grown with each disappointment. He'd snapped at Sammy and at all three kids over the last few days. He'd even made Jackie cry one time and felt awful about it for days afterward. Yet still, here he was.

"Come on," he said, looking at the guts of the light. "Come on. Everything checks out. Down to the smallest detail. There is no good reason you won't work."

He stood back and reached for the switch that powered the system. He counted to three, made a wish, took a breath, held it, and hit the switch.

Nothing happened. The light remained as dark as it had been for years.

Instead of another intense sense of disappointment, something seemed to snap in Jack's head. All the misery, all the frustration, all the loss bottled up inside of him was suddenly released. He grabbed his wrench and threw it at the machinery. It struck the wall, ricocheted off, and cracked the window. Then he ran down the steps, grabbed a crate at the bottom of the lighthouse, carried it out to the rocks, and hurled it as far as he could. It crashed down, and the contents exploded over the wet rocks. With another cry of rage, he ran down to the beach, yelling and cursing, spinning around uncontrollably before he dropped down into the sand and sat there, rocking back and forth, his face in his hands, tears trickling between his clenched fingers.

"I'm sorry, Lizzie. I'm sorry. I tried. I really tried. I just can't make it *work*. I can't make it work," he said again in a quieter voice. "I can't accept that you're gone. I can't! You should be here, not me. Not me!"

His breathing slowed. His mind cleared. The longer he sat there, the greater his calm grew. He looked out to the darkened ocean. He saw the usual distant pinpoints of light representing far-off ships making their way up or down the Atlantic. They were like earthbound stars, thought Jack. So close, but so far away.

He looked skyward toward Lizzie's little patch of Heaven... somewhere. He'd never found it. *It just swallows you up. It's so big and we're so small*, thought Jack.

Now he could fully realize how a little girl could become obsessed over a lighthouse. He was a grown man and it had happened to him. The mind, it seemed, was a vastly unpredictable thing.

"Dad?"

Jack turned to see Mikki standing behind him. She was in pajama bottoms and a T-shirt, with a scared look on her face.

"Are you okay?" she said breathlessly. I . . . I heard you yelling." She wrapped her arms around his burly shoulders. "Dad, are you okay?" she asked again.

He drew a long breath. "I'm just trying to understand things that I don't think there's any way to understand."

"Okay," she said in a halting voice.

He looked back at the Palace. "I moved all of us here for a really selfish reason. I wanted to be close to your mom again. She grew up here. Place was filled with stuff that belonged to her. Every day I'd find something else that she had touched."

"I can understand that. I didn't want to come here at first. But now I'm glad I did." She touched his arm. "I look at that photo of Mom you gave me every day. It makes me cry, but it also feels so good."

He pointed to the lighthouse. "Do you want to know why I've been busting my butt trying to get that damn thing to work?"

She sat down next to him. "Because Mom loved it?" she said cautiously. "And she wanted you to repair it?"

"At first I thought that too. But it finally just occurred to me when I saw you standing there. It was like a fog lifted from my brain." He paused and wiped his face with his sleeve. "I realized I just wanted to fix something, anything. I wanted to go down a list, do what I was supposed to do, and the end result would be, presto, it works. Then everything would be okay again."

"But it didn't happen?"

"No, it didn't. And you know why?"

Mikki shook her head.

"Because life doesn't work that way. You can do everything perfectly. Do everything that you think you're supposed to be doing. Fulfill every expectation that other people may have. And you still won't get the results you think you deserve. Life is crazy and maddening and often makes no sense." Jack paused and looked at his daughter. "People who shouldn't be here are, and someone who should be here isn't. And there's nothing you can do about it. You can't change it. No matter how much you may want to. It has nothing to do with desire, and everything to do with reality, which often makes no sense at all." He grew silent and looked out to the black ocean.

Mikki leaned against him and gripped his hand.

"We're here for you, Dad. *I'm* here for you. *I'm* part of your reality."

He smiled. And with that smile her look of fear finally was vanquished. "I know you are, baby." He hugged her. "You know I told you I was scared when my dad was dying, that I withdrew from everybody?"

"Yeah."

"Well, when my mom left me, I pulled back even more. If it wasn't for your mother, I think I would've just kept pulling back until I disappeared. I played sports and all, but I didn't have many friends, I guess because I didn't want them. Then we got married and I went off to the military. Then when I got home I picked a job that required a lot of hours and a lot of sweat."

"You had to support your family."

"Yeah, but in a way I think I was still retreating. Still trying to hide."

"Dad, you were there for us."

"I missed a lot of things I shouldn't have. I know it, and so do you."

She squeezed his arm. "There's still a lot more to see," Mikki said quietly.

He nodded. "There is a lot more to see, honey. A lifetime more."

She shivered. He put his arm around her. "Come on. Let's go in."

As they walked past the lighthouse, Mikki glanced at it and said, "Are you sure?"

Jack didn't even look at it. "I'm very sure, Mikki. Very sure."

54

After Jack got back to his room, he dropped, exhausted, onto the bed, but he didn't go to sleep. He lay there for a while, staring at the ceiling. Life was often unfair, insane, damaging. And yet the alternative to living in that world was not living in it. Jack had been given a miracle. He had already squandered large parts of it. That was going to stop. Now.

He opened his nightstand and pulled out the stack of letters. He selected the envelope with the number five on it, slid out the letter, and flicked on the light. What he'd just told Mikki, he firmly believed, because he'd once written down these same sentiments. He had just forgotten or, more likely, ignored them in his quest for the impossible. He began to read.

Dear Lizzie,

As I've watched things from my bed, I have a confession to make to you. And an apology. I haven't been a very good husband or father. Half our marriage I was fighting a war, and the other half I was working too hard. I heard once that no one would like to have on their tombstone that they wished they'd spent more time at work. I guess I fall into that category, but it's too late for me to change now. I had my chance. When I see the kids coming and going, I realize how much I missed. Mikki already is grown up with her own life. Cory is complex and quiet. Even Jackie has his own personality. And I missed most of it. My greatest regret in life will be leaving you long before I should. My second greatest regret is not being more involved in my children's lives. I guess I thought I would have more time to make up for it, but that's not really an excuse. It's sad when you realize the most important things in life too late to do anything about them. They say Christmas is the season of second chances. My hope is to make these last few days my second chance to do the right thing for the people that I love the most.

Love,
Jack

Jack slowly folded the letter and put it away. These letters, when he was writing them, were the only things he had left, really. They represented the outpouring from his heart, the sort of things you think about when the trivial issues of life are no longer important because you have precious little time left. If everyone could live as though they were in jeopardy of shortly dying, Jack thought, the world would be a much better place. But in the end they were only letters. Lizzie would have read them, and perhaps they would have made her feel better, but they were still just words. Now was the time for action. He knew what he had to do.

Be a father for my children. Repair that part of my life.

Jack rose and went from room to room, checking on his kids. He sat next to Jackie as the little boy slept peacefully, his hand curled around his monster truck. Cory slept on his stomach, his arms coiled under him. A tiny snore escaped his lips. Next, Jack stood in the doorway of Mikki's room, watching the rise and fall of her chest, the gentle sound of her breathing.

He closed her door and went downstairs and onto the rear screened porch. From here he could see the lighthouse soaring into the sky. He had built it into some mythical symbol, but it was only a pile of bricks and cinder blocks and metal guts. It wasn't Lizzie. It had no heart. Not like the trio beating in the bedrooms above. Three people who needed him to be their father.

In this last letter he had been lamenting that there were no second chances left to him. Yet that insane, unfair world that he had sometimes railed against had done something remarkable. It had given him another shot at life.

I'm done running.

Jack went back to bed and slept through the night for the first time in a long time.

55

Beginning the next day, Jack literally hung up his tool belt for the rest of the summer. Instead of going to work, he drove Jackie and Cory to Anne Bethune's camp. And he didn't just drop them off and leave. He stayed. He sat and drew pictures and built intricate Lego structures with Jackie, and then, laughing, helped his son knock them down. He instructed Jackie on how to tie his shoes and cut up his food. He helped construct the sets for a play that Cory was going to be in. He also helped his oldest son with his lines.

After camp they would go to the beach, swim, build sand castles, and throw the ball or the Frisbee. Jack got some kites and taught the boys how to make them do loops and twisters. They found some fishing tackle under the deck at the Palace and did some surf fishing. They never caught anything but had great fun in their abject failure to hook a single fish.

Jenna and Liam came by regularly. Sometimes Liam would bring his drums, and he and Mikki would practice for the talent competition. Since the Palace wasn't soundproofed, the pair would go up to the top of the lighthouse. That high up, their powerful sound was dissipated, although the seagulls were probably entertained.

At least the lighthouse was good for something, thought Jack.

He and Mikki took long walks on the beach, talking about things they had never talked about before. About Lizzie—and high school and boys and music and what she wanted to do with her life.

Mikki continued to waitress at the Little Bit. Jack and Sammy dropped in to eat frequently. And they also did some repairs for Jenna, but only because she refused to charge them for their meals. Charles Pinckney visited them at the Palace. He would tell them stories of the past, of when Lizzie was a little girl about Jackie's age. And all of them would sit and listen in rapt attention, especially Jack.

Jack took Jenna for rides on the Harley, and they were over at each other's homes for meals. They would take walks on the beach and talk. They laughed a lot and occasionally drew close, and arms and fingers touched and grazed, but that was all.

They were friends.

The summer was finally going as Jack had hoped it would. He would lie awake at night, listening to the sounds in the darkness, trying to differentiate among his children's breathing. He got pretty good at it. Sometimes Jackie would have a nightmare and would bump open his dad's door and climb into bed with him. The little boy would lay tight against his dad, and Jack would gently stroke his son's hair until he fell asleep again.

One evening he and Sammy were drinking beers out on the screen porch. Mikki and Liam were at the top of the lighthouse having one last practice before the competition. The two boys were down on the beach building the last sand castle of the day. The sun had just begun its descent, flaming the sky red and burning parts of it orange.

Sammy looked over at his friend. "Life good?"

Jack nodded. "Life is definitely good."

"Summer's almost over."

"I know."

"Plans?"

"Still thinking about it." Jack gazed at him. "You?"

"Still thinking about it."

They both turned when someone knocked on the door to the porch. It was Jenna.

"I came to pick up Liam and all his drum stuff," she said, joining them. "Big day tomorrow. They need to get their rest."

Sammy said, "I'll go help him."

Before either of them could say anything, he headed on down, leaving Jack and Jenna alone.

"So what happened?" she asked.

Jack looked over at her. "What?"

"You're a changed man, Jack Armstrong. I was just wondering why."

He finished his beer. "This will sound really corny, but sometimes when a person opens their eyes, they can actually see," he said.

"I'm happy for you; I really am."

"You were a big part of it, Jenna."

She waved this off. "You would've figured it out on your own."

"I don't know about that. I hadn't figured it out for a long time." They both looked out to the ocean and then to the lighthouse.

"Never got it to work," he said.

"Sometimes things don't seem to work unless you really need them to."

He nodded slowly. "Going to the competition tomorrow?"

"Are you kidding? Of course."

"Why don't you drive over with us? Sammy's taking their stuff over in the truck, and we can all ride in the VW."

"Sounds like a plan."

Jenna left with Liam, and the Palace settled down for the night.

Jack knocked on Mikki's door and went in.

She was sitting on her bed going over the program she and Liam were going to perform. Jack perched on the edge of her bed.

"You know that stuff by heart," he said.

"Can never be too prepared."

"Now you're starting to sound like your old man."

"And is that a bad thing?"

He gave her a lopsided grin. "I hope not. Look, you're going to do great tomorrow. Win or not."

She stared at him over the top of her musical sheets. "Oh, Dad, we're, like, so going to win."

"Nothing wrong with confidence. But don't get cocky."

"It's not that. I've checked out all the other acts. I even saw a video of Tiffany's little baton twirl from last year. She's mediocre at best. I have no idea how she won three years in a row. Well, I do have an idea. Her mother runs the show. But nobody has worked as hard as Liam and I have."

"Well, whatever happens, I'll be out there in the audience cheering for you." He rose to go. "But you do need a good night's sleep. So not up too late, okay?"

He turned to the door.

"Dad?"

He turned back to her. "Yeah, Mik?"

She got off the bed, wrapped her arms around him, and squeezed.

"Thank you, Daddy."

Jack wrapped his arms around her. "For what, baby?"

She looked up at him. "For coming back to us."

56

"Okay, we're on next to last," said Mikki, coming backstage at the Play House.

Liam looked at her. "Who's last?"

Mikki made a face. "Who do you think? Ms. Reigning Champion. That way she gets a look at all the competition and her performance is the clearest in the judges' minds."

Liam shrugged. "I don't think it'll matter. I've seen the judges. They're all cronies of her mom's."

"Keep the faith. We've worked our butts off, and we've got a terrific act."

"How's the crowd?"

"Big. With our families smack in the middle."

When Mikki turned back around, Tiffany stood there wearing a short white robe.

Mikki eyed her. "Saving the debut of the skimpy for the crowd?"

"My daddy always said you don't give it away for free, sweetie." She looked Mikki up and down. "But then if you don't have anything somebody wants, I guess you *have* to give it away."

Mikki smirked. "Wow, that's really deep. So do you do flaming batons?"

Tiffany looked at her like she was insane. "No. Why would I? That stuff is dangerous."

"Well, to beat us you're going to have to get out of your comfort zone. 'Cause the level of competition just got stepped up, big-time. *Sweetie*."

Tiffany laughed, but Mikki could tell by the sudden look of uncertainty in the girl's eye that she had done what she'd intended to do.

Freeze her opponent.

Before the competition began, she and Liam went out to the audience to see their families.

The Armstrongs, Sammy, Charles Pinckney, and Jenna were all sitting together.

Jenna smiled and gave Mikki and her son hugs. "I'm really proud of you two."

"Knock 'em dead," called out Cory.

"Yeah, dead," yelled Jackie.

Chelsea Murdoch walked by with her entourage. Her dress was too tight and too short and her heels too high for her age. She looked like what she was: her daughter, only a quarter century older.

She eyed Jenna. "Haven't seen you here before."

"Never had a reason to come before, Chelsea," said Jenna. "This is Liam's first time competing."

Murdoch smiled condescendingly. "Tiffany's going for four straight. Crowd always loves her routine. She's thinking of carrying on baton in college," she added loftily.

"Well, good for her," piped in Mikki. "It's always nice to have a career plan."

Before Murdoch could say anything, Mikki added, "Okay, we gotta go. Show's about to start."

"Good luck, Mik," said Jack.

Looking dead at Tiffany's mom, she said, "It won't be about luck, Dad. Like the sign says, it's a *talent* competition."

There were twenty-one acts, mostly younger people, but there was an older barbershop quartet that was pretty good. Mikki watched from the side of the stage, mentally calculating where the serious competition was. Liam just stayed backstage chilling and idly tapping his sticks together. She came back to him and strapped on her guitar.

"It's showtime, big guy."

"Cool. I was about to fall asleep."

"Now, that's exactly what I need: a drummer with ice in his veins."

Liam smiled. "Let's rock this sleepy little town."

"Oh, yeah," said Mikki.

57

At first the beat was mellow. Still, the crowd whooped and clapped. Sensing the rising energy, Mikki gave Liam the cue they'd practiced. She cranked her amp and stomped on her wah-wah pedal, and her hand started flying across the face of the Fender guitar. They dove right into a classic Queen roof blaster, with Liam moving so fast he appeared to be two people, alternating between drums and keyboard. The crowd was on its feet singing the lyrics.

Mikki knew that once you had the crowd right where you wanted them, and they thought you'd already given everything that was in your tank, you did something special.

You gave them more.

She unplugged her amp and pulled off her guitar. She actually pitched it across the stage. At the same moment, Liam tossed his stick in the other direction. She snagged the sticks, he caught the Fender, and they exchanged positions. Liam plugged in the amp and became the guitarist, his long fingers expertly traversing the Fender. Mikki perched on the stool and hammered away at the full array of the drum set.

The finale was a dual one, with a solo each. Mikki rocked the house with a six-minute broadside and finished up with a mighty crescendo, her hands moving so fast there appeared to be six pairs of them. And when the audience didn't have any breath left and their palms were raw from clapping, Liam performed a guitar solo that would have made Jimmy Page and Santana proud. He held the last chord for a full minute, the amp-powered beat shaking the Channing Play House like cannon fire.

And then there was silence. But only for a few seconds as the crowd caught its collective breath, and then the applause and screams and cheers came in waves. Mikki held hands with Liam and took bow after bow. They finally had to motion for the people to sit down and stop applauding.

As they went backstage, the other performers rushed up to congratulate them.

"You rock," said the fiftyish baritone in the barbershop quartet. "You took me back to my Three Dog Night days."

Breathless and wearing wide grins, Liam and Mikki moved off to the side. Tiffany passed by them, not saying a word. She loosened her robe and let it fall off. The outfit underneath did not leave much, if anything, to the imagination. She turned to them and, using her fingers, formed an *L* on her forehead.

Mikki pointed to the stage. "You're not a loser *yet*. That comes later, *sweetie*."

Other than stumbling twice and nearly dropping her baton, Tiffany did okay. The applause was polite except for the section led by her mother, which lasted so long that finally some people turned in their seats to see who was still applauding what had been a fairly mediocre performance.

A few minutes later, all the contestants were called to the stage in a single group.

Mikki found her dad in the crowd and gave a thumbs-up. Jack gave her two thumbs-up back while Sammy extended a crisp salute. Cory did an elaborate bow to his sister's dominance on the stage, and Jackie copied him.

Jenna caught Liam's eye and blew him a kiss.

The head judge stood and cleared her throat. "We have reached our decisions. But first I would like to thank all the contestants for their fine performances."

This statement was followed by polite applause.

"Now, in third place, Judy Ringer for her sterling dance performance of *The Nutcracker*."

Judy, a skinny fourteen-year-old, ran out to get her trophy and a bouquet of flowers.

"Thank you, Judy. Now, in second place, we have Dickie Dean and his Barbershop Four."

The man who had lauded Mikki and Liam's performance hustled out and received the award for his group as the crowd clapped.

"And now for the first-place champion."

The crowd held its collective breath.

The judge cleared her throat one more time. "For the fourth year in a row, Tiffany Murdoch and her fabulous baton routine."

Tiffany stepped forward, all smiles, and whisked over to get her trophy, hundred-dollar check, and flowers, while her mother beamed. Trophy and flowers in hand, Tiffany strode to the microphone. "I'm truly overwhelmed with gratitude.

Four years in a row. Who would have thought it possible? Now I'd like to thank the judges and—"

"That's a load of crap," bellowed a voice.

All heads turned, including Jack's and Jenna's, to see Cory standing up on his seat and pointing an accusing finger at the head judge.

"This sucks!" roared Cory.

"This sucks!" repeated Jackie, who was standing on his chair and pointing his finger too.

"Cor," snapped Jack. "Jackie, get down and be quiet."

But Jenna put a hand on his arm. "No. You know what? They're right." She stood and yelled, "This stinks."

Jack shrugged, stood, and called out, "Are you telling me that Mikki and Liam didn't even make the top three? You people are nuts."

The head judge and Chelsea Murdoch scowled back at them.

Another chorus came from farther back in the theater.

Mikki craned her neck to see. It was Blake and some of the other people from Sweat Town, including Fran, the woman who'd worked as a caterer at Tiffany's party.

"Recount," demanded Blake. "Recount."

Mikki grinned at him.

"Recount! Recount!" chanted the crowd.

Tiffany stood in the center of the stage trying to pretend she was oblivious to all of the criticism. She held her trophy and posed for pictures for a photographer from the local paper.

Then the crowd started chanting, "Encore! Encore!"

Mikki looked at Liam. He said, "What the heck, let's give 'em the Purple."

She nodded, picked up her guitar, cranked her amp, poised

her foot on top of her wah-wah pedal, and struck a chord so powerfully amplified that Tiffany screamed and almost fell off the stage. Mikki looked over at Liam and nodded. A moment later the heart-pumping sound of "Smoke on the Water" by Deep Purple roared across the theater.

Minutes later, as the last note of the song died away, Liam and Mikki, their arms around each other, took a bow together. This was a trigger for the ecstatic, cheering crowd to rush the stage. Tiffany had to run to get out of the way of the stampede. The news photographer and reporter joined the crowd, leaving the baton twirler all alone. Tiffany stormed off the stage and threw her trophy in the trash, while her mother followed her out of the theater, trying to soothe her furious daughter.

Later, on the drive home, Mikki and Liam sat in the back of the VW bus. The two teens glowed both with the sweat of their musical exertions and also with sheer excitement.

Liam said, "This is like the greatest day of my life. I mean I've *never* felt this good about losing before."

Jack looked in the rearview mirror at his daughter. "So what happened to alternative edgy beats with a nontraditional mix of instrumentals?"

She grinned. "Wow—you *were* listening. I'm impressed. Anyway, sometimes you just can't beat good old rock and roll, Dad."

"The best part," said Cory, "was watching Tiffany storming off."

Jenna looked in the back of the van and tapped Jack on the arm, motioning with her eyes. He gazed into the rearview mirror to see Liam and Mikki sneak a kiss.

She whispered, "I think, for them, that's the best part."

58

"Hey!" Jack yelled.

He and Sammy had just come out of the grocery store in downtown Channing when Jack saw a guy grab his tool belt out of the truck's cargo bay and run off. Jack and Sammy raced after him, Jack a few paces in front. He saw the guy duck down a side street. He turned the corner and accelerated, Sammy right behind him. The side street turned into an alley. Then they left the alley and entered a wider space. But it was a dead end; a blank brick wall faced them. They pulled up, puffing.

Jack realized what was going on about the same time Sammy did.

"Trap," Jack said.

"And we just ran into it like a couple of high school knuckleheads."

They looked behind them as five large men holding baseball bats came out of hiding behind a Dumpster. Jack could see that the man in the lead was the same one he'd thrown headfirst into the side of the pickup truck shortly after they'd arrived in Channing.

The men moved forward as Jack and Sammy fell back until they were against the brick wall. Jack slipped off his belt, coiled it partially around his hand, and stood ready. Sammy rolled up the sleeves of his work shirt and assumed a defensive stance. He beckoned them on with a wave of his hand.

"Okay, who wants to go to the hospital first?" he said.

With a yell, the biggest man ran forward and raised his bat. Jack whipped his belt, and the metal tip caught the man right on the arm, cutting it open. He screamed and dropped the bat. Sammy drilled a foot into his gut, sending him to his knees. Next, Sammy clamped an iron grip around the big man's neck.

"I don't waste my A game on the JV." Sammy crushed the man's jaw with a sledgehammer right hand that sent him to the asphalt. Sammy looked back up. "One down, four to go. Who's the next victim?"

Two more men, including the one whom Jack had beaten up before, yelled and ran forward. Jack grabbed the man's bat, pivoted his hips, and pulled hard. The man sailed past him and hit the wall, bouncing off. Groggy, he rose in time to be put back down by Jack's fist slamming into his face.

The other guy had his feet kicked out from under him by Sammy. He ripped the bat out of the guy's hands and bopped him on the head with it, knocking him out. When Jack and Sammy looked up, the other men had disappeared.

"Okay, that was fun," said Sammy.

His smile vanished a minute later when Sheriff Tammie hustled into the alley with a skinny deputy in tow. Tammie took one look at the men lying on the ground and Jack and

Sammy holding bats, and he pulled his gun, his face dark and furious.

"Put those bats down now. You're both under arrest."

"They attacked us!" exclaimed Jack as he and Sammy dropped the bats.

"Then how come they're knocked out and you two had the bats?"

"Because they were crappy fighters," said Sammy. "Is that our fault?"

Jack pointed at one of the men on the pavement. "Look, he's the same one I fought with before. He and a bunch of his guys came after us to settle the score. We were just defending ourselves."

"That's for a court to decide."

"You're really charging us?" said Jack. "What about the other guys?"

"Their butts are going to jail too."

"Well, at least that's some justice," snapped Sammy.

"And we got to let the wheels of justice do their thing. Just the way it has to be," said Tammie.

Jack and Sammy were cuffed, loaded into the sheriff's cruiser, and transported to the jail. Jack slumped down on a bench at the back of the cell, but Sammy said, "Hey, we get a lawyer, right?"

"That's what I said when I read you the Miranda card," replied Tammie.

Tammie let Jack make a call.

He said, "Jenna, it's Jack. Uh, I'm in a little bit of trouble."

Ten minutes later, Jenna and Charles Pinckney hurried into the sheriff's office and were escorted back to see the prisoners.

"My God, Jack, what happened?" she said.

He explained everything that had happened in the alleyway.

"I've talked the sheriff into releasing you on your own recognizance," she said.

"So we can go?"

"For now, yes, but it looks like the men are pressing charges, at least according to Tammie."

"But isn't it our word against theirs?" said Sammy.

"Still have to go to court."

"But we didn't do anything wrong."

"I'm sorry, Jack," said Jenna. "I'm doing the best I can."

His anger faded. "I know. And I appreciate you getting down here so fast. Didn't know anyone else to call."

"Well, for now, you're free to go. I'll get the sheriff."

Two days later, a man in a suit knocked on the door of the Palace.

Jack answered it.

"Jack Armstrong?"

"Yeah. Who are you?"

The man stuffed some papers into Jack's hand. "Consider yourself served."

The man walked off as Sammy joined Jack at the door.

"What is it?" he asked him. "Served with what? Those jerks from the alley really suing us?"

Jack read quickly through the legal documents.

When he looked up, his eyes held both anger and fear.

"No, it's a lot worse. Bonnie is suing for custody of the kids."

59

"I can't believe Grandma is doing this," said Mikki. "Why would she?"

The Armstrongs were arrayed on the couch and floor at the Palace. Sammy was there, and so were Liam and Jenna. Jack had shown Jenna the documents, and she had read them carefully with her lawyer's eye.

"I don't know," said Jack, though he actually had a pretty good idea.

Jenna looked up from the papers. "She's requested an expedited hearing to get temporary custody pending a full hearing. In non-legalese, that means she wants to get in front of a judge fast to get the kids now and then worry about the rest later."

"She can do that?" said Sammy.

"The courthouse is open to everyone. But she has to prove her case. It's difficult to have children taken away from a parent."

Jack asked, "Exactly when and where is all this going to happen?"

"In two days. In family court in Charleston."

"But we live in Ohio."

"But you have property in South Carolina and you're living here now, if only for the summer. However, I can argue that the South Carolina court lacks jurisdiction."

"*You* can argue?" said Jack.

"Do you have anyone else in mind to represent you? I've got a license to practice in South Carolina, and I've kept everything current."

"Did you practice family law?" asked Mikki.

"I've done some of it, yes. And I know my way around a courtroom." She held up the documents. "But we don't have much time to prepare."

"Jenna, you don't have time to do this. You've got a business to run."

Before she could respond, Liam said, "I can do that. Mom taught me everything about the business. It'll be fine."

Jenna smiled. "See?"

"Are you sure?"

"Heck, nice change of pace. You can only bake so many pies before you feel the need to punch somebody. Going to court gives me a chance to whack some idiots—not literally, of course, but you get the point."

"All right, but you're going to bill me for your time."

"We'll work something out."

Mikki said, "What exactly is she saying that would make a court take us from Dad?"

Jenna's face grew serious and she looked at Jack questioningly. He nodded, "You can tell them."

"Basically that your father is unfit to be your guardian. That he's a danger to himself and others."

"That's stupid," said Cory, jumping to his feet.

"Yeah, stupid," said Jackie, though, in an act of surprising independence from his brother, he remained seated, his arms folded defiantly over his little chest.

"I'm not agreeing with her, just telling you what she's alleging."

"Does she have any proof of that?" said Mikki heatedly. "Of course not, because it's not true."

"She'll be able to show any proof she has at the hearing," Jenna explained. She looked at Jack again. "And we have to show proof that you are fit."

"How do we do that?"

"You can testify. So can Mikki and Cory. Jackie's too young, of course. I can get Charles to be a character witness. And Sammy here. They can all attest to your fitness. I have no idea what angle she's using, but I can't imagine she'll be able to show the level of proof required to take children away from their surviving parent."

Later, Jack walked Jenna out to her car.

"Jack, there is one thing I didn't want to say in front of the kids."

"What?"

"I don't think the timing on Bonnie's action is coincidence. I think it's tied to your arrest for assault. She could've easily found out. And I can guarantee they'll use that to prove their case."

"But I'm innocent."

"Doesn't matter. It's all perception. And if they can convince the judge you're violent? Not good."

"Great. Guilty until proven innocent."

"Jack, if there's anything to tell me about this, now would be a good time."

"What do you mean?"

"I mean why you think your mother-in-law is doing this."

"She blames me for Lizzie's death. She came here pretending to want to reconcile, but I turned down her offer of moving in with her in Arizona. And she only came by *once* to see the kids this summer. Some grandparent she is."

"Uh, that's actually not right, Dad."

They turned to see Mikki standing behind them.

"What?" said Jack.

"Grandma came by like six times while you were out working."

"You never told me that."

"She asked us not to. Said you might get mad."

"I told her to come and visit. I wouldn't have gotten mad."

"Well, that's not what she said."

Jenna looked at her. "What did you talk about?"

Mikki shrugged. "Stuff."

"Did she ever ask about your dad?"

"Yeah," Mikki said nervously.

"Mikki, you need to tell us everything. We can't be surprised in court."

Mikki started to tear up. "It was when Dad was working so hard and he was out in the lighthouse all the time."

Jack said gently, "It's okay, sweetie; I understand. Just tell us what you told her."

Mikki calmed. "She asked what your mood was, if you were doing anything strange. If you didn't seem to be feeling well."

"And you told her about the lighthouse and...things?" said Jack.

Mikki nodded, a miserable expression on her face. "I'm sorry, Daddy. I didn't know she was going to sue you."

"It's not your fault. It'll be okay."

"Are you sure?"

"Absolutely." He looked at Jenna. "I've got a great lawyer. Now, go back in the house, Mik. Jackie's probably attempting somersaults from one of the ceiling fans."

After she left, Jack looked at Jenna. "I lost the kids once. I can't lose them again."

She put her hand over his. "Listen to me, Jack. You're not going to lose them, okay? Now, I've got to go. Lots of stuff to prepare."

She drove off, leaving Jack standing in the front yard of the Palace, looking at the ground and wondering if his second chance was coming to a premature end.

60

The kids were scrubbed and dressed in their best clothes. Jack and Sammy had bought jackets and dress slacks for the courtroom appearance. Jenna was dressed in a black skirt and jacket, heels and hose. Liam had taken time off work to join them for moral support. He and Mikki sat holding hands in the front row.

The courtroom was surprisingly small, and Jack felt immediately claustrophobic as he stepped inside. And it was very quiet. Jack didn't like such quiet. He had sensed it on the battlefield many times. It usually heralded an ambush.

The judge was not on the bench yet, but the uniformed bailiff was standing ready. Bonnie's lawyer was already seated at his table. Jack jerked when he saw Bonnie and Fred sitting behind him. Fred was studying his hands, while Bonnie was actively engaged in discussion with her lawyer, and also with another man in a suit. Other than that, the courtroom was empty.

As Jack looked at the young man, he suddenly remembered where he'd seen him before. In a car with Bonnie parked on the streets of Channing.

Jenna walked over and spoke with the bailiff for a minute or so before approaching Bonnie's lawyer. They went off to a corner to speak in private, while Bonnie stayed sitting and talking to the other man, who was showing her something on a laptop computer.

Jack watched as Bonnie's lawyer handed Jenna a packet of documents. She frowned and asked him something, but he shook his head. She said something else to him that Jack couldn't hear, but it made the other man turn red and scowl. She whipped around and marched back over to Jack. She sat down and pulled her chair closer to him and the kids.

At that moment, Sammy walked in with Charles Pinckney. Pinckney greeted Jack, Jenna, and the kids. Then he eyed Bonnie. He surprised Jack by walking over to her.

"Fred," he said. "How are you?"

Fred O'Toole looked up and seemed surprised to see Pinckney standing there. He took the other man's extended hand. "Fine, Charles, you?"

"I've been better, actually, but thank you for asking." He turned to Bonnie, who was gazing steadily at him. "Hello, Bonnie."

She nodded curtly. "Charles."

"Let's just be thankful Lizzie and Cee aren't alive to see this god-awful spectacle," he said in a tight voice.

Bonnie looked like she had been slapped. But Charles had already turned away.

Jenna held up the stack of documents and whispered to Jack. "Opposing counsel just now gave me these documents. I asked him if he would not contest an extension on the hearing date, but he refused."

"What's in those documents?" Jack asked.

"I haven't had a chance to read them, but I've glanced at a few pages. Your mother-in-law apparently has had a private detective follow you this summer." She pointed to the other man holding the laptop. "That guy."

"What?" said a shocked Jack.

"That is, like, totally insane," added Mikki.

Jack gazed nervously at him. "What's he got on the laptop?"

"Apparently some video they intend to show the judge."

"Video? Of what?"

"I don't know."

"I didn't think they could do stuff like this," said Sammy. "Surprise the other side with crap."

"Normally they can't. But this is family court. The rules are different. Everything is supposed to be done with the best interests of the children in mind. That sometimes trumps official procedures. And they're alleging that the children are in an unsafe and even dangerous environment."

"That's poppycock," said Charles.

"And we'll show it," promised Jenna. She had previously gone over with them the questions she would ask and what questions to expect the other side to throw at them.

A moment later, the bailiff announced the entrance of the judge. He turned out to be a small, thin, balding man, with thick spectacles, named Leroy Grubbs.

They rose on his entrance and then took their seats. The case was called, and Bonnie's lawyer, Bob Paterson, rose. But Jenna cut him off and asked the court for an extension, citing the late delivery of crucial documents. This was denied by Grubbs almost before Jenna finished speaking.

Paterson made his opening statement.

"Fine. Call your witnesses," said Grubbs.

The lawyer said, "Bonnie O'Toole."

61

Bonnie was sworn in and sat down in the witness box.

"You're the children's grandmother?" asked Paterson.

"Yes."

"Can you lead us through the series of events leading up to your filing this legal action?"

Bonnie spoke about Jack's illness, her daughter's death, Jack being in hospice, the children living with relatives, and Jack's recovery and his taking the children back. And, finally, she described her offer to have them all live with her because of her concerns, after consulting with doctors, that Jack's illness would most assuredly come back with fatal results.

"And what was Mr. Armstrong's response to your offer?"

"He categorically refused it."

"And what specific event prompted you to have your son-in-law put under surveillance?"

"I saw Jack beating up two men on the street in Channing, South Carolina, in broad daylight while his children were with him. The youngest, Jackie, was bawling his eyes out. It was awful. It was like Jack had lost his mind. I don't know if it was a symptom of the disease coming back or not, but I was terrified and I could tell the children were too."

The lawyer finished with Bonnie, and Jenna rose.

"Mrs. O'Toole, do you love your grandchildren?"

"Of course I do."

"And yet you seek to separate them from their father?"

"For their own good."

"And not to punish Mr. Armstrong?"

"No, of course not."

"So you're not angry with your son-in-law? You don't blame him for your daughter's death?"

"I've never blamed him. I told him that I knew it was an accident."

"But did you really believe that? Didn't you tell Mr. Armstrong that you thought he should be dead and not your daughter?"

Bonnie pursed her lips and remained silent.

"Mrs. O'Toole?"

"I've tried to move past that."

"But you still harbor resentment toward him?"

"I don't think so, no."

"And that is partly the reason you're filing for custody, for revenge?"

"Objection," said Paterson. "The witness has said she harbors no resentment."

"Withdrawn," said Jenna. "No more questions."

"Next witness," said Grubbs.

Jack and the others were surprised to see Sheriff Nathan Tammie amble into the courtroom, not looking too happy about being there. He was sworn in, and Paterson took him through his paces as a witness.

"So you warned Mr. Armstrong on the occasion of the first assault he was involved in?"

"Yes, although I warned the other guys too. Apparently Mr. Armstrong was provoked."

"And there was a second, more recent, assault involving Mr. Armstrong, was there not?"

"Yes."

"Can you tell us the circumstances?"

Tammie sighed, glanced at Jack, and explained the altercation in the alley.

"So, to sum up your testimony, Mr. Armstrong and Mr. Duvall were holding baseball bats in an alley, and three unconscious men were lying at their feet?" The lawyer glanced at the judge, presumably to gauge the man's reaction. The judge was following the line of questioning very closely. "So you arrested Mr. Armstrong and his companion, Mr. Duvall?"

"Yes. But I arrested the other guys too."

"But Mr. Armstrong will be going to court on these charges?"

"Yes."

"Could he receive prison time?"

"I really doubt that—"

"Could he?"

"Well, yes."

"No further questions."

Jenna rose. "Sheriff Tammie, why didn't you charge Mr. Armstrong on the first altercation?"

"Well, from the witness statements it was clear that he was provoked."

Jenna glanced at Bonnie. "Provoked how?"

Tammie took out his notebook. "Three witnesses said that one of the guys Mr. Armstrong went after had yelled out something about him being the miracle man and they were willing to pay him five dollars to perform a miracle on him. And he said other stuff, trying to get Mr. Armstrong's goat, I guess."

"All directed at Mr. Armstrong personally?"

"Yes."

"Did Mr. Armstrong attack at that point, when he was the subject of these statements?"

"No. He just kept walking along with his kids."

"Go on."

Tammie looked at his notes. "Then the same guy said, "Hey, Miracle, was it true your slutty wife was cheating on you? That why you came back from the dead?""

Jenna turned to look at Bonnie in time to see her glance sharply at Jack.

"And is that when Mr. Armstrong went after them? Because they insulted his deceased wife?"

"Yes."

"So he exercised admirable restraint when the insults were only directed to him?"

"Probably more restraint than I would have exercised if it'd been me."

"And the alleged second assault? Is it true that one of the men engaged in this assault was also the same man who was involved in the first altercation?"

"Yes."

"So it could have been that these men attacked Mr. Armstrong in that alley and he was merely defending himself?"

"Objection," said Paterson. "Calls for a conclusion that the witness is not qualified to give."

"Sustained," said Grubbs, but he looked curiously at Tammie and then over at Jack.

Jenna said, "No further questions."

Paterson said, "I call Michelle Armstrong to the stand."

As Mikki rose and moved forward, she stopped next to her dad. He gave her a reassuring smile and gripped her hand. "Just tell the truth, sweetie," he said.

62

"Ms. Armstrong?" said Paterson politely. "You had a number of conversations with your grandmother this summer, didn't you?"

Mikki looked at her father, but the lawyer moved to block her view. "You must answer my questions truthfully and not look to your father for instruction."

Mikki took a deep breath. "Yes, I spoke with Grandma."

"And what did you tell her about your father's...um... actions during the summer?"

"I don't understand the question."

"All right. I mean with regards to the lighthouse, for instance."

"Lighthouse?" said the judge.

Paterson addressed him. "It was apparently Mr. Armstrong's deceased wife's favorite place as a child, and he was spending most of the nights there."

Jenna rose. "Objection. Mr. Paterson has not been sworn

in as a witness, Your Honor, and has no personal knowledge of the situation."

"All right," said Grubbs. "Sustained."

Paterson turned back to Mikki. "Your statements about the lighthouse? Can you tell the court please?"

Mikki fidgeted. "I just told her that Dad was working on the lighthouse, that's all. It was no big deal."

"Would he work out there late at night?"

"Yes."

"With Mr. Duvall?"

"Yes."

"Leaving you three children alone in the house?"

Mikki's face grew hot. "I'm *not* a child. I'm sixteen."

"All right, leaving you and your younger brothers alone in the house?"

"Sometimes, but nothing happened."

"On the contrary, did you not tell your grandmother on at least three occasions that your younger brother, Jack Jr., got out of bed and once fell down the stairs?"

Jack looked shocked. He stared at Mikki. She swallowed hard. "But he was okay. Just a bruise on his back."

"And on another occasion Jack Jr. wandered out of the house and you couldn't find him for at least an hour? And he turned up walking down the street?"

Jack slumped back in his chair, totally flummoxed.

"Yes. But he was okay."

"And did you tell your father about these incidents?"

"No."

"Why not?"

"I...I didn't want him to get upset."

"Does he get upset often?"

"Well, I mean, no; no, he doesn't."

"Did you also tell your grandmother that your dad was obsessed with the house and the lighthouse because your deceased mother loved it so much there and he was trying to reconnect somehow with her?"

Mikki flushed a deep red and started breathing quickly. Tears trickled from her eyes. "I was mad at him; that's why I said those things."

"So they weren't true? Remember you are under oath."

Jenna rose. "Your Honor, counsel is badgering. I request a recess so the witness can compose herself."

Grubbs looked at Mikki. "Are you all right?"

Mikki drew in a deep breath, wiped her eyes, and nodded. "I'm okay."

"Proceed."

Paterson continued. "And did you also tell your grandmother that your father had no clue how to run a family and didn't seem to care about you and your brothers?"

Jack looked down.

Mikki teared up again. "That was before he changed."

"Changed?"

Obviously flustered, Mikki started speaking too fast. "Yes, I mean he was like that before. No, I mean, not bad. He did love us. I mean he *does* love us. He takes great care of us."

"But didn't you also tell your grandmother that you were worried about your dad's mental state?"

In a hushed voice Mikki said, "No, I don't remember saying that."

"So you've never seen your dad acting irrationally or even in a fit of rage?"

"No, never."

Paterson turned to the man in the suit sitting next to Bonnie. "Mr. Drake, if you would?" The man rose and wheeled forward a TV on a rolling stand and slid a DVD into a player underneath the TV.

Paterson said to the judge, "Your Honor, Mr. Drake is a licensed private investigator hired by Mrs. O'Toole to keep watch over the Armstrong children. The video you're about to see represents one of the results of this surveillance."

The TV screen came to life, and they all watched as Jack came running out of the lighthouse carrying the crate. He smashed it on the rocks and then raced down to the beach, twisting and turning in what looked unmistakably like a fit of insane rage. Then he dropped to the sand and wept. The next image was Mikki creeping up to her father.

On Paterson's cue the DVD was stopped, and he turned back to Mikki.

"You obviously saw your father that night?"

Mikki nodded.

"And you wouldn't describe that behavior as irrational or even a fit of rage?"

"He was upset, but he got better."

"So in your mind he was... sick?"

"No, that's not what I meant." She stood. "You're putting words in my mouth," she cried out.

Grubbs said, "Young lady, I understand that this is very stressful, but please try to keep your emotions under control. This is a court of law."

Mikki sniffled and settled back in her chair.

"If your father were to fall ill again while you were living with him, who would take care of the family?"

"I would."

Paterson smiled. "You may not be a child, but you're also not of legal age to live alone with your brothers."

Mikki looked furious. "And Sammy. He's my dad's best friend."

"Ah, Mr. Duvall. Yes." Paterson glanced at some notes. "Did you know that after he returned from Vietnam, Mr. Duvall underwent psychiatric counseling and that he also received two drunk-driving citations?"

Sammy erupted from his chair. "My whole damn unit was ordered to undergo that counseling because we'd done two tours in 'Nam and seen atrocities you never will, slick. And those DUIs were over thirty years ago. Never had a damn one since."

The judge smashed his gavel down. "Another outburst like that, sir, and you will be removed from this courtroom."

Paterson turned back to Mikki. "So, Mr. Duvall will look after you?"

"Yes," Mikki said stubbornly.

He turned to Drake again and nodded. The TV screen came to life. They watched first as Sammy drove his Harley way too fast and without a helmet. The second scene was Sammy dozing on the beach with a couple of empty beer cans lying next to him as Jackie and Cory played very close to the water.

"Quite a responsible caretaker," said Paterson dryly. "Now, Ms. Armstrong, can you tell us what you think your mother's death did to your father?"

Jenna jumped to her feet. "Relevance?"

"We're trying to determine the conditions of the children's environment, Your Honor. The state of mind of the surviving parent is highly relevant."

"Go ahead."

"Ms. Armstrong, please answer the question."

"He was devastated. We all were."

"Is he still devastated?"

"What do you mean?"

"Your father has been involved in two fights and been arrested for an assault for which he could go to prison. You saw the video of him throwing things and jumping around in a state of fury, and of your two brothers being left in the care of Mr. Duvall while he was apparently either drunk or asleep. You've given testimony that he neglected his three children to work on a lighthouse, resulting in injury to your younger brother. Do you believe those to be the acts of a rational person?"

"But I told you he's better now."

"So he was worse at some point?"

"Look, I know what you're trying to do, but my dad is not crazy, okay? He's not."

"But you're not qualified to make that judgment, are you? It really is for this court to decide if your father is fit to have custody of his children."

Mikki stood again, tears streaming down her face. "My dad is not crazy. He loves us. He is a great dad."

Paterson gave her a weak smile. "I'm sure you love your dad."

"I do," Mikki said fiercely.

"And you'd say anything to protect him."

"Yes, I would. I..." Mikki realized her mistake too late.

"No further questions."

As Paterson walked away, Mikki looked at her dad. "I'm sorry, Dad. I'm really sorry."

Jack said quietly, "It's okay, sweetie." When Jenna rose to question Mikki, Jack put a hand on her arm and shook his head. "No, Jenna, she's been through enough."

"But Jack—"

"Enough," said Jack firmly.

Jenna turned to the judge. "No questions," she said reluctantly.

Grubbs looked at Paterson. "Any more witnesses?"

"Just one, Your Honor, before we rest our case." Paterson turned toward the table where Jenna was sitting. "We call Jack Armstrong."

63

Jack was sworn in and settled uncomfortably into the witness box, hitching his suit jacket around him.

Paterson approached. "Mr. Armstrong, did you know that your illness can cause severe depression and even mental instability?"

"I don't have an illness."

"Excuse me?"

"I was given a clean bill of health. Look at me. Does it seem to you like I'm dying?"

Paterson picked up some documents and handed them to the bailiff. "These are opinions from three doctors, all world-class physicians, who state categorically that there is no cure for your illness and that it is fatal one hundred percent of the time."

"Then they'll have to change that to 99.9 percent, won't they?"

"Do you blame yourself for your wife's death, Mr. Armstrong?"

"A person will always blame themselves, even if they could do nothing to prevent it. It's just the way we are."

"So is that a yes?"

"Yes."

"That must be emotionally devastating."

"It's not easy."

"Talk to me about your obsession with the lighthouse."

Jenna said, "Objection. Drawing a conclusion."

"Sustained."

"Tell us about your reasons for working so long and hard on the lighthouse, Mr. Armstrong."

Jack furrowed his brow and hunched forward. "It's complicated."

"Do your best," said Paterson politely.

"It was her special place," Jack said simply. "That's where she'd go when she was a kid. I found some of her things there—a doll, a sign that she'd made that said, 'Lizzie's Lighthouse,' and some other things. And when she was alive she said she wanted to come back to the Palace. I guess me going there instead and fixing it up was a way to show respect for her wishes."

"All right. What else?"

Jack smiled. "Lizzie thought she could see Heaven from the top of the lighthouse."

"Heaven?"

"Yes," Jack said. "She believed that when she was a little girl," he added quickly.

"But you're an adult. So you didn't believe that, or did you?"

Jack hesitated. Jenna glanced at the judge and saw his eyebrows rise higher the longer Jack waited to answer.

"No, I didn't. But..." Jack shook his head and stopped talking.

The lawyer let this silence linger for a bit as he and the judge exchanged a glance.

"So you wanted to fix up the place?"

"Yes. The stairs to the lighthouse fell in, and I wanted to repair them. And the light too."

"Fix the light? It's my understanding that the lighthouse in question is no longer registered as a navigational aid."

"It's not. But it stopped working while Lizzie was still there. So I decided to try and repair it."

"So let me get this straight, if I can," said Paterson in a skeptical tone. "You neglected your family so that you could repair a lighthouse that is no longer used as a navigational aid, solely because your wife as a child thought she could see Heaven from there? Let me ask the question again: Did you think you could see Heaven from there?" he asked in a chiding tone.

"No, I didn't," said Jack firmly.

"We have one more video to show, Your Honor."

"All right."

Paterson turned to Drake, who worked the controls, and the image appeared on the TV of Jack standing on the catwalk around the lighthouse reading one of his letters to Lizzie.

"Could you tell us what you're doing in that picture, Mr. Armstrong?"

"None of your business," snapped Jack, who was staring at the TV.

Jenna stood. "Your Honor, relevance?"

"Again, state of mind," replied Paterson.

"Answer the question," instructed the judge.

"It's a letter," said Jack.

"A letter? To whom?"

"My wife."

"But your wife is deceased."

"I wrote the letters to her before she...before she died. I wrote them when I was sick. I wanted her to have them after...I was gone."

"But she can't read them now. So why were you reading them? You obviously knew what was in them."

"There's nothing wrong with reading old letters. I'm pretty sure people do it all the time."

"Perhaps, but not in the middle of the night on top of a lighthouse while small children are alone in the house."

"Argumentative," snapped Jenna.

"Sustained," said Grubbs.

Jack looked at Paterson and said, "I know you're trying to make it look like I'm nuts. But I'm not. And I'm not unfit to care for my children."

"That's for this court to decide, *not* you."

Jack sat there for a few seconds. The walls of the courtroom seemed to be closing in on him, cutting off his oxygen. His anger, always near the surface ever since Bonnie had filed her lawsuit, now burst to the surface. He looked at Paterson. "Have you ever lost anyone you loved?"

Paterson looked taken aback but quickly recovered. "I'm asking the questions."

Jack now looked directly at Bonnie. "You know how much I loved Lizzie."

Paterson said, "Mr. Armstrong, you're not allowed to do that."

Jack ignored him. He stood, his eyes burning into his mother-in-law's. "I would've gladly given my life so that she could have lived. You know that."

"Mr. Armstrong," cautioned the judge.

"She meant everything to me. But she died."

"Mr. Armstrong, sit down!" snapped Grubbs as he smacked his gavel.

Jack pointed a finger at Bonnie and cried out, "No one feels worse than I do about what happened. No one! It is a living hell for me every day. I lost the only woman I have ever loved. The only person I wanted to share my life with. The best friend I will ever have!" The tears were sliding down Jack's anguished face.

The judge barked, "Bailiff!"

Jack said, "The best things that Lizzie and I ever created were our kids. *Our* kids. So how dare you try to take away the only parent they have left just because you're mad at me. How *dare* you."

The bailiff forcibly removed Jack from the courtroom while Bonnie looked on, obviously shocked by his outburst.

Paterson said, "Nothing further, Your Honor." He walked back to his chair, barely able to conceal his smile.

The judge looked critically at Jenna. "Do you have anything to add, counselor?"

Jenna looked at the distraught kids and then at the judge. "No, Your Honor."

The judge said, "I'll render my judgment on the motion this afternoon."

Jack was released from the bailiff's custody a few minutes later. They didn't wait at the courthouse but drove back in silence to Channing. They waited in a small room at the back of the Little Bit. They all jumped when Jenna's cell phone buzzed. She answered the call and listened, and her expression told Jack all he needed to know.

"The judge granted the motion for temporary custody," she said.

And it's my fault, thought Jack. *I've lost my family. Again.*

64

Jack sat on his bed at the Palace holding letter number six in his hand. He hadn't read it yet. He was thinking about other things.

No matter what you do, no matter how hard you fight, life sometimes just doesn't make sense.

Bonnie and representatives from Social Services were coming this evening to take the kids away from Jack, perhaps forever. He looked down at the letter, then balled it up and threw it down on the bed next to the other five. As he looked out the window, three cars pulled into the driveway of the Palace, including Sheriff Tammie in his police cruiser. Though it was only seven in the evening, the sky was as dark as midnight. A tropical storm was just off the coast, and the wind was beginning to slam the low country with a fury. That was the major reason they were coming tonight. To move the kids farther inland. Jack had put up no fight, principally because he wanted his kids to be safe. The lights kept flickering on and off in the house.

Someone tapped on his door.

"Yeah?"

It was Jenna. "They're here, Jack," she said quietly.

"I know."

As Jack came downstairs, he stared at the three packed bags standing next to the front door. Then he looked over at the kids. Cory and Mikki were on the couch crying, and Jackie, not understanding what was going on, was crying too. He clutched his monster truck in one hand and hugged his siblings with the other, his little body quaking.

Liam simply stood by, not knowing what to do. His big hands clenched and unclenched in his anxiety. Jack went over to his kids and started whispering to them. "It's going to be okay, I promise. This is only temporary."

Jack and Jenna both answered the door. Bonnie, Fred, and the Social Services people stood there with umbrellas in hand.

"Are the children ready?" one of the Social Services folks asked Jack.

He nodded, his gaze squarely on Bonnie.

"Bonnie?" She looked at him, her face flushed. "Do we have to do it this way?"

"I'm only thinking of the children, Jack."

"Are you sure about that?"

"I'm very sure."

Sammy, Liam, Jackie, and Cory had joined them on the front porch.

Cory said, "Grandma, please don't do this. Please. We want to stay with Dad."

One of the Social Services people, a woman, stepped in and said, "This is not the time or place to discuss this. The judge has ruled." She looked at Jack. "We really want this to go smoothly. And I'm sure you do too, for the sake of the kids." The woman glanced over her shoulder at Sheriff Tammie, who stood outside his cruiser looking very uncomfortable.

Sammy eyed Jack, but it was Jenna who stepped forward and said, "We do." Sammy took a step back, and Jack looked at his two kids. "Okay, guys, you're going to be back here faster than you can say Jack Rabbit."

Cory nodded, but the tears still slid down his face. Jackie looked at Cory and started to tear up again. Jack hugged both of them. "It's going to be okay," he said. "We're a family. We'll always be a family, right?" They both nodded. "We'll get your bags. Liam, go get Mikki. I'm sure you want to say goodbye to her. They need to get on the road before the storm gets any worse."

Sammy and Jack carried the bags out to the car, and Jack strapped Jackie in while Cory buckled up next to him. When Jack looked back up at the porch, he knew something was wrong. Liam was standing there, his face pale and his expression wild.

Bonnie had seen this too. Despite the wind and rain, she got out of the car.

"What is it?" said Jack as he ran up to Liam.

"I can't find Mikki."

Jack and the others raced into the house. It took only ten minutes to search the place. His daughter was gone.

A quarter mile down the beach, Mikki was stumbling along, crying hard. The wind and rain battered her, but she kept going, leaning into the gusts swarming off the ocean. She kept weaving away from the waterline as the storm pushed the Atlantic farther landward. As upset as she was, Mikki didn't see the palmetto tree toppling over until it was almost too late. At the last possible instant, she lunged out of the way, but dodging the tree carried her too close to the waterline and in the path of a huge wave that crashed over her. Mikki didn't even have time to scream before the receding wave swept her out.

65

Jack stared out at the darkened sky from the front room of the Palace. The rain was coming down even harder. Liam had quickly driven home to see if Mikki had gone there, but he'd called to say she wasn't at his house.

Bonnie said, "Jack, what do we do? What do we do?" Her voice was hysterical.

Jack turned to her and said sharply, "The first thing we do is not panic."

One of the Social Services personnel said, "We should call the police. The sheriff drove off before this happened, but I'm sure we can get him back."

Jack shook his head and said in a crisp, take-charge manner, "There's only Tammie and one deputy, and they'll be preoccupied with the storm. We can call them, but we can't just sit around and wait for them to start looking for her. We have to start searching the area. We need to split up. Search by street and also the beach." He pointed to Fred. "Fred, you and Bonnie drive west in your car. Go slow, look for Mikki that way."

He turned to the pair from Social Services. "You go east in your car and do the same thing. Let's exchange cell phone numbers. Whoever finds her calls the others. Sammy and I will take opposite directions on the beach." He turned to Cory. "Cor, can you be a real big guy for me and stay here with Jackie? Go to the lower level and stay away from the windows."

Cory swallowed and looked terrified at his dad. "Mikki's coming back, right?"

"She absolutely is. I bet she shows up here any minute. And we need someone to be here when she does, okay?"

"Okay, Dad."

Jack headed right on the beach while Sammy went left. The rain was being pushed nearly sideways by the wind, and most of the sand was underwater. Jack swung his flashlight in wide arcs, but it barely penetrated the darkness. It finally caught on one object, and when Jack saw what it was, his heart thudded in his chest and a cold dread settled over him.

It was Mikki's sneaker floating in a pool of shallow water. He looked in all directions for his daughter but could see nothing. He called out her name, but the only thing he heard in response was the scream of the wind. He raced on to check backyards and behind dunes, but found nothing.

"I can't see a damn thing," he said to himself. He stared out at the angry ocean, engorged and rendered infinitely more dangerous by the strength of the storm pushing it against the coast. He turned and jogged back, his gaze toggling between land and sea. He had to bend forward to keep from being blown back by the powerful winds. Every ten seconds he screamed out her name. Near the Palace he met Sammy, who reported similar failure.

Jack showed him the sneaker.

"That is not good, Jack," said Sammy.

"We're running out of time. The storm is just about to really hit."

"What do you want to do?"

"We need to be able to see a big swath of land and water."

"No way you can get a chopper with a searchlight up in these conditions."

At this remark, Jack started and looked up at the lighthouse. He turned and ran toward it, Sammy on his heels. He kicked open the lower door and took the steps two at a time. He reached the top and hoisted himself through the access door. Sammy poked his head through a few seconds later, breathing hard.

"What the hell are you doing?"

"Getting a light."

"Jack, this damn thing doesn't work."

"It's going to work tonight! Because I'm going to find my daughter," Jack shouted back at him. He ripped open his toolbox, which he'd left in the corner, snatched some wrenches, grabbed the old schematic, and began to analyze it, his gaze flitting up and down its complex drawings. While Sammy held the paper, Jack worked on section after section of the mechanism, his ability to repair it having assumed a whole new level of urgency.

As Sammy watched him work, he said, "But we need a searchlight, not something that's going to—"

"There's a manual feature," Jack snapped as he squeezed his body into a narrow crevice to check the wiring there. "The light path can be manipulated by hand."

He pulled himself out of the space and hit the power switch.

"Damn it!" Jack flung his wrench down.

He peered out into the darkness, where his little girl was... somewhere.

He involuntarily shuddered.

No. I will not lose my daughter.

A burst of lightning that speared the water was followed by a boom of thunder as the storm reached its peak. Footsteps came from below, and first Jenna's and then Liam's faces appeared at the opening to the room. They were both soaked through.

"We've been searching the street and beach on our end, but there's no sign of Mikki," Jenna said to Sammy as she looked at Jack's back.

"We were trying to power up the light," Sammy explained, "but no luck."

Sammy said, "Bonnie called. And so did the other people. They found nothing either." He held up Mikki's soaked shoe. Jenna and Liam paled when they saw it. All three instinctively looked out to the frothing ocean.

Jack remained frozen against the glass, staring out into the darkness. The electricity to the lighthouse flickered, went out, and then sputtered back on. Jack was still staring at the darkness when he saw it. At first he thought it was another bolt of lightning lancing into the water, but there was no boom of thunder following it. Yet it had been a jagged edge of current; he'd seen it! Jack suddenly realized that in that second of darkness, what he'd seen had been reflected in the glass, only to become invisible when the power came back on and the lights were restored.

He whirled around and leapt toward the machinery. "Turn the light off, Sammy," he screamed.

"What?"

"Turn it off. Off!"

Sammy hit the switch, plunging them all into darkness.

Jack, his chest heaving with dread because he knew this was his last chance, stared at the machinery with an intensity he didn't know he even had. He could hear nothing, not the storm, not Sammy's or Jenna's or Liam's breathing, not even his own. There was nothing else in the world; only him and this metal beast that had confounded him all summer. And if he couldn't figure it out right now, his daughter was lost to him.

"Turn the lights back on."

Sammy hit the switch.

And Jack saw the beautiful arc of electrical current nearly buried between two pieces of metal in a gap so narrow he didn't even know it was there. *That* was what had been reflected in the window.

He dropped to his knees, scuttled forward, and hit the gap with his flashlight. Two wires were revealed. They were less than a centimeter apart, but not touching.

"Sammy, get me electrical tape and a wire nut and then turn the main power off."

Sammy grabbed the tape from the box, tossed the roll and red wire nut to Jack, and then turned off the power. While Jenna held the flashlight for him, he slid his hands in the gap, pieced the two wires together using the wire nut, and then wound tape around it.

Jack stood and called out, "Turn the power back on, and then hit the switch. Everyone look away from the light."

Sammy turned on the power and flicked the switch. At first nothing happened. Then, as if it was awakening from years of sleep, the light began to come on, building in energy until, with a burst of power, it came fully to life. If Jack hadn't told them to look away, they would have been blinded. The powerful beam illuminated the beach and ocean to an astonishing degree as it started to whirl around the top of the lighthouse.

Jack raced around to the back of the equipment, hit a button, and grabbed a slide lever. The light immediately stopped swirling across the landscape and became a focused beam that he could maneuver.

"Sammy, take control of this. Start from the north and move it slowly southward in three-second stages."

While Sammy guided the light, Liam, Jack, and Jenna stayed glued to the window, looking at the suddenly lightened nightscape.

Jenna spotted her first. "There! There!"

"Steady on the beam, Sammy," screamed Jack. "Hold right there."

Jack threw himself through the opening and took the steps three at a time. He nearly flattened Bonnie, who was coming up the stairs.

"What is—"

Jack didn't bother to answer.

He ran on.

The light had revealed Mikki's location. She was in deep water, clinging to a piece of driftwood as ten-foot-high waves pounded her. She looked to be caught in the seesaw grip of the storm. She might have only a few minutes left to live.

Then so do I, thought Jack.

66

Jack Armstrong ran that night like he had never run before. Not on the football field, and not even on the battlefield when his very life depended on sheer speed. He high-stepped through four-foot waves that were nearly up to the rocks the lighthouse was perched on. A towering breaker ripped out of the darkness and knocked him down. He struck his head on a piece of timber thrown up on the sand by the storm. Dazed, he struggled to his feet and kept slogging on. He saw the light, a pinpoint beam. But he couldn't see Mikki. Frantic, he ran toward the illumination.

"Mikki! Mikki!"

Another wave crushed him. He got back up, vomiting saltwater driven deeply down his throat. He ran on, fighting rain driven so hard by turbocharged wind that it felt like the sting of a million yellow jackets.

"Mikki!"

"Daddy!"

It was faint, but Jack saw the light shift to the left. And

then he saw it: a head bobbing in even deeper water. Mikki was being pulled inexorably out to sea.

"Daddy. Help me."

Like a charging rhino, Jack ran headlong toward the brunt of the storm. An oncoming wave rose up far taller than he was, but he avoided most of its energy by diving under it at the last possible second. He emerged in water over his head. The normal riptide was multiplied tenfold by the power of the storm, but Jack fought through it, going under and coming up and yelling, "Mikki." Each time she called back, and Jack swam with all his might toward the sound of her voice.

The lightning and thunder blasted and boomed above them. A spear of lightning hit so close that Jack felt the hairs on his arms and neck stand. He snatched a breath and went under again as another foaming wave crashed down on him. He came up. "Mikki!"

This time there was no answer.

"Mikki!"

Nothing.

"Michelle!"

A second later he heard a faint "Daddy."

Jack redoubled his efforts. She was getting weak. It was a miracle she was still alive. If that piece of driftwood got ripped from her, it would all be over. And then he saw her. The sturdy beam of light was tethered to the teenager like a golden string. Mikki was managing to stay afloat by using the driftwood she'd snagged somehow, but there was no way she could keep that up much longer. Jack swam as hard as he could, fighting through wave after wave and cursing when one threw him off course, costing him precious seconds. But the whole time he kept his eyes on his daughter.

And yet he realized that as each second passed, she was moving farther from him. It was the storm, the riptide, the wind, everything. He swam harder. But now he was fifty feet away instead of forty. He took a deep breath and slid under the water to see if he could make better time. But it was pitch-dark even just below the surface, and the current was just as strong.

When he came back up, he couldn't see her and cursed himself for taking his eyes off his daughter. His limbs and lungs were so heavy. Jack looked to the shore and then at the angry sky. He was being pulled out too now. And he wasn't sure he had the strength to get back in. It didn't matter.

I'm not going back without her.

Jack treaded water, looking in all directions as the storm bore down with all its weight on the South Carolina coast.

He shook with anger and fear and...loss.

I'm sorry, Lizzie. I'm so sorry.

What if I just stop swimming? What if I just stop?

He would sink to the bottom. He looked at the shore. He could see the lights. His family—what was left of it—was there. Bonnie would raise the boys. He and Mikki would go to join Lizzie.

He looked to the sky again. When a bolt of lightning speared down and lighted the sky, he thought he could see Lizzie's face, her hand reaching out, beckoning to him. He could just stop swimming right now. Right now.

"Daddy!"

Jack turned in the water.

Mikki was barely twenty feet from him. This time the movement of the water had carried him toward her.

Finding a reserve of strength he didn't think he had, Jack

exploded through the water. The ocean pushed back at him, throwing up wall after wall of frothing sea to keep him from her. He swam harder and harder, his arms slicing through the water as he fought every counterattack the storm threw at him.

A yard. A foot. Six inches. Every muscle Jack had was screaming in exhaustion, but he fought through the pain.

"Daddy!" She reached out to him.

"Mikki!"

He lunged so hard he nearly came fully out of the water. His hand closed like a vise around her wrist, and he pulled his daughter to him.

She hugged him. "I'm sorry, Daddy, I'm so sorry."

"It's okay, baby. I've got you. Just lie on your back."

She did so, and he put his arms under hers and kicked off toward land.

Now all I've got to do is get us back, thought Jack.

The problem was that when Jack tried to ride a wave in, the undertow snatched him back before he could gain traction on the shore. Then a huge wave forced them both underwater, before Jack brought them back, coughing and half-strangled. Jack was very strong, and as a ranger he'd swum miles in all sorts of awful conditions. But not in the middle of what was now likely a category 1 hurricane with someone else hanging on to him. He was caught in a pendulum, and he couldn't keep it up much longer. He might be able to get to shore by himself, but he was prepared to die with his daughter.

"Jack!"

He looked toward the beach. Liam and Sammy were standing there with a long coil of rope and screaming at him. Tied to the end of the rope was a red buoy. He nodded to show he understood. Sammy wound up and tossed the rope. It fell far short. He pulled it back and tried again. Closer, but still not close enough.

"Sammy," he screamed. "Wait until the waves push us toward the beach, and then toss it."

Sammy nodded, timed it, and threw the rope. Just a few feet short now. One more time. Jack lunged for the buoy and snagged it. But a monster wave crashed down on them, and Mikki was ripped from him.

He caught a mouthful of water and spit it out. As he looked down, he felt Mikki sliding past him and away from shore, out to sea. Everything was moving in slow motion, reduced to milliseconds of passing time.

"No!" screamed Jack.

He shot his hand down and grabbed his daughter's hair an instant before she was past him and gone forever. Sammy and Liam pulled with all their strength on the rope. Slowly, father and daughter were pulled to shore.

As soon as he hit solid earth, Jack carried Mikki well away from the pounding waves. His daughter was completely limp, her eyes closed.

As Jack bent down, he could see that Mikki was also not breathing. He immediately began to perform mouth-to-mouth resuscitation. He pinched Mikki's nose and blew air into her lungs. He flipped her over and pushed against her back, trying to expand her lungs, forcing the water out.

Sammy called 911 while Jack continued to frantically work on his daughter and was now doing CPR.

A minute later, Jack sat up, his breaths coming in jerks. He looked down at Mikki. She wasn't moving; her skin was instead turning blue. His daughter was dead.

He'd lost her. Failed her.

A crack of lightning pierced the night sky, and Jack looked up, perhaps to that solitary spot his wife had tried to find all those years ago. With a sob he screamed, "Help me, Lizzie, help me. Please."

He looked down. No more miracles left. He'd used the only one he would ever have on himself.

Liam knelt next to Mikki, tears streaming down his face. He touched Mikki's hair and then put his face in his hands and sobbed.

Suddenly Jack felt a force at the back of his neck. At first he thought that Sammy was trying to pull him away from his dead child. But the force wasn't pulling; it was *pushing* him back to her. Jack bent down, took an enormous breath, held it, put his mouth over Mikki's, and blew with all the strength he had left in his body.

As the air fell away from him and into Mikki, everything for Jack stopped, and the storm was gone. It was like he had envisioned dying to be. Quiet, peaceful, isolated, alone. As that breath rushed from him, the events of the last year also raced through his mind.

And now, this; Mikki. Gone.

Jack felt himself drifting away, as though over calm water, propelled to another place, he had no idea where. But he was alone. Lizzie and now Mikki were gone. He no longer wanted to live. It didn't matter anymore. There was peace. But there was also nothing else because he was alone.

The water hitting him in his face brought him back. The thoughts of the past retreated, and he was once more in the present. It was still raining. But that's not what had struck him.

He looked down as Mikki gave another shudder and coughed up the water that had been buried deeply in her lungs.

Her eyes opened, fluttered, opened again, and stayed that way. Her pupils focused, and she saw her dad hovering above her. Mikki put out her arms, gripped her father's neck tightly.

"Daddy?" she said in a tiny voice.

Jack sank down and held her. "I'm here, baby. I'm here."

67

The ambulance took Mikki and Jack to the hospital to be checked out. Sammy followed in his van with Liam, while Jenna stayed with the boys at the Palace. Jenna had made hot tea for Bonnie, who had watched Jack's heroic rescue of his daughter from the top of the lighthouse. Now she just sat small and stooped on the edge of the couch, a sob escaping her lips every few seconds.

Jenna had tried to comfort her, while Fred just sat in another chair and stared at his hands. When Sammy called from the hospital and told them they would be home shortly and that everyone was okay, Jenna had finally broken down and wept.

Afterward, Jenna had ventured into Jack's room; she wasn't sure why. As her gaze swept the space, it settled on the letters, which were still lying on the bed. She went over, sat down, picked them up, and started reading.

She emerged from the room ten minutes later, her eyes red with fresh tears. She walked over to Bonnie and tapped her gently on the shoulder. When Bonnie looked up, Jenna said, "I think you need to read these, Mrs. O'Toole."

Bonnie looked confused, but she accepted the letters from Jenna, slipped on her reading glasses, and unfolded the first one.

The storm, its fury rapidly spent after fully hitting land, had largely passed by the time they returned from the hospital. An exhausted Mikki was laid in her bed with Cory and Liam watching over her like guardian angels, counting each one of her breaths.

Jack told everyone that Mikki had suffered no permanent damage and should be as good as new.

"The doctor said she was one strong lady," added Sammy.

"Like her mother," said Jack as he looked at Bonnie.

He passed through the house and went outside and up to the top of the lighthouse. He stared out now at the clearing sky, the sun coming up in the east. He bent down and saw the wires he had spliced the night before. It was a miracle that he had finally spotted the trouble that had befuddled him for so long. Yet a miracle, thought Jack, was somehow what he, however irrationally, had been counting on.

He leaned against the wall of glass and stared out at what looked to be the start of a beautiful late-summer day.

He turned when he heard her.

Bonnie, wheezing slightly, appeared at the opening for the room. He helped her through, and they stood side by side looking at each other.

"Thank God for what you did last night, Jack."

Jack turned and looked back out the window. "It was Lizzie, you know."

"What?" Bonnie moved even closer to him.

Jack said, "I'd given up. Mikki was dead. I didn't have any breath left. She was dead, Bonnie. And I asked Lizzie to help me." He turned to her. "I looked up to the sky and I asked Lizzie to help me." A sob broke from his throat. "And she did. She did. She saved Mikki, not me."

Bonnie nodded slowly. "It was both of you, Jack. You and Lizzie. The match made in Heaven. Two people meant for each other if ever there was."

He stared at her, surprised by the woman's blunt words.

From her pocket she drew out the letters. "I think these belong to you." She handed them back to him and reached out and touched his face. "Sometimes people can't see what's right in front of them, Jack. It's strange how that works. How often it happens. And how often it hurts people we're supposed to love." She paused. "I do love you, son. I guess I always have. And one thing I know for certain is that you loved my daughter. And she loved you. That should have been enough for me." She paused again. "And now, it is."

They exchanged a hug, and she turned to go.

"Bonnie?"

She looked back.

"The kids?" he said in a small voice.

"They're right where they should be, Jack. With their father."

68

When Mikki opened her eyes, the first thing she saw was her dad. Right after that she saw Liam, peering anxiously over Jack's shoulder.

"I'm really okay, guys," she said a little groggily.

Jack smiled and looked at Liam. "Give us a minute, will you?"

Liam nodded, flashed Mikki a reassuring grin, and left the room.

Jack gripped her hand, and she squeezed back. Mikki said, "Sorry for all the excitement I caused. It was really dumb."

"Yes, it was," he agreed. "But we were all under a lot of pressure."

"So the lighthouse finally worked?"

He let out a long breath. "Yeah. If it hadn't..." His voice trailed off, and father and daughter started to weep together, each clutching the other, their bodies shaking with the strain.

"I can't believe how close I came to losing you, baby."

"I know, Dad, I know," she said in a hushed voice.

They finally drew apart.

"So what now? We still go with Grandma?"

"No, you're staying right here with me."

Mikki screamed with joy and hugged him again.

"Does Liam know?" she said excitedly.

"No, I thought I'd leave that to you." He rose. "I'll go get him."

As he turned she said, "Dad?"

"Yeah?"

"No matter what happens in my life, you'll always be my hero."

He bent down and touched her cheek. "Thanks…Michelle."

Later, as he stood by the doorway watching the two teens excitedly talking and hugging, Jack first smiled, then teared up, and then smiled again. She was clearly not a little girl anymore. And Jack could easily see how fast her life, and his, would change in the next few years.

Later, as Jack walked along the beach, a voice called out, "I'm going to miss you Armstrongs when you go back to Ohio." He turned to see Jenna walking toward him.

"No, you won't," said Jack, "because we're staying right here."

She drew next to him. "Are you sure?"

He smiled. "No, but we're still staying."

She slipped an arm around him. "I'm glad things have worked out."

"I couldn't have done it without you."

"You're way too generous with your praise."

"Seriously, Jenna, you helped in a lot of ways. A lot."

"So what are we going to do about the budding romance?"

"What?" he said in a startled voice.

"Between our kids."

"Oh."

She laughed, and he grinned sheepishly.

"I think we take it one day at a time." He looked directly at her. "Does that sound okay, Jenna?"

"That sounds very okay, Jack."

Epilogue

A little over two years later, Jack sat on the beach in almost the exact spot he and Mikki had occupied the night he'd realized he had so much to live for. The house was quieter now. Mikki and Liam had just left for college. She'd aced her last two years in high school and gone out to Berkeley on a scholarship. Liam the drummer had cut off his hair and was at West Point. Though they were a continent apart, the two remained the best of friends.

Cory was working part-time at the Play House and learning the ropes of theater management from Ned Parker. Jackie had started talking full-blast one morning about a year ago and had never stopped since. Although, Jack noted with some measure of fatherly pride, his favorite toy was still the monster truck.

He got up and made his way to the top of the lighthouse. He hadn't been up here since the morning after almost losing Mikki. He stepped out onto the catwalk and looked toward the sea. His eyes gravitated to the spot where father and daughter had fought so hard for their lives. Then he looked away and up to a clear, blue summer sky.

Lizzie's Lighthouse. It worked when I needed it to.

Jack had two very important things to do today. And the first one was waiting for him down the beach. He left the lighthouse and set off along the sand. His hands rode in his pockets; the words he would say slipped through his mind. As he drew closer, Jack realized that he had just traveled over a half mile by beach and a lifetime by every other measure.

She was there waiting for him by prearrangement. He slipped his arms around Jenna and kissed her. And much like he had done two decades before, Jack knelt down and asked a woman he loved if she would do him the honor of becoming his wife.

Jenna cried and allowed him to slip the ring over her shaky finger. After that they held each other for a long time on that South Carolina beach as a gentle breeze rippled across them.

"Sammy's going to be the best man," Jack said.

"And Liam will be giving me away," Jenna replied. "I love you, Jack."

"I love you too, Jenna."

They kissed again and visited for a while, discussing plans. Then Jack walked back to the Palace. His pace this way was not quite as brisk. The distance seemed a lot longer going back. There was a reason for this.

The first trek had been to create a bridge for his future.

This trip involved him making a painful separation from the past.

He reached the beach in front of his house and sat down in the sand. He pulled out a photo of Lizzie and held it in front of him. It was still nearly impossible for him to believe that she had been gone nearly three years. It just couldn't be. But it was.

He traced the curve of her smile with his finger while he stared into those beautiful green eyes that he always believed would be the last thing he would see in life before passing on. While Jack had just asked another woman to marry him, and this seemed fitting and right in so many ways, he knew that a significant part of him would always love Lizzie. And that this too was fitting and right in so many ways.

Bonnie had been correct about that. Lizzie and Jack had been meant to be together forever if ever two people were. Only sometimes life doesn't match what should be. It just is. And people have to accept it, no matter how hard it may be.

You should respect the past. You should never forget the past. But you can't live there.

And now he had something else to finish. Something very important.

From his windbreaker he pulled out a single piece of paper and a pen. His hand shaking slightly and the tears already sliding down his face, Jack Armstrong touched the pen to the paper and began to write.

Dear Lizzie,
   A lot has happened that I need to tell you about.

An hour later he finished the letter with, as always,

Love,
Jack

He sat there for a while, allowing the sun and breeze to dry his tears because for some reason he did not want to wipe them away by hand. He folded the letter carefully and placed it in an envelope marked with the number seven. He put the envelope and the photo of Lizzie in his pocket and walked toward the house.

When he reached the grass, he turned and looked upward. His mouth eased to a smile when he realized what he was looking at. Today, he'd finally found it, after all this time searching.

Right there was the little piece of the sky that contained Heaven. He somehow knew this for certain. Ironically, like so many complexities in life, the answer had been right in front of him the whole time.

"Pop-pop!"

He turned to see Jackie flying toward him. The boy gave a leap, and Jack caught him in midair.

"Hey, buddy."

"What are you doing?"

Jack started to say something and then stopped. He turned so they were both looking out toward the ocean. He pointed to the sky. "Mommy's up there watching us, Jackie."

Jackie looked awestruck. "Mommy?" Jack nodded. Jackie waved to the sky. "Hi, Mom." He blew her a kiss.

Then Jack turned back around and carried his son toward the house. Right before he got there, he slowly looked back at that little patch of blue sky.

Good-bye, Lizzie.

For now.

Jack's Letters

Dear Lizzie,

    There are things I want to say to you that I just don't have the breath for anymore. That's why I've decided to write you these letters. I want you to have them after I'm gone. They're not meant to be sad, just my chance to talk to you one more time. When I was healthy you made me happier than any person has a right to be. When I was half a world away, I knew that I was looking at the same sky you were, thinking of the same things you were, wanting to be with you and looking forward to when I could be. You gave me three beautiful children, which is a greater gift than I deserved. I tell you this, though you already know it, because sometimes people don't talk about these things enough. I want you to know that if I could've stayed with you I would have. I fought as hard as I could. I will never understand why I had to be taken from you so soon, but I have accepted it. Yet I want you to know that there is nothing more important to me than you. I loved you from the moment I saw you. And the happiest day of my life was when you agreed to share your life with mine. I promised that I would always be there for you. And my love for you is so strong that even though I won't be there physically, I will be there in every other way. I will watch over you. I will be there if you need to talk. I will never stop loving you. Not even death is powerful enough to overcome my feelings for you. My love for you, Lizzie, is stronger than anything.

                                                        Love,
                                                        Jack

Dear Lizzie,

Christmas will be here in five days, and I promise that I will make it. I've never broken a promise to you, and I never will. It's hard to say good-bye, but sometimes you have to do things you don't want to. Jackie came to see me a little while ago, and we talked. Well, he talked in Jackie language and I listened. I like to listen to him because I know one day very soon I won't be able to. He's growing up so fast, and I know he probably won't remember his dad, but I know I will live on in your memories. Tell him his dad loved him and wanted the best for him. And I wish I could have thrown the football to him and watched him play baseball. I know he will have a great life.

Cory is a special little boy. He has your sensitivity, your compassion. I know what's happening to me is probably affecting him the most of all the kids. He came and got into bed with me last night. He asked me if it hurt very much. I told him it didn't. He told me to say hello to God when I saw him. And I promised that I would.

And Mikki.

Mikki is the most complicated of all. Not a little girl anymore but not yet an adult either. She is a good kid, though I know you've had your moments with her. She is smart and caring and she loves her brothers. She loves you, though she sometimes doesn't like to show it. My greatest regret with my daughter is letting her grow away from me. It was my fault, not hers. I see that clearly now. I only wish I had seen it that clearly while I still had a chance to do something about it. After I'm gone, please tell her the first time I ever saw her, when I got back from Afghanistan and was still in uniform, there was no prouder father who ever lived. Looking down at her tiny face, I felt the purest joy a human could possibly feel. And I wanted to protect her and never let anything bad ever happen to her. Life doesn't work that way, of course. But tell her that her dad was her biggest fan. And that whatever she does in life, I will always be her biggest fan.

Love,
Jack

Dear Lizzie,

    Christmas is five days away and it's a good time to reflect on life. Your life. This will be hard. Hard for me to write and hard for you to read, but it needs to be said. You're young and you have many years ahead of you. Cory and Jackie will be with you for many more years. And even Mikki will benefit. I'm talking about you finding someone else, Lizzie.

    I know you won't want to at first. You'll even feel guilty about thinking about another man in your life, but, Lizzie, it has to be that way. I cannot allow you to go through the rest of your life alone. It's not fair to you, and it has nothing to do with the love we have for each other. It will not change that at all. It can't. Our love is too strong. It will last forever. But there are many kinds of love, and people have the capacity to love many different people. You are a wonderful person, Lizzie, and you can make someone else's life wonderful. Love is to be shared, not hidden, not hoarded.

    And you have much love to share. It doesn't mean you love me any less. And I certainly could never love you more than I already do. But in your heart you will find more love for someone else. And you will make him happy. And he will make you happy. And Jackie especially will have a father to help him grow into a good man. Our son deserves that. Believe me, Lizzie, if it could be any other way, I would make it so. But you have to deal with life as it comes. And I'm trying my best to do just that. I love you too much to accept anything less than your complete and total happiness.

                                                         Love,
                                                         Jack

Dear Lizzie,

    Christmas is almost here, and I promise that I will make it. It will be a great day. Seeing the kids' faces when they open their presents will be better for me than all the medications in the world. I know this has been hard on everyone, especially you and the kids. But I know that your mom and dad have really been a tremendous help to you. I've never gotten to know them as well as I would have liked. Sometimes I feel that your mom thinks you might have married someone better suited to you, more successful. But I know deep down that she cares about me, and I know she loves you and the kids with all her heart. It is a blessing to have someone like that to support you. My father died, as you know, when I was still just a kid. And you know about my mom. But your parents have always been there for me, especially Bonnie, and in many ways, I see her as more of a mom to me than my own mother. It's action, not words, that really counts. That's what it really means to love someone. Please tell them that I always had the greatest respect for her and Fred. They are good people. And I hope that one day she will feel that I was a good father who tried to do the right thing. And that maybe I was worthy of you.

                                                   Love,
                                                   Jack

Dear Lizzie,

    As I've watched things from my bed, I have a confession to make to you. And an apology. I haven't been a very good husband or father. Half our marriage I was fighting a war, and the other half I was working too hard. I heard once that no one would like to have on their tombstone that they wished they'd spent more time at work. I guess I fall into that category, but it's too late for me to change now. I had my chance. When I see the kids coming and going, I realize how much I missed. Mikki already is grown up with her own life. Cory is complex and quiet. Even Jackie has his own personality. And I missed most of it. My greatest regret in life will be leaving you long before I should. My second greatest regret is not being more involved in my children's lives. I guess I thought I would have more time to make up for it, but that's not really an excuse. It's sad when you realize the most important things in life too late to do anything about them. They say Christmas is the season of second chances. My hope is to make these last few days my second chance to do the right thing for the people that I love the most.

Love,
Jack

Acknowledgments

To Michelle, for taking the journey with me.

To Mitch Hoffman, for readily jumping in with both feet on something so different.

To David Young and Jamie Raab, for allowing me to stretch.

To Emi Battaglia, Jennifer Romanello, Chris Barba, Karen Torres, Tom Maciag, Maja Thomas, Martha Otis, Anthony Goff, Michele McGonigle and Kim Hoffman, and all others at Grand Central, for their unparalleled support.

To Aaron and Arleen Priest, Lucy Child, Lisa Erbach Vance, Nicole James, Frances Jalet-Miller, and John Richmond, for carrying the laboring oar so much.

To Maria Rejt, Trisha Jackson, and Katie James at Pan Macmillan, for so successfully building my career across the waters.

To Eileen Chetti, for a superb copyediting job.

To Grace MyQuade and Lynn Goldberg, for doing what you do so damn well.

To Lynette and Natasha, for keeping the home fires well lit and burning robustly.